CHILD'S PLAY

Also by Merry Jones

CHILD'S PLAY

AN ELLE HARRISON NOVEL

MERRY JONES

Oceanview Publishing
Longboat Key, Florida

ISBN 978-1-60809-191-1
Published in the United States of America by Oceanview Publishing
Longboat Key, Florida

www.oceanviewpub.com

10 9 8 7 6 5 4 3 2 1

PRINTED IN THE UNITED STATES OF AMERICA

To Robin, Baille, and Neely

Acknowledgments

Deep appreciation to: agent Rebecca Strauss; editors Pat Gussin and Emily Baar; the entire Oceanview team, headed by Bob and Pat Gussin; trapeze queen Maureen Krajewski; Philadelphia Police Department homicide detective Chuck Boyle (Ret.); the entire Philadelphia Liars Club; dog-and-beer buddies Kelly Simmons and Gregory Frost; venting recipients Janet Martin, Nancy Delman, and Lanie Zera; both Nicks, valiant first reader, Robin, and Baille and Neely, who make me so proud.

CHAPTER ONE

I was the first one there.

The parking lot was empty, except for Stan's pickup truck. Stan was the custodian, tall, hair thinning, face pockmarked from long-ago acne. He moved silently, popped out of closets and appeared in corners, prowled the halls armed with a mop or a broom. In fourteen years, I couldn't remember a single time when he'd looked me in the eye.

Wait—fourteen years? I'd been there that long? Faces of kids I'd taught swirled through my head. The oldest of them would now be, what? Twenty-one? Oh man. Soon I'd be one of those old schoolmarms teaching the kids of my former students, a permanent fixture of the school like the faded picture of George Washington mounted outside the principal's office. Hell, in a few months, I'd be forty. A middle-aged childless widow who taught second grade over and over again, year after year, repeating the cycle like a hamster on its wheel.

Which reminded me: I had to pick up new hamsters. Tragically, last year's hadn't made it through the summer.

I told myself to stop dawdling. I had a classroom to organize, cubbies to decorate. On Monday, just three days from now, twenty-three glowing faces would show up for the first day of school, and I had to be ready. I climbed out of the car, pulled a box of supplies from the trunk, started for the building. And stopped.

My heart did triple time, as if responding to danger. But there was no danger. What alarmed me, what sent my heart racing was the school itself. But why? Did it look different? Had the windows been replaced, or the doors? Nothing looked new, but something seemed altered. Off balance. The place didn't look like an elementary school. It looked like a giant factory. A prison.

God, no. It didn't look like any of those things. The school was the same as it had always been, just a big brick building. It seemed cold and stark simply because it was unadorned by throngs of children. Except for Wi-Fi, Logan Elementary hadn't changed in fifty years, unless you counted several new layers of soot on the bricks.

I stood in the parking lot, observing the school, seeing it fresh. I'd never paid much attention to it before. When it was filled with students, the building itself became all but invisible, just a structure, a backdrop. But now, empty, it was unable to hide behind the children, the smells of sunshine and peanut butter sandwiches, the sounds of chatter and small shoes pounding Stanley's waxed tiles. The building stood exposed. I watched it, felt it watching me back.

Threatening.

Seriously, what was wrong with me? The school was neither watching nor threatening me. It was a benign pile of bricks and steel. I was wasting time, needed to go in and get to work.

But I didn't take a single step.

Go on, I told myself. What was I afraid of? Empty halls, vacant rooms? Blank walls?

For a long moment, I stood motionless, eyes fixed on the façade. The carved letters: Logan School. The heavy double doors. The dark windows. Maybe I'd wait a while before going inside. Becky would arrive soon, after she picked up her classroom aquarium.

Other teachers would show up, too. I could go in with them, blend safely into their commotion. I hefted the box, turned back to the car.

But no, what was I doing? I didn't want to wait. I'd come early so I could get work done without interruption or distraction before the others arrived. The school wasn't daring me, nor was I sensing some impending tragedy. I was just jittery about starting a new year.

I turned around again, faced its faded brown bricks. I steeled my shoulders, took a breath, and started across the parking lot. With a reverberating metallic clank, the main doors flew open. Reflexively, I stepped back, half expecting a burst of flames or gunfire. Instead, Stan emerged. For the first time in fourteen years, I was glad to see him. Stan surveyed the parking lot, hitched up his pants. Looked in my direction. He didn't wave or nod a greeting, didn't follow social conventions. Even so, his presence grounded me, felt familiar. I took a breath, reminded myself that the school was just a school. That I was prone to mental wandering and embellishing. And that children would stream into my classroom in just three days, whether I was ready or not.

* * *

The hallways were still unlit. I hurried along the long, dark corridor, hearing only my breath and my own rapid steps until at last I came to room 2B. My room. Inside, I turned on the lights, closed the door, and worked nonstop all day, not joining colleagues for lunch, not taking breaks to chat. When Becky came by with Joyce, it was already after three.

Becky, one of my best friends, was Logan School's kindergarten teacher. Short, warm, honey-voiced, and bosomy, she was a walking, talking hug. Children and puppies were helplessly drawn to her. So were men.

Joyce Huff, on the other hand, was my nemesis. She taught the other second-grade class. Except for one year when she'd filled in for a fifth-grade teacher on maternity leave, she'd been teaching second grade since the *Mayflower* landed, and she thoroughly disapproved of my teaching style. Her pale-tan hair was fastened in its customary old-fashioned beehive. Her smile, like her skin and posture, was tight. She stepped into my classroom, lost her smile, and raised a hand to her mouth, actually swooning.

I followed her gaze to my "Wonder Work" bulletin board, twenty-three sections in varied neon colors, one for each student's best assignments.

"My God," Joyce finally spoke. "Was there a Crayola explosion in here?"

I smiled. If Joyce didn't like it, it must be good.

"It's very colorful." Becky gawked.

The room was vibrant, yes. Each zone—Art and Writing, Reading, Tech, and Science—was identified by a large bright overhead mobile. Each bulletin board display radiated a medley of tones. Shelves contained glowing colored baskets. And each desk was labeled with a student's name in a rainbow of vinyl letters.

Becky didn't say anything, just looked around.

Bright colors were stimulating. What was the problem?

"Sweetie." Joyce called other people "sweetie" and "darling," as if she were a wise adult and we were all children. "I know you're a free thinker and you intend well, but you've . . ." She paused to purse her lips. "Sometimes you've got to follow the rules."

Rules? "Sorry?"

"We're dealing with second graders, Elle, darling. At their age, children are sensitive, struggling to make sense of the larger world.

They need their classroom to be an organized haven, a safe, soothing, structured place in which they can relax and learn."

I looked at Becky, but she backed off, sank into the chair at my desk. Not getting involved.

No problem. I could deal with Joyce on my own. "My classroom is very well organized, thank you, Joyce. It's also energetic and stimulating." Joyce fancied herself the Martha Stewart of second-grade teachers. A self-proclaimed expert, the maven of oilcloth and doilies, her classroom featured monochrome pastel bulletin boards with matching fabric borders. Everything was consistent in size, color, and texture. Repetitive. Predictable. Mind numbingly boring.

"I'm only thinking of your sweet little seven-year-olds," she went on. "They need order and calm. The security of regular patterns. Look around. It's helter-skelter in here."

I bit my lip so I wouldn't lose my temper. "You and I have different styles, Joyce. So far, my students have done fine."

"But you have every color in creation, clashing and battling for attention. You have moving pieces. Incongruent shapes. There's no thematic thread in your design, no comfort in your color scheme. In fact, dear, you have no color scheme. The room has no focal point—"

"Elle?" Becky interrupted, lifted a printout off my desk. "You didn't tell me Seth Evans is in your class."

Joyce and I turned to her.

"Yeah," I said. "He completes the set."

"Who's Seth Evans?" Joyce asked.

"Ty Evans? Seth's his baby brother," Becky told her.

Joyce's eyes widened. "Oh my."

Like Becky, I'd taught Ty Evans and his younger sister, Katie. Now, I'd teach their little brother, too. I'd treat Seth the same as the other students. I picked up a marker, began tracing letters for a poster board. Eventually, it would be titled, "Mrs. Harrison's Superstars," decorated with the children's glowing names glued onto colored stars.

"He's out," Becky said.

"What?" I asked.

"Ty," she answered.

"Out?" Joyce grabbed the chain holding her reading glasses. "He is? So soon?"

I kept tracing.

"I saw it in the paper the other day. He turned twenty-one, so they sprung him."

They sprung him? I looked up and smiled at Becky, her attempt at talking gangsta.

"So what did he serve, five or six years?" Joyce frowned. "They call that justice?"

I pictured Ty, a skinny, scrappy second-grader, knees scuffed, hair unkempt. Acting tough, picking fights, taunting other kids, making them cry. How many times had I tried to meet with his parents? His father never showed. His mother, Rose, came reeking of eau de booze. I could still see her, a small, bone-thin woman with leathery skin and inch-long dark roots, crimson glue-on nails, a broken front tooth. She'd insisted that her son was a good boy, that the other kids must be singling him out, lying about him.

I'd wondered about her tooth, how she'd broken it. And the thick makeup under her eye looked kind of green. Was it masking a bruise? I'd asked her if Ty had ever been exposed to violence, and she'd denied it so vehemently that I suspected his bullying behavior mimicked what went on at home. I'd recommended that Ty get counseling, brought Rose to talk to Mrs. Marshall, the principal. But without clear evidence that he was being abused, there wasn't much we could do. Ty kept on bullying and getting suspended. Years later, when I heard he'd been arrested, I was sorry but not surprised.

Truth was, I'd let him down. So had his mother, his other teachers, Mrs. Marshall—every adult in his life. We'd let him slide, passing him and his troubles along year after year, until finally, at the age of fourteen, Ty had grabbed a knife.

I pictured his father's blood pooling on a linoleum floor. Ty, standing beside him, watching it spread. Had he been relieved? Shocked? Sorry? Scared?

"Elle?" Becky nudged my arm.

Oh dear. I'd lost track of the conversation.

"You just pulled an Elle," she whispered.

Damn. "Pulling an Elle" was the cutesy term my friends had for my mental wanderings. Actually, those wanderings were anything but cute. They were a symptom of what a shrink diagnosed as a dissociative disorder usually brought on by stress or intense emotion. In other words, when there was trouble, I escaped by slipping off into the safety of my mind. But until that day, I'd never "pulled an Elle" at school. So I was worried. Was my condition getting worse? Would I drift during class, abandoning the children? Would I have to quit teaching?

Joyce was still talking. "—but I had his sister, Katie, in class— that year I filled in for Jill Kaminsky and taught fifth. And that girl was an angel. Prettiest little thing."

"Elle and I taught her, too."

"So you know what I mean. She's a darling, yet her brother's a cold-blooded killer. Same family, opposite natures. Shows you that some children are just bad seed. Something rotten in their genes. Remember that boy in Myra Ellis' class? The one with the gerbils?"

"That was before our time," Becky breathed.

"But you heard how he was burning them with matches and cutting their bellies open. Imagine. In fourth grade. His parents— well. On the surface, they were lovely people. They sent him to a psychiatrist, but you can bet that, wherever he is today, he's still just as bad inside. You can't change a person's nature. I bet this Ty's just the same as that boy."

I blinked at her. To my knowledge, Ty had never tortured gerbils.

"I don't know," Becky said. "People can change."

Joyce tsked. "You can't change heredity, and mark my words, there's a hereditary factor involved. I bet it's sex-linked—you know, affecting only the Y chromosome. That would explain why Katie's sweet as pie, not a bit like Ty. Either way, Elle, you better watch out for their brother. What's his name again? Gabriel?"

Gabriel? Where had she gotten that?

"Seth," Becky answered.

"I'm serious, sweetie. You have hamsters in here, don't you? Keep an eye on that boy."

"I'm not going to hold Seth responsible for someone else's actions. Even his brother's."

"I agree," Becky said. "I don't think Elle should have preconceived notions about Seth."

I resumed tracing an "S."

"I didn't say she should," Joyce bristled. "But she'd be crazy not to watch him. After all, where's his big brother, Ty, now? Living at home with the family? So the younger boy has a killer in his house? As his male role model? How is that even allowed?" Joyce shook her head, wrung her freckled hands. Held onto her reading glasses as she looked around the room. "And seriously, Elle, given that boy's likely predispositions, you really should tone this room down. You don't want to overstimulate him—"

"Joyce, stop. Elle will handle it." Becky's hands were on her hips. "You don't even know Seth or Ty."

"No, but after teaching for almost thirty years, I know their like. Once in a while, maybe every six or seven years, you run into a child who's different."

"Every child is different," Becky countered.

"Not just different. Plain down-to-the-core bad. Soulless. Devoid of conscience. Capable of who knows what. And genetics has got to be part of it."

I shook my head. Refused to engage. Started a "U."

Becky rolled her eyes.

Joyce crossed her arms, raised her voice. "I'm right and you both know it. Take your boy Ty. The court said he was too young to be tried as an adult. But he wasn't too young to eviscerate his father. Where does that kind of brutality come from in someone so young? It's got to be inbred. In his genes."

Becky met my eyes, shook her head. "So, Elle. What about them Phillies?"

"You're changing the subject because you know I'm right."

Becky smiled at her. "I'd say it's time to call it a day. You heading out, Elle?"

She was giving me a chance to escape. But before I could respond, Joyce gave a harrumph and waved her pointer finger at us. "Okay, as usual, you two are trying to ignore me. But if you're smart, you'll think about what I've said. Trust me. Some people are bad from birth. Pretend otherwise at your own peril." With that, she stormed out of the room.

Becky stared after her. "You've been warned, Elle. You might have a second-grade psychopath."

"And you might have a kindergarten killer."

I expected her to continue, come back with something like seven-year-old strangler, so I was trying to think of a retort, something better than kindergarten criminal. But Becky didn't continue. She frowned.

"What?"

"Nothing."

"You're frowning about nothing?"

"No."

I waited for her to continue, finished tracing an "R."

"Just... What if Joyce's right? What if bad behavior is genetic?"

Was she serious? "Then there's nothing a teacher can do about it. We tell kids what the rules are and hope they'll follow them." I put down the stencil. Reached for scissors.

"Why should they follow the rules when their teacher doesn't? 'It's helter-skelter in here.'" Becky mimicked Joyce. Looked around the room, frowning. "'Everything's clashing and competing for attention. You don't even have a focal point.'"

I grinned. "Focal point? What the hell does that even mean?"

"No idea."

We laughed. Becky looked around. "It really is bright in here, Elle."

I tried to be objective. "Too much?"

"No," she managed. "It's perfect." Still laughing, she hugged me good-bye, reminded me of our weekend plans, and left me contemplating colored markers, letters, and star-shaped cutouts.

I worked another hour, finishing the Superstars sign, fending off images of Ty and his dead father. It was around four thirty when I closed my classroom door. On the way out, I noticed the lights on in the principal's office and stopped in to say hello, somehow not noticing the dark red smudges on the floor.

* * *

Mrs. Marshall sat at her desk, arms at her side. Head tilted. Blouse drenched with blood.

I stopped breathing. The walls swayed and, for the briefest moment, Mrs. Marshall became Charlie, my late husband. Her office became our study. Just as he had two years before, Charlie sat on the sofa, a knife in his back. Dead. I grabbed the doorframe, bit my lip, and the flashback faded. Charlie vanished, but Mrs. Marshall remained, her head slumped to the side, exposing a deep gash in her neck. Her empty eyes gazed at blankness, and her cheeks oozed crimson clots. Wait—had her face been cut?

I didn't move closer to find out. Didn't move at all. My heart pummeled my ribs, adrenaline flooded my veins. I stood stunned, frozen, absorbing the sight. *Move,* I told myself. *Do something.* Finally, I did. I spun in a circle, looking for a killer, finding no one, just a dead elementary school principal with a mop of dyed dark curls and blood, lots of blood.

Okay. I knew what to do: call the police. Right. My phone was somewhere in my bag. I opened it, started digging. Remembered that there were landlines in the office. Phones on the desk. I dropped my bag, took two steps forward, reached for Mrs. Marshall's phone. Pushed a button for a dial tone, then 9-1-1.

When someone picked up, I told him who and where I was, what had happened. My voice sounded disconnected, far away. The operator said that police were on the way. That I should stay on the line with him until they arrived. But no. I hung up, wasn't comfortable staying there with Mrs. Marshall. Sarah Lorraine. Those were her names, not that I'd ever used either one. No one had, as far as I knew. No, staying there with her was way too intimate. Mrs. Marshall wouldn't want a staff member with her at such a private moment. She didn't mix with staff, didn't warm up and chat or even celebrate birthdays. She kept everything coldly professional, rarely even smiled.

Oh God. Was that what was cut onto her face? A smile? I looked at her again, saw slits extending from her mouth to her ears. A wide grin carved onto her face?

I backed up, bumped into the door jamb, knelt to get my bag. Spun around and dashed out of the office into the lobby. Scanned the vacant seats, the "Welcome to Logan School" banner. Where was the killer? Was he still around, watching me? My skin itched. I had to get away, somewhere safe. The lobby was too open, exposed. The double doors—I could run outside. Leave. But the 911 operator had told me to stay. Did that mean stay inside? It made no sense. Why should I stay inside with a murderer? Why couldn't I think straight? Thinking was oddly difficult, taking too long. But I couldn't stay in the open lobby, vulnerable. I hurried up an empty hallway, along polished linoleum floors, under long fluorescent lights. I passed stairways and classroom doors, away from what I'd seen. Getting nowhere. Surrounded by silence.

Lots of silence.

What was I doing? The police would arrive and go to the lobby. I should stay where they could find me. I looked over my shoulder, saw no one. Started back.

I moved slowly, making no sound, and stood against the wall outside the lobby, watching, listening. Clutching my bag. Wait— what was that metallic clank? An old water pipe? What about that faint clicking, crackling? Shoes slapping the floor? I pressed against cinder blocks, teeth clenched, stomach knotted. The school was quiet, hollow, and the hollowness grew, echoed, roared so loudly that it drowned out the clamor of my breathing, my heart pounding, my blood rushing. Was that a shadow or a flicker of the fluorescents? Was someone across the room? Watching me? Yes, I could feel it, the heat of his eyes.

Forget the 911 operator. I needed to get out of the building. I moved unsteadily toward the doors, certain that someone was behind me, sensing his body heat. Oh God. I should take off and full out run. Yes. On three. I took a breath. One. I readied myself, bent my knees slightly. Two. I recalled the morning, the school's odd sinister aura. Three. I started to run, and a hand clamped onto my shoulder. I smacked it and whirled around, yelling and swinging my bag, expecting to confront the killer.

And faced Stan Olsen.

* * *

Stan didn't flinch when my bag struck his head. He eyed the floor as if it hadn't happened, mumbled. Something about not meaning to frighten me, about locking up. About security.

I backed away, readying my bag for another swing. Maybe he had a knife. Maybe he'd killed Mrs. Marshall. After all, he had motive. She'd berated him a thousand times in front of faculty, even more in front of students. Maybe she'd criticized him once too often.

Except that his hands weren't bloody. And his clothes had no red splatter.

Maybe while he'd stabbed her, he'd covered his shirt with a trash bag. Maybe worn work gloves.

"You're the last one." He ran a gnarled hand through his sparse hair and stepped toward me, eyes aimed at the floor to my left. "The rest are gone."

I kept stepping backwards, inching toward the doors. Where were the police? I was chilly, shivering. Alone with a possible killer.

"No." My jaw was clenching. "Someone else is here."

He frowned. "Who?"

"Mrs. Marshall." Why had I said that?

"So late? It's almost five." He peered into the office. Saw her light. Stomped toward it, muttering. "She knows it's still summer hours. Why's she still here? How am I supposed to lock up?"

Did he really not know that she was dead?

"Stan, wait. Don't go in there."

He kept going. Maybe he was playing dumb to cover his crime.

"Mrs. Marshall is dead."

He stopped, rotated slowly until he faced me. Didn't say a word.

"Someone killed her."

For a full second, his gaze actually flickered directly onto me. His eyebrows raised. Not surprised enough. Not upset or curious or scared. "For real?"

I shivered, nodded. "Yes."

His eyes moved away. "Is there a mess?"

Did he think he'd have to clean it up? To Stan, was a murder the same as a kid throwing up or spilling milk?

There was a mess, but I didn't say so. Instead, I told him we shouldn't touch anything. "The police are on the way."

"They're coming now? So I guess I can't lock up even though it's already past time." He headed out of the lobby, down the hall to his custodian's closet.

As soon as he did, I ran out the front door to my car. Except for the principal's car and Stan's truck, it was alone in the lot. I turned on the engine, put on the heat, and sat there trying to get warm, not looking at the school. Afraid that it would grin.

CHAPTER TWO

I remembered him well. Nick Stiles was the same detective who'd questioned me after Charlie's murder. He was married to a friend of my friend Susan's. Despite the big scar crossing his face, he was even better looking than I remembered, and his eyes were a disarming shade of blue. They watched me gently now, but two years ago, those same eyes had been steel blades, slashing me with accusations. Not that I blamed him. I'd been the obvious suspect; statistically, the spouse was pretty much always the killer. Especially when the marriage was troubled, which ours had been. Very. Charlie and I had been separated. I'd filed for divorce. Detective Stiles must have thought he had a slam bang easy case.

Of course, he'd learned otherwise.

But that was two years ago. Now, he greeted me with a crooked smile, took my hand, and asked in a caring tone how I was doing after that "tragic affair" with my husband as if he'd never personally tried to crucify me. As if he and I were old friends. His hand was large and solid, and it held onto my unsteady fingers longer than it should have. Maybe he was trying to put me at ease? In that case, why was he talking about Charlie's murder? No, Stiles didn't give a damn about my ease or lack of ease. More likely, he was letting me know that he hadn't forgotten me, even hinting that I might be a suspect in this murder, too.

Except that, this time, he had no reason to suspect me. I wasn't the victim's spouse or even her friend. I was one of dozens of teachers at the school, had no particular conflict with Mrs. Marshall. No motive. Detective Stiles needed to take my statement. He took a seat opposite me in the lobby, waited for me to start.

But I didn't start. Wasn't sure what to say, didn't quite trust him. Maybe I should call Susan. She wasn't just a close friend; she was a criminal defense lawyer. But if I put off giving my statement until I talked to a lawyer, I'd appear to have something to hide. Better if I just told him what had happened.

"Mrs. Harrison? You all right?" Stiles leaned forward, uncrossed his legs.

Of course I was all right, I told him. But I wasn't. I fidgeted, picturing Mrs. Marshall's vacant eyes.

He asked if I wanted coffee or a cold drink. Told me to start when I was ready. "Why don't we start at the beginning? Tell me about your day. Did you notice anything out of the ordinary?"

Well, for starters, the school building had threatened me. But Stiles wouldn't be interested in that. I closed my eyes, remembering. Sifting through hours of moving desks and arranging bean bag chairs. Greeting a few teachers who popped into my room to say hi. Hanging mobiles, decorating bulletin boards, organizing shelves, labeling cubbies. Listening to Joyce criticize my color scheme. And to Becky, interrupting. "Why didn't you tell me Seth Evans was in your class?"

Seth Evans, brother of Ty Evans, who had recently been released from prison.

Where he'd been serving time for murder.

Should I mention that?

I looked at Stiles.

"You thought of something." It wasn't a question.

I looked away. "It's not related."

"It might be."

"I was just thinking about a student. I taught his sister and brother, too."

"And?" Stiles' eyes hardened, waiting for me to get to the point.

"And." I folded my hands. "The student's brother is Ty Evans."

Stiles' eyes glimmered as he repeated the name. He took a pen and notebook from his jacket pocket. Fired questions. How well did I know Ty? Had I seen him since his release? Had I heard from him while he was in juvey? To my knowledge, had Mrs. Marshall heard from him? How had he and she gotten along? He jotted down my answers as if they were important.

As soon as I mentioned Ty, I regretted it. He had been released just days before the murder, but surely that timing was just a coincidence. He had no reason to kill Mrs. Marshall—hadn't attended Logan in a decade. But because of me—because I'd said his name—he'd undoubtedly be hounded and questioned about the murder. Maybe accused of it. My stomach churned. I knew what it was like to be a suspect.

I tried to minimize the damage I'd done. "But there's no reason to think Ty had anything to do with this. I shouldn't have even mentioned it." I heard myself sounding idiotic. Stopped talking, closed my mouth.

Stiles kept jotting notes. Looked up. Asked me to continue going through my day. "Anything else of note?"

Just a blood-drenched blouse. A clown-like smile carved into the principal's face. Creaks and clanks, shadows flitting in an empty school.

And Stan appearing from nowhere, his hand grabbing my shoulder.

"Nothing worth mentioning."

Stiles finally walked me out of the building. The press was waiting. News reporters, lights and cameras. Shouted questions. "Detective Stiles, can you comment on the murder?" "Is it true the principal was maimed?" "Do you have a suspect?" "Ma'am? What's your connection to the crime?"

Stiles put a hand up, cleared a path through the confusion, and led me away, past the Medical Examiner's van, the jumble of police and their cars, the gaggle of neighbors gathered in the parking lot. He walked me to my car, noticing that I was unsteady, asking if I was okay to drive.

I said I was even though I wasn't. I just wanted to get away. But in the car, my hand shook as it tried to fit the key into the ignition. And my mind drifted, unfocused. I wasn't sure how I got to the parking lot exit, but somehow, I had. Turning onto the street, I looked in my rearview mirror. Detective Stiles was still standing there, hands in his pockets. Watching.

* * *

I parked out front, hurried past the "For Sale" sign, up the steps to my door where I fumbled with the key, kept missing the keyhole, jabbing the key to the left or the right. I scolded myself: *What's wrong with you? Slow down. Watch what you're doing.*

So I slowed down, watched the key and the hole, carefully lined them up, and inserted one into the other. Turned the key, heard the click. Opened the door. And dashed inside where I slammed the door shut and fastened the bolt with still-trembling hands, stayed there for a few heartbeats, leaning my head against the solid wood. Then I wheeled around, went to the wine rack in the study. Opened a bottle of Syrah. Poured myself a glass. Took a hefty swallow before taking the bottle and my glass to the living room and plopping onto the sofa. Leaning back, I let soft throw pillows and overstuffed cushions engulf me.

No sooner had I settled down than my phone rang.

Damn.

Maybe I wouldn't answer. The phone was in my bag, all the way in the hall. Whoever it was could leave a message. I'd call them back.

But the phone kept ringing, repeating my ringtone, Elvis Presley's "Suspicious Minds."

Probably it was Becky, calling with details for Saturday's class. Four of us had signed up for circus school. I pictured Mrs. Marshall's grotesque clown-like grin, and circus school seemed abhorrent. I should take the call and tell Becky about the murder. I stood up, took my glass and bottle to the hall. Put them on the table beside the door, picked up my bag, dug inside to find the phone. Braced myself for Becky's shock and tears.

But it wasn't Becky.

"What the hell?" Susan greeted me. "Are you crazy or just stupid? Why didn't you call me?"

Call her?

"You should know better. After everything I've said to you—"

Wait, where did she get off calling me stupid?

"—haven't you learned anything?" Susan paused but not long enough for an answer. "How many times have I told you: Never, I mean, never ever talk to the cops without an attorney. Never. Not under any circumstances."

She had to be talking about the murder. But how could she know about it? Who'd told her? Stiles? No way.

"But you completely, totally, absolutely ignored me and sat down to blab to Nick Stiles."

"I had no choice," I began. "I only told him—"

"Of course you had a choice. You shouldn't have told him any-thing. Other than maybe your name. Which, as you recall, he already knew from the last time I told you not to talk to him." She sputtered. Fumed. "Imagine my surprise when I turn on the six o'clock news and see none other than my dear friend Elle Harrison being escorted from the school by homicide detective Nick Stiles."

Oh man. I picked up the wine glass. "We were on the news?"

"You bet you were. They said they didn't know your connec-tion to the crime, but they said police were talking to you, and they identified you. By name. And occupation. Elle Harrison, who teaches second grade at Logan Elementary."

They identified me? That couldn't be good. Didn't it imply that I might a suspect? Or that I was somehow involved? That the po-lice had reason to spend time with me?

I put the glass to my mouth, emptied it. Worried that my neg-ative publicity would infuriate Mrs. Marshall. Then remembered that, no, nothing would infuriate her ever again. I pictured her soaked red blouse. The gaping wound on her neck. Poured more wine. The reds almost matched.

"Okay?" Susan asked.

Damn. I'd missed what she'd said.

"Elle, are you there?" Susan barked. "Did you just pull an Elle on me? Not now, damn it, Elle. Come back to earth. Pay atten-tion. I'll be there in half an hour? Okay?"

I told her, yes. I'd see her then. Ended the call. Took the wine and the phone back to the living room, planted myself on the sofa, and made the dreaded call to Becky. It went as predicted. Shock, fear, questions. I got off the phone feeling drained and sank back against the cushions.

And noticed ever so slight indentations in the carpet. Shaped like shoes.

* * *

But that was impossible. I'd vacuumed just the day before and hadn't gone into the living room afterward, not until now. I'd walked across the carpet to the hall a couple of times, but hadn't gone into the rest of the room. And these footprints made a circle with a second small loop near the window.

I swallowed more wine, stared at the carpet. At the slight indentations shaped like shoes. Men's shoes. Or maybe women's flats?

Maybe I'd missed spots in the carpet when I'd vacuumed. Or maybe the vacuum didn't have enough suction to erase old footprints. Or maybe there were no footprints. Maybe I was imagining them the same way I'd imagined the school glaring at me. Maybe I was so upset about Mrs. Marshall that I was inventing intruders who'd snuck around my house, leaving shoe prints.

I closed my eyes. Counted to three. When I opened them, the footprints remained, subtle, but as real as my wineglass. My mind slogged ahead, analyzing the implications of the depressions in the pile. Realizing that, if the shoeprints were real, then the person who'd left them must be real, too.

And that, oh man, that person might still be in the house.

I sat frozen, moving only my eyes, scanning the room. Seeing no one. Hearing nothing but a quiet refrigerator buzz floating in from the kitchen. Was someone hiding in the pantry? In a closet?

Well, if he was, he'd be sorry. Gripping the wine bottle, ready to clobber, I hopped to me feet, dashed to the coat closet, flung the door open. Faced my winter jackets, a cleaning bag with Charlie's old cashmere coat. Skis. Boots. No intruder.

But that didn't mean he wasn't in the house. I moved on, cautiously opening the pantry, linen and bedroom closets, checking under Charlie's desk, beneath the bed, inside the cabinets under the sinks.

Finally, I decided that I was alone. Whoever had been in the house was gone. But what had he wanted? To rob me? I had very little of value—just standard stuff. Televisions and computers. A tea set from my mother's mother. A couple of rings and bracelets Charlie had bought me. Was anything missing?

Again, I searched the house, scanning shelves, opening drawers. Nothing was gone. Nothing was even out of place. In fact, the house looked immaculate, neatly staged, ready for real estate showings.

Showings. Of course. There had been no strange intruder. Jerry O'Malley, my realtor, must have come by. Must have used the key from the lock box.

Except that he'd had no reason to come by. We hadn't scheduled a showing that day. Had he brought a potential buyer by without an approved appointment? I stood in the living room, still clutching the wine bottle, studying the footprints. Following them in their circle, feeling my face get hot, resenting the invasion by a stranger inspecting my shower tiles for mold and my cupboard for crumbs and mouse turds.

Jerry had no business taking people through without permission. He wasn't supposed to show up unexpectedly, leaving footprints.

Especially not on the same day that someone had slit Mrs. Marshall's throat.

I downed my wine, clutched the empty glass and the half-empty bottle. Thought of Charlie. Pictured him stabbed to death just down the hall in the study. Would someone find my body there, too?

Enough. I needed to collect myself. I was in no danger. Mrs. Marshall's killer, whoever it was, had no reason to harm me. And Charlie's killer was dead, no threat to me or anyone else.

Fine. So what about the footprints?

Jerry. He'd simply taken someone through without permission.

I should take the key out of the lock box and tell Jerry and his bands of high-stepping carpet-crushing potential buyers to keep out.

Except, no. I had to sell. The place was riddled with my past. With Charlie. Even now, I sometimes heard his voice whispering my name, saw his shadow lingering near the wine rack. Smelled his aftershave wafting through the bedroom. As long as I stayed in the house, I would keep imagining Charlie's presence and be unable to move on. And, two years after his death, it was time to move on.

All I had to do was make it clear to Jerry that he must not bring anyone by without first confirming the visit with me. Good. Settled. I'd email him right away. I took my glass and bottle to my laptop on the kitchen table. Opened my email account. Saw that Jerry had sent me about eight messages.

I'd read about three when I heard a key turn in the front door lock. Damn. I wasn't imagining it. Someone had a key and was coming in. Jerry? Just in case it wasn't, I pulled a butcher knife from a kitchen drawer with one hand, gripped the wine bottle in the other, and waited just inside the kitchen door. Ready to strike.

* * *

The scent of Chanel No. 5 wafted by.

"Think she's awake?"

"She's not in the living room."

Good God.

I stepped into the hallway, the knife and bottle still in my fists. Met my three best friends, Jen, Becky, and Susan on their way to the kitchen. The rescue squad, the cheer-up team, showing up to make everything all right.

"Look at her. She's pale as a frickin' ghost." Jen leaned close, eyeing me. I felt her breath on my face, heard the tiny whistle of air passing through her remodeled nose. "I bet she hasn't eaten a fucking thing." Not eating was unthinkable to Jen. She wore a size zero but ate—and talked—like a linebacker.

"At least she's been drinking." Becky entered the kitchen, nodded at my wine. "Most of a bottle's gone." My friends had an inexplicable habit of talking about me as if I weren't there.

"Well, can you blame her?" Jen took the bottle from me, swirled it under the light to see how much was left. Produced a shopping bag with replacements. "Cabernet or Pinot?"

Susan walked by holding a bag of groceries. Without comment, she took the knife from my hand as she passed.

"Any of you ever hear of door bells?" I managed. "I thought you were burglars. I could have stabbed somebody—"

"Chill, Elle." Jen took three glasses out of the cabinet. "You're way too frickin' tense."

"We thought you might be lying down, so we didn't want to bother you by ringing," Becky explained. She had a key. Actually, they all did. I had keys to their houses, too. But those keys were supposed to be for emergencies, not for walking in any time at will, unexpectedly. I thought of Jerry. Apparently everyone I knew felt free to waltz into my house.

Jen put the wineglasses and a new bottle on the table, put her arms around me in a hug. Her synthetically enlarged breasts pressed against my chest. They were softer than I'd imagined. "Shit, Elle, what a nightmare. Thank God Becky told me what happened. Otherwise, I'd have found out by seeing you on goddamn TV news?"

Oh Lord. Was Jen in a snit because I'd talked to Becky first?

"Let it go, Jen," Becky said. "Elle told me because I teach at the school. I needed to know."

"I didn't have a chance to call, Jen. I just got back from talking with the police—"

"Which you had no business doing without consulting me." Susan unloaded her grocery bag onto my countertop. Swiss cheese, onions, French bread. "Now, tell me everything that you said to Stiles. Everything." Eggs, peppers, tomatoes, mushrooms.

Jen poured wine. Becky passed the glasses around. Susan made a frittata. I sat at my kitchen table, surrounded by three people I'd loved since childhood, smelling dinner cooking. And I told them about finding the body, about running into creepy Stan. About Stiles' interest in Ty Evans.

Susan stopped shredding cheese, turned to face me. "What? Ty Evans? For God's sakes why?"

"Who the eff is Ty Evans?" Jen broke a chunk of crust off the bread, bit into it.

"Remember a few years ago, that kid who killed his father? That was him," Becky said.

Jen shrugged, chewed. Didn't remember.

But Susan wasn't finished with me. Her hand ran through her hair, landed on her hip. "Elle, how did Ty's name come up? Did Stiles ask you about him?"

She was interrogating me. I squirmed. No, Stiles hadn't asked me about him. Not exactly.

She noticed. "Wait. So you brought up Ty's name? I don't get it. Was there a reason to associate him with Mrs. Marshall's murder? Did you see him at the crime scene? Or hanging around the school? Had Mrs. Marshall recently mentioned him to you? Did you have any evidence implicating him at all?"

My face got hot. I already regretted mentioning him, and Susan's questions made me feel even worse. "Susan, I had to say something. He's a convicted killer who got out of jail just days before the murder. And he hated Mrs. Marshall. The whole time he was at Logan she repeatedly punished and humiliated him, made an example out of him. She suspended him every time she looked at him."

Susan shook her head, picked up the cheese, and resumed grating. Vigorously. "Of all people, Elle, you should know better. You know what it's like to be unjustly accused."

I did, yes.

Becky, Jen, and I stared at our wineglasses, silent. When Susan got mad, we regressed, became the little neighborhood girls she'd babysat thirty years earlier and behaved as if she were still in charge. But she wasn't, and I resented her scolding me. I sat with my insides burning, trying to justify what I'd done. I hadn't actually accused Ty Evans of anything. And, knowing that he'd had motive and opportunity, wasn't I right to tell Stiles?

Maybe not. Maybe I was a rat.

Nobody spoke. Susan fried onions in butter. Becky cut mushrooms and tomatoes. Jen chewed on a chunk of red pepper.

They waited for me to say something. When I did, it was an attempt to justify myself. "Susan, he hated her. Everyone at the school knows that."

Susan worked her spatula. "He might have hated her seven years ago. But that's a long time ago—a third of his life. So the kid's been locked up for all those years—misses high school and college and any chance for a normal life. Finally he gets out only to have the cops pounce on him about another murder."

"Just because I mentioned him?"

"Believe me. It doesn't take much once you've been convicted. The cops bring you in for everything."

My stomach clenched. I'd messed up but couldn't undo it. "Was I supposed to hide what I knew?"

"That's my point. You don't know anything. You had no business bringing up Ty's name."

She was right. I had no excuse. Shouldn't have done it. My eyes felt swollen, head throbbed.

"Susan, don't yell at her." Becky put a hand on my arm.

"I'm not yelling."

"She's already had a horrific day."

"Yes," Jen agreed. "We came here to comfort her. Telling her what she shouldn't have done won't help. Whatever she did, she did. That's the end of it." The scent of Jen's Chanel No. 5 mixed with fried onions.

I lifted my wineglass, tried to believe that I hadn't done much harm. That if Ty were innocent, he'd be fine.

"Whoa!" Jen leaned over to look at my computer screen. "What's this?" She began reading aloud. "'We have lots to talk about. Drinks or dinner? You name the night, the sooner the better.' Sizzle sizzle. Elle, why haven't you told us about him? Who is this effing guy? JerrO?"

* * *

I'd forgotten about my email, had been reading it when I'd heard the key in my lock and grabbed a knife.

"He's not a guy. He's just my realtor."

"Really." Jen's eyebrows raised. "Then 'just' your realtor 'just' has a thing for you."

Six eyes stared at me, waiting for a reply.

"No, he doesn't." Did he? "He wants to get together to talk about the house."

"He could talk about the house on the phone. The dude wants something more."

"He's hitting on you, Elle."

Was he? "Look at another one," I told Jen.

I got up, stood behind her as she opened one email, then another, and read them aloud. Jerry wanted to show me new staging ideas for my living room. Or to discuss market strategy. Or to review comparable properties and pricing. All kinds of reasons to have wine or cocktails, coffee or dinner.

"He's certainly persistent." Susan dumped chopped vegetables into the frying pan.

"And pushy." Becky washed the cutting board.

"Of course he's pushy," Jen huffed. "The man's in real estate."

"They aren't all pushy," Becky said.

"Of course they are." Jen brushed her bangs out of her eyes. The bangs were part of her new look, and she kept touching them, not used to them yet. "And if this guy wants Elle, he'll keep pushing. He'll do anything to try to get her."

Yikes. "He's not trying to get me." I felt the need to defend him. "He only contacts me about the house." But what if they were right? Had Jerry been trying to date me? Had I been too obtuse to notice? Would he really do "anything" to get me—like sneak into my house and leave shoeprints on my carpet?

"This one was just sent today." Jen opened an email. "'While we talk, we can have a picnic by the river. I'll bring wine.' You can't think that's just business, Elle. The guy is after your tail."

A picnic? Seriously? I took a step back and rubbed my arms, felt crowded.

"So tell us about him." Becky was drying the knife, putting it back in the drawer. "Is he cute?"

Cute? Jerry? I'd been focused on selling my house, not on my realtor's looks. But I tried to decide. He was tall and beefy. His hair was graying, held in place with gel. His nose was imposing and prominent. Eyes light blue. Jaw strong. Lips full. Was he "cute"? Maybe, in a slick kind of way. I didn't know.

"Cute isn't everything." Susan didn't look up from the stove. She ought to know, married to Tim with his protruding belly and weak jaw. "More important, is he single?"

I conjured up Jerry's left hand. Saw no ring. But that didn't mean anything. Men took their rings off when it suited them. Lord knew Charlie had.

"He sounds single," Jen said. "You can tell from the emails. He's lonely and has tons of free time. Hell, he's ready to get together with Elle any time of day, any day of the week. No wife would put up with that."

"Okay." Susan sprinkled cheese into the pan. "So he's aggressive and single. And interested."

"So?" Becky asked. "Why doesn't she go out with him? No chemistry?"

"I think she ought to give him a chance." Jen blew the bangs off her forehead. "Lord knows she could use a new man."

"So what's the problem?" Susan wiped her hands on a towel.

I emptied my wineglass. Then I told them about the lock box and the shoeprints.

* * *

Predictably, they wanted to see them. Susan lowered the heat on the stove, and we clustered in the hallway outside the living room, stooping, squatting, kneeling, even lying on the floor to get a better view of the indentations on the carpet.

"You're sure they're not yours?" Susan asked.

"Of course I'm sure. My feet aren't that big. And I'd know if I'd walked there."

"But it looks like you did walk there. There are at least two sets of prints."

Oh, right. I'd forgotten that I'd walked around the living room, following the intruder's trail. Even so, the first set was unexplained.

"I bet it's him. Jerry. He's obsessed and he's stalking her." Jen spoke with certainty. "She didn't respond to his emails, so he's escalating. Moving in on her, penetrating her territory whether she likes it or not."

"Or," Susan said, "if it's him, he might have come in to measure the floor."

"No way. Son of a bitch already has the measurements," Jen argued. "When you list your house, they put room dimensions in the brochure—"

"Don't be so literal, Jen. I meant he might have come in for innocent reasons."

"If it was him," Becky said.

"It was him." Jen got up off the floor. "She should check her bedroom. See if anything's amiss."

Amiss?

"Like what? You think he stole her panties?" Becky climbed to her feet.

"Maybe. Or he left her a gift on them. Or on her towels or sheets. Sometimes these perverts get off by fantasizing about the person they're stalking—"

"Jen—" Susan put up a hand.

"And they jerk off onto their stuff."

"—that's really enough."

Yuck.

"Eww!" Becky winced.

"Who knew Jen was an expert on stalkers?" Susan asked.

"I watch all those effing crime shows. You can learn a lot."

Susan didn't comment. No doubt, she'd defended more than a few stalkers.

"So if he's coming into the house and wandering around fantasizing, what's he going to do next?" Becky asked.

"Hold on." Susan put a hand up. "We don't know that he's doing any of that."

"But if he did. Do you think he'll get violent?" Becky took hold of my wrist.

Violent? Jerry? I couldn't imagine it.

Then again, I hadn't imagined him coming into my house without permission.

"I don't think Elle's safe here." Becky tightened her grip. "She needs to take the key out of that lock box to keep him from coming back."

"No point," Jen said. "Any good stalker would have made copies. If she wants to keep him out, she needs to change the locks."

I did? We stood in a circle outside my living room. I looked at Susan. She usually had common sense. I expected her to say that, as far as we knew, Jerry was just a realtor. That, if he'd come into the house, it had likely been for benign reasons. That his emails were indicative not of an obsessed stalker, but of an aggressive salesman trying to schmooze his single, probably lonely widowed client.

But Susan didn't say any of that. She shouted, "Oh shit," and spun around, racing back to the kitchen.

The rest of us followed. The frittata wasn't burned, but one side was dark and crispy. We sat at the table, eating and, by tacit agreement, not talking about Jerry, Ty Evans, the police, or Mrs. Marshall's murder. Instead, we drank too much wine and focused on lighter topics. Susan's three daughters and their teenage hormones, their unanimous dread of the new school year. The numbness of Jen's nipples, an aftereffect of her recent enlargement surgery. And our upcoming circus classes.

Jen had conditions. "No way am I wearing an effing clown nose. Not after the money I spent getting this one remodeled."

"It's not a clown class," Becky reminded her. "It's tightrope, aerial work, and tumbling."

"Tumbling? Jen, what if you tumble onto your new boobs?" Susan asked. "You better be careful."

"Why, you think they'll pop?" Becky chewed frittata.

"You guys are just jealous." Jen sat straight, thrusting her chest out. "If I fall, they'll cushion me."

"If you land on them, you might bounce," I said.

"Unless Becky's right and they pop." Susan smirked.

I pictured them smashed, hanging limp and deflated on Jen's chest. Oh dear. Could they really pop? Maybe Jen shouldn't go with us.

Jen stuck her tongue out. "Wait 'til you see me in a leotard, you bitches. My girls aren't going to pop, but your eyes will."

Susan shook her head.

"Seriously," Becky said. "Maybe we should cancel."

"Because of my boobs?" Jen asked. "Don't worry, I'll be fine."

"Not everything is about you and your body, Jen. I meant because . . . you know." Becky lowered her voice and eyed me. "Because of what happened today. Elle might not be up for it."

They all looked at me, assessing whether I would be up for it. I tried to smile, to act as if I wasn't seeing Mrs. Marshall and her open throat as the centerpiece of the table.

"I'm fine," I insisted. "Besides, we've already paid."

"Big fucking deal," Jen said. "It's only money."

Becky and I looked at each other. We lived on teachers' salaries, didn't have a rich husband like Jen.

"No, we have to go," I insisted. "Becky chose circus school. The deal is that we try each other's choices, no excuses."

They watched me, still uncertain, still deciding.

"Besides," I went on, "it'll be good to focus on something besides the murder."

"Good point," Becky agreed. "So we'll go."

"We should be proud of ourselves," Susan said. "People never follow New Year's resolutions. But we have. Eight months and, so far, nobody's canceled even once. So, if Elle's okay with it, I say we go ahead."

I raised my glass. "To circus school. It's got to be better than hot yoga."

"You fucking wimps whined through the whole class," Jen complained.

"It was hellish."

"Becky almost passed out."

Jen's perfect nostrils flared. She poured herself another glass of wine. "My ass. You're a bunch of losers."

Becky lifted a glass, cheerful. "Here's to us losers. And to keeping our New Year's resolution."

Each month, we'd taken turns picking new experiences to share. So far, we'd taken wine tasting, ceramics, sailing and dragon boat classes. Attended an opera, toured an archaeological museum, ridden in a hot air balloon, and sweated through hot yoga.

Next was circus school. I didn't like heights and had been privately dreading it. But a promise was a promise, and I'd be with my friends. Compared to the day I'd just had, how bad could it be?

* * *

The dishes were almost done, the third bottle of wine finished. I poured coffee and passed a mug to Susan.

"Elle." She met my eyes. "About before. Sorry. I shouldn't have been so hard on you."

At first, I didn't know what she was talking about.

"It's just that I've always felt bad for Ty."

Oh, that. I swallowed coffee. "Susan, why don't we just let it go?"

"Fine, but I want you to understand why I reacted like I did." She paused, cleared her throat. "At trial it came out that Ty's father had been abusing him. Ty committed the murder to protect himself and his family. That fact should have helped his defense, but Ty got the maximum sentence for a juvenile because his attorney blew it and didn't emphasize the history of violence. Ty endured a brutal childhood, and then he got a rotten defense attorney and a raw deal."

Susan went on talking. I recalled Ty the second grader with scabby knees. At seven years old, already a bully, mocking and hurting other kids. I saw myself consoling his victims, sending Ty to the principal's office. Banishing him so I could restore order in the classroom.

I tried to remember talking to Ty. Had I ever done more than just punish him? Had I tried to find out why he was so angry, asked about his scabs and bruises? I must have. Of course I had. And he must have made up stories, hidden his abuse. Claimed he'd fallen off his bike. Been smacked in the face with a baseball. And since he'd kept the truth from me, how could I have known what was happening to him? I'd consulted the principal, contacted his parents. What else could I have done?

Oh, hell. I could have done a lot more. I could have made sure he was safe.

He'd been a little boy in my charge, and I hadn't helped him. I'd left him to his abuser, so that his desperation and rage had continued to build. Until finally, with no one else to protect him, he'd protected himself.

And, since I'd overlooked his desperation, wasn't I partly to blame for what had happened? Weren't all the adults who'd let him down? His mother. His teachers. And Mrs. Marshall. Had Ty killed her because she'd failed him back then? And, if so, was she just the first in a series of revenge killings? Oh God. Was I on his list?

No. Ridiculous. Ty wasn't tracking down and killing every adult who'd ever neglected him—there must be hundreds of us. Probably he didn't even remember most of us, least of all some woman who taught him fourteen years ago when he was just in second grade.

I drifted back to the conversation. No one had interrupted me, telling me I was pulling an Elle. But somehow, without my noticing, the coffee mugs had been washed, the dishes put away, and Becky and I had both received texts and emails formally notifying us of Mrs. Marshall's death and informing us that Logan School's opening would be delayed for a week so that staff and students could grieve. And besides, the building was closed; it was an active crime scene.

The buzz that the wine had given me was gone. My friends were ready to go home. Jen asked if I'd be all right alone in the house. Becky offered to stay the night. Susan offered me her guest room.

I thanked them all, declined the offers, promised to bolt the door. And did as soon as they left.

Then I grabbed my cell phone and, just to be safe, the carving knife. I went upstairs, filled the bathtub. Got in and soaked, but not before taking a fresh towel from the closet. And examining it closely, making sure it was clean.

* * *

I slept so deeply that, when the phone rang, I didn't know what it was. Didn't recognize my own ringtone. I slapped the nightstand randomly, trying to turn off some radio. When I finally identified the sound, fumbled for the phone, and answered, I thought I heard a faint, high-pitched giggle, but no one was there.

What time was it? The screen on the phone said 2:47.

Who calls someone at 2:47?

I tried to go back to sleep, but the phone call had jangled me. I kept hearing noises. A continuous electric hum. The occasional tiny thunk of an insect against the window. A passing car, a distant train, a police siren. All normal. But wait, what was that creak? A floorboard? Was someone in the house?

Of course not. I'd bolted the doors. The creak was just beams or eaves settling, something like that.

But there it was again. Coming from downstairs.

I sat up, grabbed my knife. Listened. Heard nothing.

Was it Jerry? Getting up the nerve to come upstairs? But I'd bolted the doors. No one could come in, even with a key.

Unless he'd broken a window and climbed in.

Another creak, quieter this time. Almost inaudible.

It's nothing, I told myself. *Go back to sleep.* But I knew I wasn't going to sleep. Clutching the knife in one hand, the phone in the other, I got out of bed, crept out of the bedroom along the hall to the stairs. If someone was there, what would I do when I confronted him? Assuming it was a him. How sexist of me, to expect a burglar to be male. But probably he was male. Could it be Jerry?

No, not in the middle of the night. Jerry wasn't that crazy. Was he?

I tiptoed down the steps, pausing at each level, peeking down into the darkness, trying to see a moving shadow or a shape. At the bottom of the steps, I stopped, body rigid. Was someone watching me? Waiting to pounce on me from behind?

Was it Mrs. Marshall's killer?

Her bloody grin hovered in front of me, her eyes aimed behind me. I raised the knife and whirled around, bellowing, "Back off!"

Even the empty stillness of the hallway didn't persuade me that I was alone. I stood ready to strike, waiting. Heard the clunk of the refrigerator making ice cubes. Bit my lip.

Nobody's here, I told myself. *Relax. You're hearing normal sounds. The phone call rattled you.*

Still, I had to check. I stepped along the hallway, looking not just ahead, but also behind me and to the sides. Peeked into the powder room. Stopped at the door to the study where, two years ago, I'd found Charlie slumped on the sofa. My stomach clenched, remembering.

"Turn on the lights," I whispered aloud. *Nobody's here. You'll see. It's just your imagination.*

My limbs were stiff, unwilling to move, but I forced my hand, the one holding the cell phone, to lift itself and flip the light switch. Light flooded the room, and my eyes, accustomed to the dark, reflexively clamped shut.

"Elf!" Charlie sounded jolly. "Come in. Join me."

I blinked, saw the empty room. The new plush sofa. The desk, bookshelves, mahogany bar.

"There's plenty of Syrah," Charlie's voice said. "Open a bottle. You can use a drink."

"Go away, dammit," I said out loud. "Get out of my head."

I'd been told the phenomenon wasn't uncommon. That widows and widowers sometimes talked to their lost loved ones for years. But I couldn't continue. I needed to stop imagining Charlie. Had to sell the house and free myself.

I left the study, went from room to room, double-checking windows and doors. Making sure everything was intact and locked. I opened the door to the basement, looked down into its empty blackness, felt its dampness and chill. Didn't go down. Never did. No one could be down there anyway—the only windows were in the back of the house, under grills.

Finally, I decided that there had been no unusual noise, that the phone call had jarred me and, already shaken by the murder, I'd overreacted to some benign sound. I went back upstairs to bed.

When I closed my eyes, Mrs. Marshall's corpse greeted me. Her smiling lips didn't move but she gurgled, "See you soon."

What?

She nodded, her carved grin fixed. "No point hiding. Killer's already got you."

I sat up, turned on the light. It had only been a dream. But weren't dreams messages from the subconscious? So my subconscious was warning me that I was in danger. But from whom? Ty? A harsh scrape at my window startled me. I grabbed the knife.

Probably it was the oak tree. Its branches had been trimmed, but might still hit the window in the wind. Or it might be a squirrel. Did squirrels climb trees at night? I didn't think so, wasn't sure. Maybe it was a bat, then. Or a raccoon.

But what about my dream? Was it about Ty? I saw Mrs. Marshall towering over him. "Why do you continue to defy me with this behavior?" she demanded. "You can't win, you know." His eyes gleamed with hatred. Had that hatred endured all these years? He would have come into the office, found her at her desk, unsuspecting. Would have chatted with her until she'd been comfortable enough to let him come close. His knife must have come fast, slashing before she could resist. And the smile—why would he have carved it? Why not just run away?

But it might not have been Ty. Could have been anyone. Stan, for example. He'd had opportunity. And so had the assistant principal, Mr. Royal. Or what about an angry parent—Ty's mother, Rose Evans, for example? How many times had she accused Mrs. Marshall of singling Ty out, punishing him unfairly?

And what about Mrs. Marshall's husband? Statistically, the killer was usually the spouse. Hadn't I been accused of killing Charlie just because I was married to him? So maybe her husband had done it. I tried to remember his name. Fenton? Philip? Something unusual with an "f."

So many possibilities. I closed my eyes, saw Mrs. Marshall lecturing the suspects. They sat in a classroom, and she stood before them in her blood-drenched blouse and skirt, demanding to know, "Who did this? Come on, whoever it was, admit it. Raise your hand." She paused, waiting.

No hand went up. Stan looked at the floor. Ty, seven years old again, picked a scab on his arm. His mother examined her fake nails. Mr. Royal drummed his fingers on the desktop. Fenton or Philip gazed at the window.

"If the guilty person doesn't admit it," Mrs. Marshall warned, "I'll have to punish all of you." She paused. "Okay, that's it. Line up against the wall. I'm going to measure your shoes and compare them to the footprints."

Footprints? Wait—the ones in my rug? I was getting mixed up. Dozing. It was after three when I reached over and turned the lamp off. A few minutes later, the phone rang. The screen said, "Unregistered number," and when I answered, no one was there.

It's possible that I nodded off for a while. But when the sun came up, I was wide awake, staring at a crack in the bedroom curtains, watching light fade into the sky.

CHAPTER THREE

On Saturday morning, our class was held in an open field in Bucks County. As we drove up, we saw an expanse of high ladders, platforms, and complicated multileveled nets.

My head ached, hungover. The day before, trying to numb the shock of what had happened to Mrs. Marshall, I'd imbibed too much wine. And the last few nights, I hadn't been able to sleep. Even though I'd dozed in the car while Susan drove, I was still unquestionably woozy when we arrived at circus school. I stared up at the platforms, imagined being high off the ground standing on a narrow plank. Rode a wave of dizziness.

"WTF, Becky," Jen gasped. "What have you gotten us into?"

Becky beamed. "This is going to be great." She bounced, almost skipped ahead to meet the instructor.

His name was Shane. Shane was about five foot eight, solid like a gymnast, maybe twenty-six years old. His hair was golden and he wore tight Spandex. He welcomed us warmly and promised an experience we'd never forget, led us to a grouping of folding chairs. Then he gave some background information about the trapeze.

"As you probably, know," he said, pointing up high in the nets, "a trapeze is a short horizontal bar hung by ropes or metal straps from a support. You've no doubt seen it at the circus. But there, you usually see the flying trapeze. There are other forms—static, spinning, swinging, as well as flying."

We were signed up for the flying kind.

Flying? I swallowed, looked up at the nets. A woman was swinging high above the ground, hanging from the trapeze by her arms, gaining momentum, going higher and higher until, poof, she let go and flew, somersaulting, whirling head over heels in the air, finally landing in the net below. Good God. Were we supposed to do that? My stomach hopped into my throat, splashed the morning's coffee back into my mouth.

Shane was still talking. Telling us about the flying trapeze. A French acrobat named Jules Leotard had invented it in his father's gym, over the swimming pool. Who the hell cared who'd invented it, let alone where? Then again, we were all wearing tight clingy garb obviously named for the guy. I'd never heard of him, but he was evidently very famous. Oh man. My stomach was still flipping. I eyed the ladder leading up to the platform. Was I the only one who felt physically ill? Were we seriously going to go ahead with this?

Jen stood to my right, unfazed, focusing on Shane, posing to display her surgically tightened tummy and enhanced bust. On my left, Becky glowed with anticipation, and Susan stood next to her, frowning in concentration, as if memorizing Shane's every word. Were they all crazy? What were we doing there, four forty-ish women with, except for Jen, our belly bulge and midriff flab? We weren't acrobats. We weren't even athletic. True, Susan had been on swim team in high school almost thirty years ago. But the rest of us? We sometimes went to the gym. Jen did occasional yoga. And I had zero upper body strength, had never been able to do two consecutive push-ups. Could barely even do one.

Shane talked on. Listed things we were going to do. In the next eighty minutes, we were going to learn to take off from the platform, to swing, to transfer to the catcher, Velda—apparently—the woman I'd seen swinging before, and finally, to drop to the net. Velda was up on a platform again. She was going to demonstrate the first moves we were going to learn. She held the trapeze, hopped off the platform, swung her legs up and back a few times, and finally dropped to the net.

As she dropped, so did I. My body caved and I bent forward, head on my knees. I smelled moist soil and sweet weeds. Sensed insects scampering in all directions around me. My gut lurched.

"You all right, Elle?" Becky asked.

Everyone looked at me.

"Fine. Just tired." What else could I say? That heights made me dizzy? That I felt sick and terrified and wanted to get in the car and speed away? That I'd spent the last few nights listening for prowlers and dreaming of my murdered principal? I got to my feet, asked if there was a lady's room nearby.

Shane smiled at the term, pointed out a row of portable toilets.

I had no choice. Took off toward them, stomach wrenching, I told myself that there had to be worse things than throwing up in a Porta-Potty, even though I couldn't imagine what they might be. As it turned out, I didn't make it there, got sick behind a bush.

When I emerged, Becky was waiting with a water bottle. Asking if I was all right.

I thanked her for the water, rinsed my mouth. Assured her, then the others, that I was fine. And except for being embarrassed, I was. I felt a lot better, well enough to join in some warm-up exercises and climb the ladder thirty feet or so up to the platform. Determined to be tough, I didn't look down. The whole way up, I kept my eyes on Jen's ankles and the prongs of the ladder. Finally, we crowded onto the platform. I clung to the rope fence, told myself that the breeze wouldn't blow me off. Took deep breaths. Told myself not to get dizzy. Wondered how nobody else had a problem being up there.

"Holy effing smokes." Jen gazed around. "Look at this goddamn view."

Susan moved to the very edge of the platform. "Wow. Must be incredible when the leaves turn."

Becky agreed. "We should come back in a few weeks. The leaves will be brilliant by then." She noticed me, tilted her head. "You look kind of green, Elle."

I forced a smile. "No, I'm fine."

Shane rubbed chalk onto his hands. Spoke quickly, vigorously, explaining what we were going to do. First, we were going to learn to take off. "When you're ready to swing off the platform, you say, 'Hup.' It's the signal that you're about to go."

"Hup," Jen and Susan echoed, grinning.

"Hup." Becky tugged my arm. Urging me to be more enthusiastic.

"Hup." My belly did a flip turn.

Shane took the trapeze off a hook, held it up. "This is your fly bar. You're going to chalk your hands and grip it like this." He demonstrated. "For the takeoff, you'll use three movements, just like Velda did. First, the force out. That's when you kick your legs forward to gain height. Next is the hollow. That's a neutral position, and it's followed by the sweep, which is when you kick your legs backwards. So. You move from force out to the hollow, the hollow to the sweep, and then you reverse. Sweep to hollow to force out. They're kind of the same moves as swinging in the playground."

"How do we stop?" The question came from me.

Everyone looked at me. Was it a stupid question?

Shane paused, as if the answer were obvious. "You slow down the moves and release into the net. Velda will help you climb out." He watched me. "Any more questions?"

No. Nobody else had questions. The four of us exchanged glances, chalked our hands. The others were pumped, ready to go. Jen asked if she could go first.

And she did. Graceful as a high diver, Jen cried out, "Hup," and swung off the platform, legs propelling her forward and back. Becky and Susan cheered. Even I managed to shout, "Go, Jen!"

Finally, the arc of her swing decreased and she let go of the bar, falling gracefully into the net. No smashed boobs. We clapped and hooted as Velda helped her to the ground.

Becky went next. She wasn't as lithe as Jen, but her movements were crisp and efficient. She swung high, didn't seem to want to stop. When she dropped to the net, my stomach leaped, heart fluttered. I looked at the ladder, considered climbing down.

"You go next, Elle," Susan offered.

She must have seen the panic in my eyes.

"If you feel well enough," she added. "Do you?"

She'd given me an out. I could claim to be sick. But I wasn't sick; I was scared.

I stalled. "Go ahead, Susan. I can wait."

"No, no," she insisted. "I want to go last."

She did? Shane held the bar out to me. I could still back out. But the ladder was steep. And I'd be descending alone. Oh God. I looked from the ladder to the trapeze, back to the ladder. Finally, I let go of the fence and took a wobbly step toward Shane. Grabbed his arm to steady myself. Shane took my hand off his arm and placed it on the trapeze. When I'd grabbed it with both hands, he nudged me to the edge of the platform. "Ready?" he asked.

Was he serious? Had he never witnessed raw terror before? Would I be the first student to have a heart attack midair? I could still back out.

But Shane had his hand on my back. "Got your grip?"

I nodded.

And when I didn't say, "Hup," he did.

In a heartbeat, I was off the platform, hanging on by my arms.

"Force out," Shane yelled.

My legs froze, refused to move. I dangled, swaying in the breeze. The ground beneath me zoomed away. Oh God.

"Kick," Susan shouted.

"Swing your legs!"

Voices screamed, telling me what to do.

My body became rigid, refused to move. How long had I been hanging there? *Okay, okay.* I closed my eyes. Told my legs to swing.

Nothing. They were stiff.

I dangled, tried again.

Swing. I concentrated. Bent my knees an inch or two, then relaxed them. The trapeze wiggled a little bit forward, a little bit back. I repeated the movement, trembling from head to toe.

Shane yelled again. "Raise your legs. Force out."

My shoulder joints burned. Fingers ached. Oh God. I couldn't hold on, was going to fall.

"Force out!" Shane repeated.

I couldn't hang on much longer. *Damn it, Elle,* I told myself. *Just do it.* I took a breath, closed my eyes, locked my knees, and shoved my feet up, then down. Bent my knees and kicked backwards. The trapeze responded. Swung forward and back. I repeated the movements, lifted my legs higher, felt the pressure shift in my shoulders. Susan and Shane, Jen and Becky—maybe

Velda—everyone was yelling, cheering. Air swirled in my face and the ground blurred. My body flew back and forth, up and down, the arc of my swing increasing.

Until, at the peak of a force out, my grip loosened, and I slipped off the bar. I lost hold and soared, swimming through air, trying to position myself to hit the net. Limbs flailing, I noticed a dog-shaped cloud in the sky, silence. And speed.

When I landed, I didn't feel pain right away. In fact, I didn't feel my left arm at all. Velda was there, tugging at me, working to free my arm from the netting. Shouting to Shane to call an ambulance. As she helped me off the net, I looked down at my shoulder, saw a bone-shaped lump jutting out below it, dislodged, in the wrong spot. Confused, I tried to move it back where it belonged. And white-hot pain exploded.

* * *

The doctor's name tag said Singh. "You're lucky," Dr. Singh told me.

Lucky? I clenched my jaw, trying not to wail, almost unable to hear her through the screaming of my shoulder. By what standard did she consider me lucky? If she'd said I was stupid, I'd have understood. After all, I'd jumped off a platform thirty-odd feet off the ground. That was stupid. But lucky?

She was explaining what she meant, but the pain screeched and hollered, and all I understood of her message was that my X-ray showed no fracture and no need for surgery. At that point I didn't care. Surgery would have been fine. Anything, even amputation. I just wanted the infernal pain to stop.

"I'm going to help you relax." Dr. Singh stuck me with a needle. Great way to relax somebody, jabbing them with sharp objects. But I was in no position to object, unable to move my arm, unable to think for the pain. Where were my friends? Shouldn't they be here, advocating for me? Then again, Susan hadn't taken her turn yet. Maybe they were still at circus school.

I leaned back, watched Dr. Singh's face. Her eyes were huge and warm, and they smiled at me, reassuring me while her hands reached out for my shoulder.

"I'm going to be as gentle as I can," she promised. "When I finish, you'll feel much better."

She manipulated my shoulder, maneuvering cartilage and bone. I winced. I gnashed my teeth.

"Take deep breaths." She spoke softly. "It won't be much longer."

And it wasn't. With a sharp actual pop, the bone slid back into the socket. Instantly, the pain subsided. I almost cried.

Dr. Singh smiled. "Better?"

I wanted to hug her, but she told me not to move my arm. To rest it in place with a sling and ice it for a few days, then gradually exercise it. She prescribed pain medication. A nurse placed my arm in a sling. And that was it. Presto. I was done.

Becky, Susan, and Jen were waiting in the lobby. When I walked in, they surrounded me, clucking and fussing.

"I'm so sorry." Becky grabbed my good arm. "It's all my fault. I shouldn't have suggested something so dangerous."

"I knew someone would get hurt," Jen said. "I thought it was going to be me."

"No, Jen. You were a natural," Becky told her. "Totally graceful."

Jen smiled. "I did look fucking hot up there, didn't I." It wasn't a question.

Susan started for the door. "I wonder how often stuff like this happens. They made us sign a liability waiver, but still, if they have a significant number of injuries—"

"I'm not suing them, Susan."

"Still. I'm just saying."

"Susan's right, though. The circus school should offer you some kind of compensation." Becky held onto my uninjured arm as we walked to the car. "I bet they'll at least offer us free lessons. Plus they owe us a makeup session."

Was she serious?

"I'm in," Jen agreed. "How about you, Elle? Want to try for the other shoulder?"

"I thought it was fun." Becky pouted. "Didn't anyone else? I mean, Elle, except for falling, didn't you like it?"

I opened my mouth. Remembered hanging in the air while the earth spun away.

"I liked it," Susan said. "And if I hadn't been so worried about Elle, I'd have liked it a lot more."

Wait. Had Susan gone ahead with her lesson after I'd been hurt? "So you guys finished the class while I was in the hospital?"

Susan unlocked the car, tossed her bag in. "Elle, think about it. I was up on the platform. To get to you, I could either climb down that rickety ladder or swing on the trapeze and drop. So guess which one I chose?"

They went on about how Shane had promised to show us four skills, but we'd been able to try one. How swinging had felt like flying. Their voices became a buzz of chatter as my pain medicine kicked in. Nothing hurt anymore. I floated among friends, mellow and relieved, lulled by the motion of the car. I'd dozed on the way to circus school, and I dozed on the way home.

* * *

Everyone came back to my house.

Jen went straight to the kitchen and opened the fridge. "WTF, Elle? How the hell do you live? There's nothing in here. No, I lied.

You have old cheese, mustard, and mayo. A perfect feast." She was always hungry, and hadn't eaten in hours.

I came into the kitchen, sat at the table. Told her there was peanut butter in the cupboard, bagels in the freezer.

She squinted as if she didn't understand.

I explained that I'd planned to go to the supermarket the other day after work but hadn't because of finding Mrs. Marshall. And it hit me that I hadn't thought about Mrs. Marshall or her murder for almost the whole day. Fear of heights and pain from a dislocated shoulder had completely absorbed my attention. Now that we were home, the murder shoved its way to the front of my mind again, upstaging all other topics.

"What about you?" Susan asked. She held a pencil and notepad, waiting.

What? Damn. Evidently, I'd missed something. I scrambled to cover my lapse. Um, what did she mean? Oh. They must have been talking about going back again to circus school, finishing the class. "No way I'm going anywhere near the place," I said. "But you guys go ahead."

Susan blinked. "What are you talking about?"

"She pulled an effing Elle," Jen said. "She has no idea what we're talking about."

"Well, who can blame her?" Becky took a seat beside me. "She's been through hell in the last couple days."

"Yes, and we all feel awful about it." Jen pushed her bangs aside. I noticed she'd broken a fingernail, probably on the trapeze. "But I need food."

Food? Oh. They hadn't been talking about circus school.

"Elle?" Jen pulled a box of graham crackers out of my cupboard. "How old are these?"

"Old." I'd bought them at the beginning of the summer, hoping to make s'mores.

"We're ordering Chinese." Susan hadn't moved. She waited, her pencil at the ready. "So far, we're getting General Tso's chicken, shrimp with broccoli, hot and sour soup." She watched me.

I added Moo Shu pork. She wrote it down and began to call in the order.

Now that I thought about it, I was hungry. Hadn't eaten much all day, and it was—I looked at the oven clock to check the time. Susan stood in the way, talking to the restaurant. Never mind, I'd check the time on my cell phone. But where was my bag? I'd had it in the hospital—had taken my insurance card out of it. Then what had I done with it? I had no idea.

"Where's my bag?"

"Shrimp and broccoli," Susan said. She pointed toward the hallway. Becky wouldn't let me get up, insisted on going for me.

I asked Jen what time it was.

She munched a graham cracker, glanced at the clock. "Almost five."

Five? Wow. The whole day was gone. Becky came back with my bag, and even though I already knew the time, I used my right arm to dig out my cell phone. I'd turned it off before circus school, as Shane had wanted no distracting ringtones.

"Anyone want one?" Jen offered graham crackers smeared with peanut butter.

Nobody did.

"How about some wine?" I suggested.

"Good idea." Susan headed to the wine rack in the study, Becky got glasses. Jen licked peanut butter off her fingers. I watched my phone screen come back to life. Telling me that I had nineteen messages and twenty-three missed calls. In one day.

I checked the messages, scanned names and numbers. Joyce. Detective Stiles. The assistant principal, Mr. Royal. Lots of numbers I didn't recognize. And Jerry. A whole bunch from Jerry.

* * *

I wished I hadn't turned the phone on. I considered turning it off again, pretending I hadn't seen the messages. But what if Detective Stiles had something important to tell me? And Jerry might have arranged more showings. I hadn't spoken to him yet about boundaries, needed to take care of that.

Susan opened a bottle of Pinot Noir. Talked about red not being right for chicken and fish, but who cared.

I turned my phone off. The messages could wait.

We drank wine until the food arrived. Talked about the day, began to laugh about it. About how it had at least been a memorable experience, even more than hot yoga. We talked about what we'd do next month, when it would be my turn to choose the adventure. Skydiving? Bungee jumping? We named activities we'd never want to try, argued about which would be the worst. And somehow, the conversation shifted, became not about the worst experiences we might have, but the worst we'd already had. And that morphed into the worst things we'd ever done.

Jen went first. "In high school, I was a regular little klepto."

"We know," Becky said. "You used to give us sweaters and lip gloss."

"I didn't know," Susan said. "Holy hell, Jen."

"I know. It's amazing I never got caught. If I saw it, I took it. I didn't even want half the stuff I grabbed. I guess it was just the thrill of getting away with it."

Susan ate with chopsticks. "You were an adolescent. Research shows that adolescents don't have the capacity to understand the effects of their actions."

"Bullshit." Jen swallowed shrimp. "I knew full well I could get caught."

"But you didn't really realize the full impact of that. You didn't grasp that what you were doing might change the course of your life, get you a criminal record, keep you out of college, erase your chance of meeting let alone marrying a guy like Norm, and so on. Teenagers' brains aren't fully developed."

"She's right," Becky said. "We learned about that in Child Development classes, remember, Elle?"

"Of course I'm right. I have full-fledged teenagers at home. Their cerebral cortexes work about a tenth of the time. Plus they're full of hormones that trigger the brain. Bottom line, they can't control their impulses or think out the potential consequences of risky behavior. That's why kids binge drink, have unprotected sex, do drugs, drive like maniacs, shoplift—whatever. They do stuff that only seems like a good idea if they don't think it through. And they can't think it through."

Like Ty? He'd been a teenager when he'd killed his father. "So when Ty committed murder, his brain wasn't developed yet?"

"Oh, shit, here we go," Jen moaned. "After what a bitch today was, I thought we'd for once have a nice pleasant dinner conversation—"

"But that would be like pretending there's no elephant on the table," Becky said.

Jen blinked at her. "What?"

"A pleasant conversation won't undo what's happened. The elephant's still on the table."

"Not the table," I said. "The room. I think the expression is 'there's an elephant in the room.'"

"Whatever," Becky said. "He's still here and we can't pretend he isn't."

"Who?" Jen asked. "The elephant?"

"The murder. Or Ty Evans." Becky put her chopsticks down. "Choose your elephant. We've been pretending all day that everything's just peachy. But it isn't. Mrs. Marshall was murdered. And Ty Evans is back, and he might have killed her."

"I don't think he did." I wasn't sure why I didn't. I just didn't. "But if he did kill her, he can't blame it on being a teenager. He's twenty-one now."

Susan had a wad of General Tso's in her mouth. "Technically, he's still an adolescent. The brain isn't developed until about age twenty-five." She swallowed some wine.

"Oh, bullshit," Jen said. "It wasn't his age that made him kill anyone. He killed his father because he effing hated him. And if he killed Mrs. Marshall, he must have effing hated her, too. Given the right motive, anyone can do something awful no matter what their age."

"You think everyone would cross any line?" Becky asked. "Including committing murder?"

"Hell yes. Any one of us, in certain situations, would commit murder."

"I wouldn't." Becky bristled.

I thought about it. "Of course you would, Becky," I said. "To defend your life? Your friends? Your students?"

"That's different," Becky said. "That's not murder. That's justified homicide, something like that."

"Not necessarily," Susan said. "Let's say you do it preemptively."

"Like Ty did," I added.

"Besides, don't act so above it, Becky. We've all, each one of us already crossed lines. Like I did with shoplifting. Not just lines of law. Sometimes just right and wrong. Remember what a bully I was in middle school? I was effing cruel. I kept that kid Melissa out of cheerleading squad. I wouldn't let anybody sit with her at lunch."

We all looked at her.

"Oh get off it. She was a bitch. Besides, I'm not the only one who did stuff like that. You've all done your own shit."

"I sure have," Susan said. "When I was just starting death penalty cases, I messed up. My client went to death row because I let him go on the stand."

"Was he innocent?" Becky asked.

"Doesn't matter. I don't know or want to know. But I never should have let him testify. And then there's Porter Thomas, accused of killing his girlfriend's mother. Deep down, I knew he was guilty as hell, but I got him off."

"That's your job. You're a defense attorney."

"Even so, as soon as the trial was over, he killed his girlfriend and her new boyfriend. It's my fault."

Wow. "You had to do your job, Susan," I told her.

"No, I think it is her fault if she got him off when she knew he was guilty." Jen diddled with her bangs.

"Don't make her feel worse, Jen." Becky's face was blotched with scarlet. "I've done bad stuff, too."

We stared at her, waiting.

"I dated a married man."

"Good God." Jen's eyes popped. "Sinful and shocking."

"Stuff it, Jen," Becky said. "I broke it off when I found out he was married, but still."

"What about Elle?" Jen grabbed the shrimp, refilled her plate. "She's been awfully silent."

I had been indeed. I was making a list of the worst things I'd done. Starting with the little boy Ty. If I hadn't been so concerned with maintaining a peaceful classroom and had worked with him more one-on-one, I might have helped him before he got so mad that he killed someone. And what about Mrs. Marshall? If I hadn't been so compelled to finish my Superstars poster and had stopped by her office a few minutes earlier, I might have prevented her murder. Not that her murder was my fault, but my compulsiveness might have indirectly allowed it. And what about Charlie? Granted, he'd provoked me, but I'd been awfully cruel to him, rejecting him outright, refusing to hear his apologies and promises. Even his death was partially my fault. Because if I hadn't been divorcing him, I'd have been with him the night he'd been killed so the murder couldn't have happened. I went on, tracing chains of effects back to their causes, identifying the roles I'd played in drastic outcomes.

When I tuned back in, our plates were empty. The others were still talking about the worst things they'd ever done. I thought about people I hadn't saved, about actions I should have or shouldn't have taken. I couldn't decide which was worst, there were too many contenders.

CHAPTER FOUR

The sling was inconvenient. For the next few days, managing with one arm, I was actually glad the opening of school had been delayed—I'd never have been able to teach. Anyone who's ever injured an arm must know how awkward the simplest tasks become. Dressing, undressing. Fixing coffee. Showering and drying off. Using the computer. Doing anything at all, especially while talking on the phone, which seemed to be all the time. I became expert at balancing the phone between my chin and my good shoulder while using my good arm to, for example, fold laundry or make tuna salad. Or pour myself a drink.

Which is what I did whenever Shane called. He called almost every day, checking on my shoulder, offering free classes to our group as soon as I was ready. He sounded nervous, no doubt worried about a lawsuit. I thanked him for his concern, assured him that I was fine and that Becky would reschedule the class. Didn't mention that I'd rather drink drain cleaner than go back on a trapeze.

I heard from Stiles, too. He had more questions about Mrs. Marshall. Did I know her family? Her husband, her friends? Anyone who disliked her? I answered no, no, and yes. As far as I knew, Sarah Lorraine Marshall had been disliked by pretty much everyone. He asked if I knew of former students other than Ty who might have had a grudge against her. The constant flow of questions pulled at me, a vacuum sucking details from my head. I had little information for him, and promised to call if I remembered anything even remotely relevant.

That week I'd expected to be in school, so I'd made no plans. Days passed sluggishly. Hotter than usual for September. I reviewed my lesson plans, my class list. I read novels, sent emails, clicked back and forth between daytime television shows. Met Becky and Jen for lunch a couple of times. Talked on the phone at least once a day with Jen and Susan, at least twice with Becky.

Jerry called repeatedly, his booming voice leaving messages about a property near mine that had just been listed, a comparable sale that had just fallen through, another that had been completed. Most of all, about the need for us to get together over dinner or drinks and discuss curb appeal or changes in the marketplace. Each message was pushier than the last.

I didn't take his calls. Didn't return them. I'd decided to lay down the law with him and define clear limits, but lacked the energy to deal with him or his predictable reaction and kept putting it off. Meantime, he continued to schedule showings. Almost daily, I had to leave the property from ten to eleven or twelve to one or five to six or whenever while potential buyers tramped through the house, commenting on my wall colors, my bathroom light fixtures, my closet space. My home.

Sometimes, watching the front door from across the street, waiting for a realtor and his clients to leave, I wondered how the house felt about being open for strangers, being up for sale. Could it sense that change was coming? Did it care? Of course it wouldn't care in the sense that people care, but in a more silent, nuanced way. Before Charlie and I had lived there, an old woman had owned the place. She'd raised her children there, been widowed there. Had still owned it when she'd died. When I'd first seen the house, I'd felt its stable, homey nature. It was warm like an embrace or fresh cookies. The memories of comfort and love held by its walls had been almost tangible.

But Charlie and I had added our own mix of memories. Betrayal. Lies. Murder. Had those memories altered the house? Could the people wandering its rooms sense lingering darkness and pain? Or did the house feign cheerfulness, putting on its best false face for visitors? Because, surely, homes were more than just walls and ceilings. They must take on the qualities, reflect something of the natures of those who dwell within their beams.

I thought about the house every time I left for a showing. I wondered if it was angry with me for leaving, or glad to get rid of me and my sadness. I never doubted that it had opinions. Or that it had a soul.

But even if it didn't, I couldn't allow Jerry to wander through at will. At the beginning of the week, I called a locksmith who said he'd come by to change my locks Tuesday at one. He didn't show at one. Or one thirty. I called him at about two. He said he'd been tied up, offered to come by Wednesday at one. Again, he didn't show. That night, I Googled locksmiths and wrote down a bunch of numbers. Called one and left a voice message.

Overall, the week passed quietly, without incident. A few times, mostly at night, the phone rang and, when I picked up, no one was there. But that was no big deal. Those calls sometimes happened to everyone.

* * *

Sunday was supposed to be the last day before school started. I'd left it open, planless, so I could relax and prepare for the semester's first day. But in fact, I'd had the whole week to prepare, so the day offered lots of free time. I began by grappling with uncertainty. I didn't know where I was going to live. Wasn't sure I could sell the house. Didn't know who'd killed Mrs. Marshall. Plus my shoulder was tender, so I was still relying on the sling part-time, pain medication occasionally. That morning, I sat at my kitchen table with a coffee mug, watching the stove clock until 8:17 became 8:18.

Maybe I'd call Becky. Good idea. We'd go shopping. Or see a movie. I got my phone, turned it on. Saw a staggering number of texts and voice messages. And before I could punch in Becky's number, as if the caller had been waiting for me, my ringtone sounded. A number I didn't recognize, but I answered anyway, the phone already in my hand.

"Elle Harrison?" The caller used my full name. Obviously a stranger.

"Yes." Why was I identifying myself to a stranger?

"Rory Reich from the *Inquirer*."

Oh God.

"I wonder if you'd answer a few questions regarding last week's murder at Logan Elementary. I understand you discovered the body—"

"I'm sorry," I began. "I can't talk about the crime."

"Understandably. I wouldn't ask you to. We're approaching this from the human side of the tragedy. We want to focus on your experience of finding your principal dead in the school. Your thoughts on school safety. And your memories of the deceased, Mrs. Marshall, the effect her death will have on you and the children because of the kind of person she was."

The kind of person she was? I recalled her yanking Ty by his shirt collar, hissing at him.

"I'm sorry." I clutched my phone. "I can't do this."

Rory Reich persisted until I interrupted him to wish him luck and pushed the END button. I sat for a moment, staring at the phone, wondering how much of my voice mail was from the media. No way was I going to talk to them. I didn't want the attention, had no desire to discuss the murder or Mrs. Marshall. I would call Becky, make a plan, escape for the day.

But my phone rang again.

Eight twenty-three a.m. On a Sunday. And I'd already had two calls.

This time it was Detective Stiles. He was sorry to call so early but wanted to catch me before I got busy. Once again, he asked if I'd remembered anything else about the murder. Anyone lingering around the administration office? Anyone leaving the area? What did I know about Stan the custodian? Had Mrs. Marshall mentioned any personal conflicts or worries? Was she an Eagles fan?

"Mrs. Marshall?"

"An Eagles cap was on the floor of her office."

Oh God. Had the killer dropped it? Because no way Mrs. Marshall would own it. I told him I had no idea what it was doing there, but I'd let him know if anything came to mind.

After the call, what came to mind was the hallway of Logan Elementary. I saw myself leaving my classroom late, after everyone else had gone. Following fluorescent lights down the hall. Seeing no one. I strained to remember. Had I noticed an unnatural quiet? A tension in the air? Had I had even the trace of an inkling of what waited in the principal's office?

No. Unless I counted the morning, when the building itself had seemed sinister. Had that been a premonition? Was there even such a thing?

I poured a second cup of coffee. Stood at the kitchen window, looking out at my little patio, staged with potted geraniums and a few Adirondack-styled chairs. Jerry's idea. Which reminded me I still had to call him.

Before I could, amazingly, the phone rang again. A news team from Channel 6 wanted to stop by for a short interview. Sorry, no, I told them. That wasn't going to happen. But another call followed and, before ten a.m., producers from all three major news stations had phoned for interviews. The timing of their calls confused me.

"Why are you calling now?" I asked one of them. "The murder happened more than a week ago."

"School reopens tomorrow." That was his explanation.

"So?"

"The public cares about what happened," he said. "We're committed—actually, we're obligated—to respond to their concerns and to focus on the implications of the murder, how the violent death of a school principal impacts students and the community."

He spoke in media babble. Apparently, the media—not just one, but all of the local news stations—shared his view of commitment and obligation.

I turned him down. In fact, I turned all of them down. That guy was persistent. He told me to think about it and called back a few minutes later to urge me to change my mind. Another one—I don't remember which channel she worked for—became outright aggressive.

"But, Elle." She used my first name. "You have to do this."

I did?

"If you don't, you'll be letting Mrs. Marshall down." She talked as if she'd known Mrs. Marshall personally, as if they'd been friends. "One of the best ways we can honor her memory is to tell people about her on our program. And, as the person who found her, you are vital to that tribute."

"I don't think so."

"Really? Interesting." Her voice lost its sweetness. "Most people are eager to appear with us. Those who aren't usually have something to hide. Do you, Mrs. Harrison?"

Mrs. Harrison? Not "Elle" anymore? Was she threatening me?

I hung up on her. Wondered if I'd be sorry. Of course I wouldn't be. I mean, what could she do? Declare on the air that second-grade teacher Elle Harrison had refused to appear on her show and actually hung up on her? That Mrs. Harrison had been uncooperative and impolite? Probably she wouldn't mention me. But if she did, what repercussions could there be? I didn't have time to think about it because my ringtone began again.

I glared at the phone. It was so small, looked harmless. But then, so did a hand grenade. It kept singing my ringtone. "We're caught in a trap. I can't walk out . . . because I love you too much, baby . . ." I considered tossing it out the window onto one of the knockoff Adirondacks. Instead, I answered it, deciding to change my ringtone. Elvis' "Suspicious Minds" was another leftover from my life with Charlie, the sound track for our marriage.

Caller ID told me Shane was calling. I didn't pick up. Wasn't ready to reschedule circus classes. But immediately, another call came through.

"Was it horrible, Elle, dear?" Joyce Huff used her most sympathetic tone. Kind of like fingernails on a chalkboard. "I would have called earlier, but my husband swept me off to Block Island for the week to get me away from the horror of it. Poor, poor Mrs. Marshall."

I told her I was busy, trying to end the call.

"But, sweetheart, rumors are flying, ghoulish ones, and I don't know how to respond. People are saying her face was mutilated. Ellen Gallagher said that her ears were cut off. Tell me that isn't true." She paused, waiting for me to respond.

"Which part?"

"Oh dear God, so it's true! What did they do to her?"

I assured her that when I saw her, Mrs. Marshall still had her ears.

"But they mutilated her face? My God. How?"

I told her I couldn't give details. That the police had asked me not to talk about it.

She went on, thrashing me with questions. Was it terribly bloody? How had the killer gotten into her office? Did I think Mrs. Marshall knew her killer? Who did I think had done it? Because she'd been thinking about that boy who'd just gotten out of jail. How the timing was simply too big a coincidence. How it very likely could have been him.

She went on until my phone beeped with another call and I managed to escape.

The calls went on all morning. Apparently the media had been contacting others who wanted to put a lid on what was being aired. I got worried calls from Assistant Principal Frank Royal, Superintendent Dr. James Higgins, school board president Philip Wang, and president of the PTA Evelyn Wright. Jen and Susan also called. So did my anonymous breather. I wondered if it was Jerry. Which reminded me again to call him.

But that would involve yet another conversation on the phone, and I was done with it. I left it on vibrate and went upstairs to get dressed, still using one arm. I struggled with my bra, perplexed by the avalanche of phone calls about Mrs. Marshall. I fastened the clasps in front and shimmied and twisted them around to the back, slid my right arm through the strap. Tried to lift my left arm to slide it through but, with each movement, my shoulder moaned and hurt, so I gave up, yanked the bra around, undid the clasps, and tossed it onto the bed. I pulled on a loose t-shirt and cutoffs, came downstairs. Found two new voice messages.

One was from Jerry, a reminder that he was showing the house at noon, which meant I had to be out from noon to one. The other was silence. No message, just a few seconds of quiet breathing.

* * *

By a quarter to twelve when the sun was nearly at its highest, I was out walking my neighborhood, the Fairmount section of Philadelphia. Heat shimmered off the asphalt on tight streets packed with parked cars. Rows of townhouses slumped as if melted together. An elderly man wearing a sweater and heavy wool pants hobbled along with his elderly dog. A glistening lithe man jogged by, and a woman bicycled around me, calling out, "On your left" too late for me to figure out which side she meant. I looked around as she whooshed by and thought I saw people a few yards behind me. But when I turned, no one was there.

By the time I got to Kelly Drive, sweat was trickling down my midriff, and my shoulder bothered me. I hadn't worn the sling both because of the heat and because I was determined to begin using my arm before school started, which was the very next day. Anyway, my left shoulder ached, I was dripping sweat, and I couldn't go home for an hour. But walking was a relief. I focused on moving through humid, smothering air. On people passing by. On the present moment, nothing else. At the Museum of Art, I watched eager tourists line up to take selfies with the Rocky statue, and maniacs running up and down the museum steps under the midday sun. At Lloyd Hall, I saw dancers on roller blades, surrey riders, families snacking on the patio. Was I the only one sweltering? The heat weighed on me, slowed my body and mind. I wondered about all those marches in history where people were forced to walk themselves to death. Were they Native

Americans? Prisoners of war? If it weren't so hot, I'd remember, but my thoughts evaporated before I could reach them. I trudged past Boathouse Row and then along the Schuylkill. Its shady path didn't offer much relief. I stood watching the river, rowers slicing the water with their long, thin sculls. Was it cooler on the water? Did the rowers feel even the slightest hint of a breeze? I smeared sweat across my forehead. Checked my cell phone for the time. Refused to look for messages.

Forty minutes left.

In forty minutes, I'd have heat stroke. I'd be like those dehydrated apples they sold in the grocery. Enough walking. I'd go to Lloyd Hall, buy a cold drink, sit in the shade. I turned around to go back. Someone a few yards ahead darted into the bushes.

Wait. Could someone be following me?

I stopped in the middle of the path, shivered despite the heat. Reasoned with myself. Even if I'd seen someone dart into the bushes, why should I assume that the darting had anything to do with me? The person might have darted for any number of reasons—to catch a ball, for example. I tried but couldn't think of another reason. Besides, I was probably mistaken. No one was likely to be darting anywhere in this ninety-plus-degree weather from hell. More likely, the bushes had been disturbed by a startled squirrel or pigeon. I walked a few careful steps, passing those bushes, looking into them. No one huddled there. Not a pigeon or a dog. Not a squirrel.

But so what? Clearly, no one was following me. Why would anyone follow a sweaty fortyish-year-old woman with a not entirely slim figure?

Stupid question. Obviously, it was because of the murder. Because the media had named me, had announced that I was the one who'd found the body, had alerted the killer to the identity of a possible eyewitness named Elle Harrison.

So the killer knew who I was. Was that who was following me? Was he coming for me? I looked around. Was that guy with the fishing pole looking my way? Was his pole just a prop? How about that jogger? Hadn't he run past me a few minutes ago? Why was he coming back?

My right hand grabbed my left elbow. What an easy target I was. I was alone in the middle of a crowded path, vulnerable to passing bikes and streams of pedestrians. I did a 360, scanning the area, looking for a killer. The couple seated in the sculpture garden. The family in their rented surrey. Men and women, together and alone, walking and running and riding and sitting. Were any of them killers? What was I actually looking for? What did a killer look like?

Eventually, I convinced myself that the murderer wasn't following me down Kelly Drive. That, even though the news media reported that I'd found Mrs. Marshall, the killer had no reason to think that I'd seen him. I was perfectly safe. To celebrate, I went to Lloyd Hall and ordered a strawberry smoothie. Sat under an umbrella, watching geese waddle along the riverbank. When the air stirred, I held still, savoring the breeze, which, in an eye blink, was gone. A family arrived at the table next to me with a hot, red-faced toddler and a baby, both crying.

I checked the time again. A quarter to one. The showing should be almost over. I could head for home. I waited at the stoplight along Kelly Drive. Cars whizzed by. A woman came up to the curb, brushed against my arm. She stood too close, especially in the heat. I stepped away from her and, the moment I did, she took off, flying into the street, making a solid thunk against a Range Rover. And a softer crunch under its wheels.

Brakes screeched. The Range Rover swerved over the curb, onto the grass, scraping a tree trunk before stopping. Cars behind it stopped, but the other lane kept moving, horns honking, drivers annoyed that with traffic slowing, they might not make it through the light before it turned red again.

I didn't move, stared at the mass of legs and arms and bloody flesh that had just been the woman standing next to me. Why had she jumped in front of a speeding car?

A crowd was gathering, gaping, commenting. A man in running shorts rushed to the victim, felt her wrist, her throat. I wanted to shield her from everyone, felt protective.

"What happened?" someone asked.

"That car over there hit her."

"Was she crossing against the light?"

"The way those cars speed around that curve it's amazing more people don't get hit."

"Who is she?"

The man stood and shook his head, as if pronouncing the patient dead.

"Do you know her?" Someone put a hand on my arm, offered me a tissue.

A tissue? The woman's face was wrinkled and kind. She wore a flowered dress, smelled like Shalimar, too heavy a scent for such a hot day. "It's all right," she told me. "Don't cry."

I wasn't crying. Was I?

"Was she your sister?"

I touched my face. It was wet, not just with sweat. I took the tissue, thanked her. Shook my head, no. She wasn't my sister. Why would she ask that?

Someone else—the guy in running shorts—asked me who she was.

Me? Why would he think I knew? I looked at her again.

She'd been about my size, wearing a gray t-shirt and blue shorts kind of like mine. She'd had dark hair, cut shorter than mine. Did others think we looked alike?

"Oh God." A woman moaned. A girl, really. She stepped close to me, stared at the body, holding car keys. Repeated "Oh God," over and over, louder and louder. "It wasn't my fault. I swear, she jumped in front of my car, and I couldn't stop. I couldn't." She turned to the people in the crowd, one at a time, horror radiating from her eyes. Her hands clawing at her face.

"You're right." My voice sounded hoarse. "I saw it. It wasn't your fault."

She spun around to face me, met my eyes. Repeated what I'd said. "She saw it. It wasn't my fault." Her eyes screamed that she'd just killed a woman. That, her fault or not, she would never be the same.

Sirens sounded.

"Of course it wasn't your fault, dear," the flowery dress woman said. "I was right over there, and I saw it, too. At first, I thought he was going to push her." She pointed my way.

I looked around. No one was behind me. No question, I was the one she was pointing at.

"But it was the woman next to her. He shoved her right in front of that car. I saw him, just like this." She mimicked the shove, hands open, flabby arms extended.

"Who are you talking about?" someone asked. "Who did it?"

"Where is he? Did you see where he went?"

"You must have seen him," Flowery Dress insisted. "He was right here. He has long hair, light colored. And he's wearing baggy clothes."

"I saw a guy with long hair," a woman said.

"See? That was him!"

They spun in circles, searching for the guy with long hair.

The sirens got louder. The bereft driver wailed. Horns honked. Leaves shuddered above us as the breeze picked up, and I shivered, scanning the crowd for a killer. The woman who'd been standing beside me lay silent and broken on the road, her gray t-shirt smudged and bloodied.

* * *

Another violent death. This time I didn't know the victim. But for the second time in nine days, I was talking to police, answering questions.

The officer's name was Wilson. He was young, early twenties. His hat, too large for his head, hung over his eyebrows.

I stood under a sycamore tree, answering his questions. No, I didn't know the woman. No, I had no idea why she'd flown in front of the car, hadn't seen anyone behind her.

"Do you have any idea why someone might want to push you in front of a car?"

"Me?" Apparently he'd talked to the woman in the flowery dress. "No."

"Other witnesses saw a man push her." Wilson's face was flushed. Was he new to the cop business? Was this his first fatality? "One said that the man had been aiming for you, but the victim got in the way."

I shook my head. Knew nothing about it.

"Ma'am." Officer Wilson lowered his eyes. "The dead lady. Do you recognize her?"

No, I didn't.

"She's dressed almost the same as you. Her hair's fixed like yours."

I glanced at her. She was still in the street, surrounded by cops and a guy from the coroner's office. Again, I heard the thunk of the collision.

Oh man. Maybe Flowery Dress was right. Maybe someone had intended to push me into traffic and gotten mixed up, accidentally pushed the wrong woman. The killer—had he followed me on my walk, hoping to eliminate the only possible witness to Mrs. Marshall's murder? I looked again at the dead woman. Her body morphed into Mrs. Marshall's, and she turned to me, beaming her blood-drenched clown grin. I shuddered. Were the deaths related? Did the killer know he'd pushed the wrong woman? Because if he did, he might come back—

"Ma'am?" Officer Wilson watched me.

What? Oh damn. I must have missed a question. "Sorry."

He eyed me. "Why don't we sit? You look a little pale."

He looked around for a bench, didn't see one, led me to the curb. We sat. Around us, lights flashed from police cars, ambulances, a coroner's wagon, a camera crew. A crowd chattered, pointed, gawked. Officers moved spectators back, separating them from witnesses. People craned their necks to see the dead woman. The driver stopped wailing. She sat at the back of an open ambulance, wearing a blanket and a dazed expression. Someone—an EMT—handed me a water bottle. My hands shook as I opened it. I took a sip.

"Feeling better?" Office Wilson asked.

I nodded. It seemed to be the appropriate answer.

"So. Let's try again. Do you have any idea why someone might want to harm you?"

"No." The answer came out automatically, reflexively. And I'm not sure he heard it because he stood, greeting someone. I turned.

Detective Stiles stood behind me.

Once again, Detective Stiles questioned me about a homicide. I told him what I'd told Officer Wilson, that I hadn't seen anyone push the woman. But I still wondered about what Flowery Dress said. What if the killer had been aiming for me, not for the dead woman? What if he was Mrs. Marshall's murderer and thought I could identify him? Was he following me, waiting for a chance to eliminate the threat? I looked around, scanned faces in the crowd.

If he was there, I couldn't tell. No one looked familiar, and none of the men had long hair. No one was looking my way. All eyes were on the body being zipped into a coroner's bag. No, the two deaths were most likely unrelated. Coincidence. I repeated that word to myself like a mantra until the dark red pool glimmering on the asphalt became Mrs. Marshall's blood-soaked blouse. I closed my eyes, hugging myself. And saw my living room carpet.

Someone had walked on my carpet, making footprints in the pile. Had those shoe prints been not Jerry's, but the killer's? Had he been in my house? Was he playing with me? Stalking me?

"Mrs. Harrison?" I'd slipped away again, pulled another Elle. Detective Stiles had stepped away without my noticing. He joined me again at the curb, studied me. His eyes were a disarming shade of blue. He had new information. The woman had been identified. She was a dental hygienist. Forty-one years old. Lived nearby on Green Street. Her name was Patsy Olsen. He listed each fact separately, watching for my reaction. Finding none. I hadn't known her. And I hadn't seen what happened leading up to the collision.

I heard the thunk of impact, watched the wheels roll over her.

"Mrs. Harrison?"

Damn. I'd missed what he'd said.

"It's important."

What?

"Even if I'm wrong and there's no connection, it's best to err on the side of caution."

I nodded. Of course it was.

"Frankly, from behind, it would have been difficult to tell the two of you apart."

The two of us. Me and Patsy Olsen.

"And with your connection to the Marshall case, I'm tempted to think Patsy Olsen was an unlucky bystander. And that you were the intended victim."

So it was true? Someone had tried to kill me. And Patsy Olsen, dental hygienist, was dead because she'd happened to stand beside me, wearing blue shorts and a gray t-shirt.

Detective Stiles helped me to my feet. His arm felt sturdy. I didn't want to let go of it. But I assured him that I was fine, set to go. I nodded when he reminded me that he had no proof for his theory, again when he advised me to take precautions nonetheless. I kept nodding when he told me to be alone as little as possible, even when he said that I could go and that he'd be in touch. When he went to talk to other witnesses, my head was still bobbing.

I walked across the street, passing parked police cars. Officer Wilson lifted his hand in a wave. When I looked back, Detective Stiles was standing with Flowery Dress, taking notes.

* * *

All the way home, I repeated Stiles' warnings. I might have been the intended victim. I kept looking over my shoulder to make sure no one was following me. I slowed at corners, peered around hedges or brick walls to see if anyone lay in wait. And when I got home, I jammed the key in the lock, rushed inside, slammed the door behind me, bolted it, and headed for the living room. I sank onto my sofa, sorting through my jangled thoughts.

That poor woman. Patsy Olsen. Poof—gone.

Was it supposed to have been me? Had someone—a guy with long hair—pushed her by mistake, aiming for me? Was he the same person who'd killed Mrs. Marshall?

My hands covered my eyes, and I leaned back against the cushions. Replayed the moments before and after I'd found Mrs. Marshall's body. I hadn't seen anyone. Wouldn't know the killer if he was standing next to me. How could he think I could identify him? He simply plain out couldn't. Which meant he'd have no reason to come after me.

Which meant that the two deaths were completely unrelated.

And that Stiles' theory was just plain wrong.

Fine. So why didn't I feel better?

I chewed a hangnail. I needed to get back into my life. Maybe make some coffee. Maybe have something to eat. Maybe call Susan or Becky.

But I sat, unmoving. Hearing thunks. Seeing crushed limbs, puddled blood.

I sat. Stared at the carpet, the indentations where people had walked during the showing.

And boom, it hit me: even if the two murders were unrelated, I wasn't necessarily out of danger. Mrs. Marshall's killer might not be after me. But someone pushed Patsy Olsen in front of a Land Rover, and a witness thought he'd been aiming for me.

A shiver slithered up my back, around my throat, down again.

But who would want to kill me? I had no enemies.

None that I knew of.

Unless it was the same person who'd come into my house uninvited and walked on my freshly vacuumed carpet, leaving indentations.

Jerry?

But no, Jerry couldn't have been the guy. He didn't have long hair.

Never mind. The very fact that I could suspect him meant it was time to sever our relationship. I needed to make sure he couldn't get into the house and then fire him. But the locksmith had never called back. I had to call another one, change my locks, dispose of the lock box and of Jerry. In fact, I'd do part of it right then. I sat on my overstuffed sofa preparing a severance speech. Taking control. Spurred on by offending footprints from the day's showing. They lingered in my living room carpet like insults, like bruises. I had to vacuum, to erase them.

But first I'd deal with Jerry. I wouldn't accuse him of prowling or misusing the lock box key. I wouldn't even mention my suspicions. I would simply end it. "Our relationship isn't working for me," I would say. "I've decided to move on with another agent." I wouldn't defend my position or engage in discussion. I wouldn't let him coax me into giving him another chance. I would simply repeat my decision until he accepted it.

I practiced the speech until I was confident, and then I called his number.

He answered with a booming, "Hello."

"Jerry, it's Elle." I talked fast, spitting out my speech, not giving him a chance to respond. "Listen, our relationship isn't working for me. I've decided to move on—"

Jerry interrupted. "Leave your name and number. I'll get back to you."

I'd delivered a full half of my speech to his voice mail.

At the beep, I hung up. I sat for a moment, telling myself it was no big deal. I'd call back and fire him later. Meantime, I'd call another locksmith. Where had I left that list of numbers? I picked at my hangnail, heard a thunk, saw a crushed body on the street. Finally, I went to the utility closet, got my vacuum, took it to the living room. Began to erase the footprints in the carpet. Stopped when the phone rang.

It was Jerry.

My stomach did a quick flip. Why was Jerry calling? Never mind—didn't matter. I'd give him the speech and get rid of him. How did it start again? I scrambled to remember. Stood straight. Took a breath. Answered the phone.

"I'm glad you called," I told him, and I began. Said that I'd been thinking. Things weren't working out. I wasn't happy.

He cut me off. His voice was big, loud. Impossible to interrupt. He said that he was calling to reassure me. He'd sensed that I was discouraged, especially given the trauma of recent events. He talked about the housing market, the unpredictable nature of buyers. He reminded me of the shortcomings of my house, its dire need for a kitchen upgrade, its history as a crime scene. He claimed that he was the only realtor who understood the complexities of the place. That he was highly motivated, that he personally cared about my success and future. He promised to do better if I'd give him another chance.

I strained to remember my speech. What had I planned to say? How had I intended to counter his arguments? Oh, right—I would simply repeat myself. Insist that I was going to move on.

"Jerry, thanks," I began. "I understand what you're saying, but even so—"

"Great. That's great. You won't be disappointed, Elle. I mean it. I'm personally invested in this sale. It's not just another house to me. I consider you a close personal friend. That's why I'm calling. To reassure you. I have plans. I want to redo some staging and hold an open house. What do you say we talk about it over lunch?"

I explained that I wasn't up to it. That I was too upset about the car accident.

"What car accident?" He sounded alarmed.

I wasn't aware of crying, but tears poured down my face as I told him about Patsy Olsen and the Land Rover.

"Good God," he boomed. "Elle, what are you wearing?"

What?

"Go put on one of those pretty sundresses. I'll be there in ten minutes. I'm taking you for a drink. You need to be taken care of, after what you've been through."

Oh Lord. I told him no, that wasn't happening, but he persisted. "Come on, Elle. You'll feel better. Let me do this for you. Let go for once. I'll help you relax."

Somehow, I managed to make him understand that I wasn't going anywhere. When I got off the phone, I hadn't fired Jerry, but at least I'd avoided having a drink with him. I'd fired him next time we talked, though. And I'd get a locksmith.

I finished vacuuming, but didn't turn the vacuum off. I left it running while I sat on the sofa. Its motor was almost loud enough to drown out the repetitive deadly thunks, but not quite.

CHAPTER FIVE

Monday morning, school opened. And clearly, Mrs. Marshall wasn't around.

Dozens of children pressed against the front doors in a writhing, shapeless mass. Mrs. Marshall always had students line up quietly, in an orderly fashion according to grade and classroom. She'd hung signs for each classroom on the outside walls of the building, had upper-class monitors help organize the lines. But today there were no signs, no monitors, no lines. Children crowded around the doors in a noisy, swelling mob. Mr. Royal stood on the steps red-faced and frantic, waving his arms and shouting, attempting to get kids to follow directions.

"People!" His voice was lost in the din. "People!"

Kids shrieked and pushed. Some laughed. Some cried. None seemed to notice him. I gaped, readying myself. Teachers would have to rescue him.

I parked, got out of my car.

And saw Joyce Huff rushing my way. She grabbed my hand, led me away from the school toward the playground.

"Joyce?"

She pointed past the swings to the ball field. The Jolly Jack's ice cream truck was parked there. At 8:35 in the morning, it was already open for business. Parked on the far end of the ball field, on school property. Mrs. Marshall had made it repeatedly and abundantly clear to the ice cream man that he couldn't park his truck there. That he had to keep it off school grounds. Now that she was dead, as if to spite her, Duncan Girard—that was the ice cream man's name—had parked his truck right where she'd told him not to, at the end of the playground.

"He has nerve. How dare he take advantage of Mrs. Marshall's death to defy school policy!" Joyce ranted. She dragged me by the arm.

"Joyce, wait. Did you see all the kids at the front door?" I looked over my shoulder, back at the school. "Mr. Royal's there alone—"

"Serves him right." She marched on. "I sent him a detailed plan for opening day and he ignored it. Let him sweat."

I explained that the children needed our help, but Joyce was unmoved, focused solely on the Jolly Jack's Frozen Treats truck. "This will only take a minute. Just help me for one minute, will you?" I wasn't wearing the sling. My shoulder was still tender, and I worried she'd pull my arm too hard as she led me past the slides, the climbing wall, the swings. Onto the ball field.

"Duncan Girard, what do you think you're doing?" she called from fifty yards. "You ought to be ashamed, using the principal's death as an opportunity to break school rules. Do you have no respect?"

I was right beside her, and her shrill shouts ripped at my eardrums. As she ran the last several yards to the truck, I yanked my arm from her grasp, triggering a pang in my shoulder. Joyce banged on the hood of the truck.

"Come on out here, Duncan."

Before she finished saying his name, he stepped out from the rear of the truck, smiling.

The smile was dazzling. His teeth gleamed white. His eyes twinkled brown. His shoulders stretched the seams of his Jolly

Jack's shirt. He nodded at Joyce, then at me. I'd heard about Duncan Girard from Mrs. Marshall and other teachers, but I'd never met him. He looked into my eyes so directly that my face heated up.

Joyce told him that if his truck wasn't gone in ten minutes, she'd call the police.

Duncan's smile didn't fade, but his gaze moved past us. "Yo, Brodsky. That you? You grew a foot. How was your summer?" I turned. Saw Dennis Brodsky, a fifth grader, much taller than I remembered, walking toward the school. He yelled back that his summer had sucked.

Duncan laughed. "Come by later. I'll give you a free water ice."

Dennis waved, shouted, "Sweet!"

Joyce sputtered. "I meant what I said. I'll have the police here. You have no business on school property!"

"Easy, lady. Don't get your panties in a knot." Duncan eyed her, head to toe. Then, still speaking to her, he turned to look at me. "You'd think I was a damn drug dealer the way you're carrying on. But the fact is, I have every right to be here. It's a public street."

"You're in defiance of school policy—"

"Yo—Shelly! Linda!"

Two fourth-grade girls walked past, giggling and waving when he called their names. "Hi, Duncan."

"Stop by later. Free water ice today!"

"You see how he acts with them?" Joyce turned to me. "Ingratiating himself to them. Gaining their trust."

I frowned, didn't want to take part in Joyce's squabble. "I'm heading back to the school."

"No, listen to me." She grabbed my wrist, whispered urgently. "Elle. That's what pedophiles do. Oh my God. That explains everything. I bet he's a pedophile."

What? "Joyce, stop. You don't know—"

"What did you say?" Duncan Girard stepped over to Joyce, leaned down, and put his nose into her face. "I'm a what? I heard you. Now, say that to my face." His voice was a growl.

Joyce's mouth opened. He took hold of her shoulders.

"Okay, that's enough." I sounded puny. "Let go of her."

He held on, breathed into her eyes so that she kept blinking. "Don't go making accusations about me, ma'am. In fact, don't even say my name out loud. Ever. You get that?"

I grabbed his arm, tried to pull it off of Joyce. But my left arm had no strength, and his was steely and muscled. Indifferent to my efforts. It didn't budge, held onto her, stared into her eyes.

"Tell me what she said about me." He gave Joyce a shake. Another.

"Who?" Joyce's eyes bulged.

"You know who," Duncan scoffed. "Obviously, she said something to you. Bitch was after my blood. I thought I was finally done with all the hassles and accusations."

Bitch? Finally done? Wait—was he talking about Mrs. Marshall? I knew they'd had words, but not that she'd accused him of anything, let alone of pedophilia. Oh Lord. Was that why she'd wanted his truck moved away from school property?

I kept pulling his left arm, to no avail.

"Whatever that witch told you was bull. She had no proof—no complaints. Not one reason to think anything happened—"

Joyce was ashen, trembling in his hands. I thought she might faint.

"—and I warned her to shut her face." He paused, glaring first at Joyce, then at me. "Now she's gone, and do I get left alone? Even for a day? No. First day back, you two start hounding me." He released Joyce so roughly that she almost fell over.

"Hey, Duncan!" A bunch of kids ran over to the truck. "Guess what? We got an extra week of vacation!"

"Because of our principal. Know what happened? She got killed."

"Yeah. Someone chopped her to pieces."

Duncan beamed an instant smile, reached out and tousled a redheaded kid's hair, welcomed them all back to school, said that, yes, he'd heard about their principal, and offered them free water ice. As he talked to them, his eyes remained on Joyce and me, cold as the coldest of Jolly Jack's frozen treats.

* * *

Joyce trembled all the way across the ball field. "I'm calling the police."

I suggested that we go to the teachers' lounge and have a cup of hot tea, collect ourselves. We still had a few minutes before school started.

"He assaulted me. You saw it—and did you hear what he said about Mrs. Marshall? He did it, Elle. I tell you. He's the one. He killed her. She found out he'd been molesting the children, and he killed her so she wouldn't reveal the truth—" She slipped on some loose gravel near the swings, fell flat onto her butt.

"Joyce!" I helped her up. "Are you okay?"

Her face was crimson, body shaking. She brushed dirt off her dress, bit her lips, checked her beehive for loose hairs. Her chin was quivering, her eyes filling. "Elle dear, did you see the way he strong-armed me?"

I nodded, yes, I had. "Well, that was after you called him a pedophile."

"Of course it was. What pedophile wants to be exposed?"

"Joyce," I began. "We don't actually know—"

But she continued as if I hadn't spoken, repeating her theory. "And the way he talked about Mrs. Marshall? The names he called her? He all but confessed to killing her. She found out about him, and that's why he did it. I know I'm right. That pervert needs to be stopped!"

The ten-minute bell rang. I looked across the playground to the front of the building. Students still flocked in disorder around the front door. Mr. Royal still stood on the steps, waving his arms and shouting for attention. Several teachers made their way through the crowd, attempting to sort students into groups by grade.

Joyce recovered from her fall, and we walked back. She continued to rant, insisting that Duncan Girard shouldn't be allowed anywhere near children, that the police needed to be informed of his pedophilia. That he was the one who'd killed Mrs. Marshall.

As we approached the building, half a dozen cheerful children ran our way. Former students greeting us, chattering, grinning. Telling us what room they were in this year, who their new teachers were.

Joyce and I welcomed them, patted heads, herded them back toward the school. As we approached the other teachers who were trying to organize the pint-sized mob, Joyce once again took hold of my arm, aggravating my sore shoulder.

"Elle?" She looked even paler than before. "What if I'm right?"

I freed my arm from her grasp, rubbed my shoulder. "Joyce, please listen. He was rude and out of line, but we have no reason to think—"

"Elle, stop defending the brute. Think about it." She stepped close, put her mouth to my ear. "If Duncan Girard killed Mrs. Marshall to keep her quiet, what do you think he'll do to quiet us?"

Our eyes met. Joyce's looked feverish. As I thought about the answer to her question, a wave of excited, noisy children engulfed her. Her eyes didn't leave mine, even as they swept her away toward the school.

* * *

What Joyce said jarred me, but I didn't have time to dwell on Duncan Girard. Twenty-three seven-year-olds demanded my attention. They swarmed into the classroom where I helped them find their desks, locate their cubbies, and store their lunches. We introduced ourselves as I took attendance, and each child talked a little about his or her summer. I told them about the exciting year they would have, what we were going to study in class, what our daily schedule would look like. I led them through the different sections of the classroom: computer tables, cozy reading corner, writing and art tables. I answered questions, tried to memorize names. Noticed Seth Evans. Ty's brother was short for his age, thin and dark-eyed.

I passed out textbooks and workbooks, helped the children write their names in each. In a heartbeat, it was time for gym class, and they lined up. I marched them single file to the gymnasium. As we passed the main office, a boy said, "That's where Mrs. Marshall got killed."

Another boy was doubtful. "How do you know?"

"Because. My brother Trevor told me."

"Shh," I told them.

"Is there blood? Can you see?"

A few children stepped out of line to find out and pressed their noses against the glass windows outside the office.

"Get back in line," I said.

"But how does your brother know?"

"He just does."

"Children." I put my finger over my lips. "No talking in the hallway."

They obeyed, eyeing me warily. Not yet sure how strict I was. But even though they were silent, their curiosity persisted, hummed in the air like electricity. I decided to address it and talk about what had happened openly. After all, the loss of Mrs. Marshall was theirs as much as anyone's. Their questions and worries needed to be addressed.

So, after a few games of dodgeball with Mr. Lyons, we returned to room 2B. And I plunged right in.

"On the way to gym, some of you were talking about Mrs. Marshall."

The room fell silent. All eyes turned to me. A girl with blond hair—the name on her desk was Elana—gasped and covered her mouth as if I'd uttered an unmentionable word.

"As you know, something terrible happened, and she's no longer with us."

"She was killed," Trevor's little brother said. "Somebody killed her."

Forty-six eyes watched to see how I would respond. My credibility was at stake. If I tried to deny or soften the truth, they'd never trust me. But if I gave too many gory details, I'd scare them. And creep them out.

"She was killed, yes. And it's very sad."

"Who killed her?" "Was she really cut into little pieces?" "How come she got killed?" "Will the killer come back and kill somebody else?"

Questions poured. I was honest with them. I explained that I didn't have the answers, but that the police were working hard to find the killer, and that the police, the other teachers, Mr. Royal, and I would all make sure they were safe at school.

They weren't satisfied.

"What if he comes back and shoots us?" "He doesn't shoot people. He cuts them." "I heard Mrs. Marshall's head was chopped off." "I want to go home." "There was a shooter at a school and he killed kids. I saw it on TV."

The class was flying out of control, fast. The little girl named Elana was crying, and seeing her cry, a girl named Stella began crying, too.

"Okay. Everybody." I clapped my hands, interrupting the comments and tears. "You have nothing to worry about. Nobody wants to hurt you. The killer was angry with Mrs. Marshall, not anybody else."

They watched me, clearly doubted what I said. Well, they should have doubted it. I wasn't sure anything I said was true.

"So here's what we're going to do." I assigned an art project. Asked them to draw pictures of their families, a task that would allow them to express themselves and focus on something other than the murder.

I passed out construction paper and crayons to those who'd forgotten to bring their own. As they worked, I tried to concentrate on the moment, not on Mrs. Marshall's murder or Joyce's encounter with Duncan Girard. I watched my students lean over their work, concentrating and creating. I heard them breathe and grunt and sneeze and cough, smelled the energy of children.

I collected the pictures at lunchtime and looked through them while the kids were in the cafeteria. Some were more detailed, more skillfully drawn than others. Some showed a mom and dad, a sister or brother, a pet or two. Some showed just mom and children. One showed two moms, a couple of dads, and a gaggle of siblings—I counted seven. Some had trees and flowers in front of the house. Puffy clouds and the sun in the sky. The pictures seemed happy enough, except for one that was different. It showed the outline of a house, but the outline wasn't colored in. It was covered with jagged slashes, all of them bright red.

* * *

Seth's name was scrawled on the back.

I wasn't a psychologist, but the picture didn't demand one. Clearly, the red slashes represented violence and rage. Maybe even blood. Was Seth that angry? He was only seven years old. How could he have so much fury? I heard Joyce insist, "Some children are just bad seed."

No, I didn't accept that. Maybe Seth's picture wasn't about his anger. Maybe it was about his distress at Mrs. Marshall's murder. After all, hers hadn't been Seth's first brush with violent death. He'd been just a baby when Ty had stabbed their father, but the death and its aftermath would have affected him deeply. The drawing might reflect Seth's collective trauma.

For the rest of the day, I kept an eye on him. Paid attention to his interactions with the other children. His apparent mood.

Seth seemed quiet, a little shy. But he completed his arithmetic exercise, concentrated on the computer. Read out loud when called on.

Still, his drawing disturbed me. At the end of the day, while fifth-grade hall monitors led the class out to waiting parents and buses, I called him aside.

"Seth." I stooped to match his height. "So how was your first day of second grade?"

"Good." He avoided my eyes. Looked uncomfortable.

"I taught your sister and brother. Did you know that?"

"Yes." He fidgeted, a bird trapped in my hand.

I waited a moment, not sure how to approach my concerns, not wanting to make him even more self-conscious. "So how are they? Ty and Katie."

His eyes moved from the wall to me, back to the wall. "Good."

"And your mom?" I pictured her screaming at Mrs. Marshall for picking on Ty.

"Good."

Good and good. "That's good." I nodded, realized I couldn't talk to him about his drawing yet. He didn't know or trust me enough. I'd have to wait, assign more drawings, see if the imagery repeated.

"Katie's going to take me home from school. I'm supposed to meet her." He volunteered that information. Spoke without prodding. Maybe he was beginning to relax?

"Good." That word again.

"Mrs. Harrison!"

I swiveled, stood. Three girls hurried toward us. If I hadn't known that the blond one was Katie, I wouldn't have recognized her, but there she was, now fifteen. And still with her two best pals—the three had been inseparable even in second grade—kind of like Jen, Becky, and me. They gathered around me for hugs, asking how I'd been, saying that the classroom hadn't changed, which startled me, since I'd worked so hard to innovate my decorations.

"You've still got the cozy corner. That was my favorite," Katie's friend said.

"Yeah, Maggie. You always liked the pillows."

Maggie—of course, that was her name. I remembered now. Last name was Floyd. She'd been and still seemed to be the ringleader of the three, had strong bones, a blunt nose, red hair cropped short. A tough, impulsive nature. I remembered her as bossy, always nearby when someone fell or started crying. And the other one's name was Trish. Even in second grade, Trish had had a tired, worn-down look, as if she'd dabbled too deeply in alcohol or drugs. As if, as a child, she'd already been deeply, irreversibly disappointed.

"And oh my God, the colors. Remember that?" Trish scanned the room. "Neon everything."

Katie nodded, laughing. "And everything clashes."

Damn. I eyed my classroom. Heard Joyce declare, "See what I mean?" Criticism.

"I loved all the craziness," Maggie said. "And look—she's still got that bulletin board where you can hang whatever you want."

"You used to put up your poems, Trish."

"Right. You were the poet laureate of Room 2B," Katie teased.

"Your poems were very good," I told her.

"Really? You remember them?"

"Of course." Well, sort of. Maybe. Not really. "Are you still writing?"

She shrugged, glanced at Katie. "Not so much."

Seth stood silent, watching his sister. She ignored him, started telling me about high school. How she was going to try out for junior varsity cheerleading. Maggie and Trish chimed in that they were, too.

"How cool will it be if we all make it? We'll rule the squad."

They agreed, giggled. Declared that they'd definitely all make it. That together, they were unstoppable.

Of the three, Katie was actually the unstoppable one. Unlike the others, she had a glow, a lightness. A contagious grin. I suspected that, given her family history, she clung to the other girls for security. And that they clung to her, holding her back.

Katie finally glanced down at Seth. "So. How was your day, squirt?"

"Good," he said. He stood stiff and straight, like a small soldier.

Katie smiled, showed straight shiny teeth. "He's shy," she told me. "But once he gets comfortable, he doesn't shut up." She nudged him. He stared at the floor, turning crimson.

"Nice to see you, girls." I ushered them out the door. Told them I hoped they'd stop by again.

"Oh, we will. At least, I will. I'll be here every day to escort Prince Seth home." Beaming another smile my way, Katie adjusted her backpack and set off with her chattering girlfriends, leaving Seth to trail behind.

* * *

I walked them a few steps down the hall, then went back to my classroom and sat at my desk to go over the next day's lesson plan. But instead, I sat alert. The air, the room felt altered. Uneasy.

My skin tingled. I put down my pencil, listening. Sensing that I wasn't alone.

But I'd been gone for only a few seconds. How could anyone have snuck in so quickly? Who could it be?

Maybe Duncan Girard. But no, he was outside giving away water ice. No. It wasn't him. Then who was it? And what did they want?

As if to answer, Mrs. Marshall's carved-up corpse popped to mind, smiling its grotesque grin.

Oh God. The killer? Was that who was there?

"Hello?" I reached behind me, grabbed my yardstick. "Is somebody here?"

No answer. Of course there was no answer. No one was there.

Except that I was sure someone was. Oh God. Maybe it was the guy with long hair, the one who'd pushed Patsy Olsen under a Land Rover.

"Who's there?" I stood behind my desk, scanning the room. No one was in the computer zone or the cozy reading corner. The writing and art tables were empty. Chairs sat upside down on desktops, making it easier for Stan to come in and sweep.

Stan. Was he lurking somewhere in the room, maybe near the cubbies?

"Stan? Is it you?"

No response. Why would Stan hide? Was he dangerous—had he killed Mrs. Marshall?

I edged toward the supply closet, yardstick raised, ready to strike, aware that it was flimsy, unlikely to protect me against an actual weapon. I should have grabbed something else. But what? The scissors were blunt-tipped. Maybe a stapler? Never mind. I wasn't going to staple an intruder. The yardstick was all I had, and I was prepared to swing it hard and run screaming for help. I took a breath, counted to three, and flung the closet door open.

Confronted stacks of textbooks, chalk boxes, and construction paper.

Okay. I was mistaken. On edge. Overly suspicious. Probably no one was there.

Even so, I headed to the cubbies, nearly tripped on a forgotten lunchbox. And found Ty Evans hunkering in the corner, clutching a pair of blunt-tipped scissors.

* * *

I recognized him instantly. "Oh God. Ty?"

He hadn't changed much since the trial. His hair was longer and he hadn't shaved. But he had the same feisty gray eyes, the same ready-to-run tension. Ty blinked rapidly at the names on the cubbies, at the ceiling, at anything but me.

"Did I scare you, Mrs. H? I didn't mean to."

Yes, he'd scared me. I was still scared, but didn't dare let on. I was a teacher in my own classroom, and I had to remain in charge. Frowning, I ordered myself to act calm, lowered my yardstick, and took away his scissors. "What were you planning to do with these?" I held them up, ran a finger over the harmless round tips. Ignored the memory of Mrs. Marshall's sliced grin.

Ty let out a single "Ha." A laugh?

"I'm serious, Ty."

"Well, obviously I couldn't do much. But they were the only weapon I could find."

Weapon? I swallowed. "Why would you need a weapon, Ty? What do you want? Why are you here?" I told myself to pivot and run, but my body was stuck. *Go*, my mind repeated. *You're maybe ten steps from the classroom door. If you don't trip again on the lunchbox, you might make it. Count to three and go.*

Wait, I argued with myself. *In at most three steps, Ty will catch up with me*. Forget running. It would be better to talk to him, calm him down. Distract him until help came. Unless—oh God. Could I reach the fire alarm? Yell for help? Joyce might hear me from across the hall. Or Becky. In fact, Becky should show up any second. She always came by at the end of the day.

"Mrs. H?"

Ty had been talking, and I'd missed what he'd said.

". . . couldn't really blame them," he continued. "But I'd need something in case they called the police. You know."

I did? I had not the slightest idea. "Call the police?" Why would he expect that they'd do that?

He let out a breath. "Like I said. I'm trespassing, Mrs. H. Don't you get it? I'm not allowed on school property."

What?

"I'm a convicted felon." He glanced up at me. "If anyone but you saw me, they'd kick me out, especially after what happened to Mrs. Marshall."

Mrs. Marshall, who used to scream into his face and drag him by his shirt collars, and who'd been viciously murdered right after Ty's release. I hugged myself, tried to sound stern. "Even so, you had no business hiding in here and startling me."

He shrugged, raised his eyebrows. Not exactly an apology. I needed to get out of the cubbies space, into the open. "Come on, Ty. Let's go sit down."

When he smiled, his dimples showed. Gave me a flash of the little boy he'd been. But he wasn't that little boy anymore. He was a convicted felon. Ty followed me into the classroom, sat on a desk top. "Actually, the real reason I hid wasn't because of the cops. It was that I wasn't sure how you'd be."

"How I'd be?"

"You know. With seeing me."

"What do you mean?" I tried to sound as if seeing him after the seven or so years of his incarceration was no big deal. Normal.

"Mrs. H. It's not like people have been glad to see me come home."

Right. "Give them time." It wasn't helpful, but it was all I could think of to say.

"Time? They've had years of time. Nobody's over it. Christ, my own mother's scared of me. If I walk into a room, she finds a reason to walk out. She sits up at night. I think she thinks I'll kill her in her sleep." He let out another short "Ha."

Maybe his mother had reason to worry. After all, Ty had killed her husband. And he'd spent years locked up in the company of criminals, possibly learning tricks of the trade. Prison had certainly changed him. His face was broken out in angry red welts, his complexion had a pasty, sickly tone. And though he was long and thin, his belly swelled, reminded me of a lumpy loaf of white bread.

"Everything's different because of juvey." On his lap, his hands tightened into fists. "Other kids graduated high school and went to college. They partied. Got girls. Me? I got juvey. No friends, not one. My own mother wants me out of her house. She says I'm twenty-one and should be out on my own. Oh yeah. It's been a grand welcome home."

He paused. Blue veins popped in his forehead, pumping anger. "When I first got out, I came here to see you. Did she tell you?"

"Who?"

"Who else? Mrs. Marshall. She threw me out and promised to call the cops on me if I came back, but she promised she'd tell you I'd come by to see you."

"She must not have had the chance."

Wait. Mrs. Marshall had thrown him out. That must have made Ty angry. Angry enough to kill her? I tried to picture it, Ty sneaking into her office, waiting for her, but in my imagination Ty kept turning into the feisty little boy he used to be, the one with bruises, scrapes, and unruly hair, the one who had been neglected by his mother and abused by his father. The one Mrs. Marshall had shrieked at, who'd tensed at the sight of her.

I'd wandered again, missed part of what he'd said.

". . . but didn't have the nerve to ring your doorbell."

My doorbell? He'd been to my house?

"So I just stood outside, across the street. I wished you'd come in or out and I could just bump into you. But you never did."

Ty was sounding creepy. Had he been stalking me? Was that why I'd felt someone watching me? Was he who'd called me and breathed into the phone? My skin itched. I looked at the clock. Ten after three. Where was Becky?

"But then I found out you were teaching Seth and figured I'd come by the school." He flashed a dimpled smile, lost it quickly. "It's funny. He's my brother, but I don't really know him. He was just a baby when I went away." He paused, met my eyes.

I shifted positions, uncomfortable.

"Hell, I might as well say it. The fact is, Mrs. H, I've been trying to see you ever since I got back." His stare was too direct. Too long.

I cleared my throat, recrossed my arms. My shoulder ached. I fidgeted, reminded myself to remain calm and in charge. "Well, here we are. You're seeing me." Oops, that sounded cold. I smiled, hoping to soften my words. "What can I do for you, Ty? Why did you want to see me?"

"You don't have to do anything for me, Mrs. H. I wanted to see you because in my whole life, you're the only adult who was ever nice to me." His eyes were intense, didn't waiver.

I smiled again, trying to lighten the mood. "Oh, Ty. That can't be true."

"Oh, Mrs. H. You know it is." His mouth twisted, formed a smile. Or a grimace?

"I can't believe that." I tried to think of some examples. But his parents had abused him. Mrs. Marshall had, too, in a way. "You had some very fine teachers—"

"No one gave a rat's ass about me. Only you. You were the only one who tried to help me. You had talks with my so-called parents.

And with the Marshall herself. You stood up for me lots of times, talked to me after school."

"Of course I did, Ty. It was my job. You were just a little boy—"

"Not just back then. You came to my trial."

Well, yes. So had half the town. "I was concerned about what happened—"

"There. See? You were concerned. Don't play around with words. We both know it's true. You cared. You cared about me." His gaze drilled into my eyes, made me blink.

"Of course I cared about you. You were a child. And my student."

"It was more than that. I could feel it."

He could feel it? His eyes pierced mine. Oh Lord, why was I so clueless? Ty had a crush on me. While he'd been locked up, he must have created some fantasy about me. Great. Fabulous. Finally a new man had come into my life. Never mind he was half my age and a convicted murderer. So what was I supposed to do? What could I say? Should I try to set him straight, explain that I'd cared about him a long time ago, when he was a little boy with problems? Or deny that I'd ever cared about him? Or insist that, to me, he'd been just another student, one of hundreds, and I cared about them all?

He sat on the desktop, pupils dilated, eyes overly bright. Was he on drugs? Was he dangerous? Why was I even wondering. Of course he was dangerous. He was a murderer. But no, not a real murderer. As Susan had pointed out, he'd killed his father after years of abuse, but he'd never been dangerous to anyone else. Unless you counted all the kids he beat up. And unless he'd killed Mrs. Marshall. Dammit, what did he want from me? Did he imagine that I'd return his crush and fall into his arms? What could I say without hurting him and making him mad? I glanced at the door. Where the hell was Becky?

"Ty—" I began, but he interrupted.

"I had lots of time to think these last years, Mrs. H. And a lot of that time, I was thinking about you."

Oh God. Stop. "Ty, sorry. I just noticed the time. I have an appointment. An important meeting. I'm late. So, maybe we can finish talking another time—"

"Like I said, you were the only one who ever was good to me." He kept talking as if I hadn't spoken. "The only one who listened. Even now, you're the only one I can to talk to." He stood, stepped over to me. His eyes never left mine. "That's why I'm here."

His hands engulfed mine. They were bony and moist. I took in a breath, held it. Needed to escape. But how? Could I just thank him for stopping by? Tell him it was great to see him? I worked my hands out of his, grabbed my bag, edged toward the door.

Ty edged along with me.

"Like I said, I've got to go," I blurted.

"So how about we talk another time?" His eyebrows lifted. "Maybe tomorrow?"

"I don't know. Maybe." What? Why had I said that? I kept moving toward the door.

Ty grinned. "Okay, cool. Tomorrow." He moved with me, matched me step for step.

Never had the classroom seemed so long, the hallway so far away. I kept walking, picturing my car waiting in the lot.

"What time?" Ty asked.

Damn, seriously?

He watched me, waiting.

"I don't know. After school." Good God, what was wrong with me?

He tilted his head, dimples popping. "Great. How about I meet you at Pete's. Three o'clock?"

The classroom door was just feet away. I was practically running now. So was Ty. Was I never going to get away from him?

I had my hand on the light switch when his arms closed around me, awkward and long. I stiffened, bit my lip. Put my hands lightly on his arms, trying to brush them away, but they wouldn't brush off. His head lowered against my shoulder, pressed against my neck. I felt his breath. His weight. As he clung to me, an unfamiliar darkness rolled through me, waves in an ocean of tension, loneliness, despair that made me shudder. The shudder hadn't ended when Ty released me and stepped back. Putting his hands together, he bowed to me. Without another word, he sped out of the room.

* * *

I called Becky on her cell. Her "hello" was a whisper.

"Where are you?"

"What do you mean? Where are *you*? I'm at the faculty meeting."

Shit. Of course she was. Everyone was in the cafeteria for the first-day-of-school ritual.

"I saved you a seat. Are you with Joyce?"

"No—"

"Cuz she's not here either. So are you on your way?"

"No, I can't make it."

"It's mandatory—"

"What will they do, fire me? I just can't get there." I wouldn't be missing anything. The meeting would be the same as it was every year. Attendance forms and permission slips handed out, parents' night schedules reviewed. Same old same old.

Becky sighed. "But the cops are here, telling everyone more about the murder. And asking questions."

Really? The cops were there? They'd been just down the hall when Ty had snuck in and cornered me in my classroom? How reassuring. He could have killed me, and they wouldn't have noticed.

"You ought to be here, Elle. Detective Stiles is here. He'll wonder where you are."

No, he wouldn't. Why would he? Anyway, I wasn't going, needed to be far away from the school, off the roads, safely behind my own locked doors. Besides, I was already in my car, driving out of the parking lot. "Call me after," I whispered. "Let me know if they say anything interesting." Why was I whispering?

"Why are you whispering?"

"I'm not." Well, I wasn't anymore.

"Are you all right? You sound weird."

"Call me after."

I ended the call, raced home. Wanted to get inside, curl up on my overstuffed sofa cushions with some hot tea, a bag of cookies, and a daytime talk show. I wanted to pretend I hadn't seen Ty. That he hadn't fixated on me or scared the bejeebees out of me.

That I hadn't agreed to see him again.

I felt sullied. As if I'd done something wrong. But I hadn't, had I? Yes, of course I had. I'd managed to encourage him by not refusing to meet him for a soda. But I hadn't meant to encourage him—I'd just said anything to get away from him. Besides, how bad could it be to have a soda in a public place in the middle of the afternoon? Why was I so nervous about it? I'd see him and explain that, while I hoped he was doing well, I wasn't going to spend more time with him.

I stopped at a light. Heard Ty saying that he'd thought about me in juvey. Oh God. What if he didn't have just a crush on me? What if it was an actual obsession? If so, he might not be able to tolerate a rejection. He might lose it, might even try to kill me. I heard a loud thunk, saw Patsy Olsen fly into the street. Ty's hair was kind of long. Had it been Ty who'd pushed her, thinking she was me? No, of course not. He'd had no reason to harm me. And he hadn't tried to even when he'd had me alone at the school. No. It hadn't been Ty. Ty wasn't dangerous, and I wasn't in danger. It just felt like I was.

I pulled onto my street, up to my house. Grabbed my bag, my phone. Ran up the path, the steps. Unlocked the door, threw it open, dashed in, slammed and bolted it. Closed my eyes and let out a breath.

"Hell, Elle. Are you all right?"

I jumped and screamed, not sure which came first, but the scream lasted longer. At the same time, I threw my phone, dropped my bag, spun around, and groped for the doorknob so I could run.

"Elle?"

I glanced over my shoulder. The afternoon light glared through the living room windows, but I saw a silhouette. A man was in my house, coming at me. I turned the knob, but the door was still bolted. Wouldn't open.

"It's okay." He spoke softly, almost a whisper.

His hand grabbed my shoulder. Oh God. He turned me around to face him. And there I stood, panting, nose to nose and eye to eye with Jerry.

* * *

"Jerry?" Fear instantly morphed into fury. "What the hell? What are you doing here?" I pushed him, sidestepped to move away.

"Calm down, Elle." He moved with me, still talking in that raspy, unfamiliar whisper. His breath smelled like whiskey and onions. "It's only me."

I stammered, couldn't articulate my thoughts. Words of outrage scrambled on my tongue. "Jerry. What—How—I can't—No—" *Wait*, I told myself. *Slow down.* Maybe it was my fault. Maybe I'd forgotten an open house? A scheduled showing? But no. I knew I hadn't. What I'd forgotten was to call a locksmith.

Jerry rubbed his chin, shifted his weight from one leg to the other. His eyebrows furrowed. "I know, I know. I should have let you know I'd be here. You're right. But honestly, Elle, I didn't intend to scare you."

"Then what did you intend?" I shoved him away, temper flaring. No longer too stunned to speak. "Get out. You need to leave. What did you do, use the key in the lock box? That's unethical and illegal—"

"Elle. Relax. We're friends."

"No, Jerry—"

"Okay, cool down. I confess. I was going to surprise you. I hired a staging consultant—on my own dime."

"A what?"

"Elle, we've talked about how to make your house more appealing to buyers, and I've suggested better staging. But so far, you haven't had the time or inclination to make changes. So I talked to a colleague—"

"Bullshit. No. Stop making excuses. You have no right to come in here without my permission."

"Well, technically, when you hired me as your agent, you gave me permission to do what I have to—"

"No. No. I gave you permission to show my house. Nothing more. Real estate agents aren't given carte blanche to come and go—"

"Elle." He moved closer, lowered his voice again. "To be honest, I thought that by now, I was more than just your real estate agent."

Good God. "Actually, Jerry." I stepped back. "Right now you aren't even that. You're fired."

"What? You can't mean that. Elle, I have your best interests at heart. I came here to measure walls for the consultant, that's all. Why don't I take you to dinner? We can talk." Again he came closer. Again I smelled booze. He reached out to touch my arm. I moved out of reach, stepped back, into the living room.

"There's nothing to talk about, Jerry. We're done."

"Come on, Elle. Don't pretend you don't feel a connection."

I didn't know what to say, just put up a hand and shook my head. No.

"Dammit, Elle, what's the deal? You and I—you've been giving me signals from the start. We both know it. So, let's cut the playing-hard-to-get act. I'm here for you, babe." He came at me, lips parted. Oh God. He was about to kiss me.

I dodged. Turned my head and put my hands up to fend him off. "Jerry, you need to leave."

He stood, staring at me, bereft. He blinked a few times, and I worried he might cry. But he didn't cry. He looked away, jaw clenched and rippling. When he looked back at me, his eyes were ice. "Look, honey, I've done a lot for you. Spent my own cash on brochures and ads, spent dozens of hours trying to sell this dump when I could have been earning huge commissions on my other properties—I've got plenty of listings for over a million dollars each—"

"Nice. Now you'll have more time for those."

He glared. "Do I have to remind you that I've not just been trying to sell your place? I've also been busting my butt searching for a home for you to move into? And that we've still got three properties to visit."

"Forget it."

"They're already scheduled and confirmed."

"So what?" My God, didn't he get it?

"Just one more outing. Then you'll be free of me." His eyes looked wounded, puppy-like.

"Okay, fine. We'll look at those." God help me, I was a sucker and a fool.

He looked hopeful.

"But that's it. After that, we're done."

He watched me, bit his lip. "We'll see," he said. Then he whirled around, unbolted the door, and left.

I watched through the living room window as he stomped to his car. Then I sank onto my sofa, noting the impressions of his shoes on my newly vacuumed rug.

* * *

So it had been Jerry, after all. Jerry coming into my house uninvited, unauthorized, abusing the realtor's lock box key. But why? What did he want? Jen's voice popped to mind with an extensive list of perversions Jerry might have committed in my home. Oh man. Did I have to reexamine my towels and sheets? My lingerie? Had he gone through my photos and private keepsakes? I recoiled, eyed his footprints in the carpet then sat back and surveyed the room. The two antique wingback chairs carefully arranged at specific angles and distances from the fireplace. The coffee table polished to a gleam, the single nonimposing—no, not just nonimposing—the boring pale-green porcelain vase on its surface. Jerry had dictated the whole living room presentation, had made me remove pillows, afghans, knickknacks, mementos. Had called it "clutter." But now, without the clutter, nothing looked real. The room looked hollow and soulless, like no one lived here. Like a movie set. Or, Jen's voice suggested, like the setting for a pornographic fantasy.

I cringed again. The room felt stained. I looked out at the entranceway. This time, Jerry had gone way too far. I could still smell his whiskey-onion breath. Never mind. I was finished with him. The locks were going to be changed today. I got up, looked around the kitchen for the list of locksmiths. Couldn't find it. Started over. Opened my laptop, logged into Google, searched again for locksmiths, cursed Jerry the whole time. What was wrong with him? I should have called the police. Should report him to the Realtors Association, whatever that was. If there even was such a thing. I clicked on Safety Lock Company. It had a nice website. Fine, I wrote down their number. Went back to the Google list and, as a backup, wrote down the number for Lock and Safe. Good. Even if Jerry had made a copy of my key, he wouldn't be able to use it.

I called Safety Lock and got voice mail. Left a message. Called Lock and Safe. The woman who answered said Mr. Johnson would be at the house at seven thirty that evening.

Good.

Next, I searched for a new realtor. Or I began to search. There were hundreds, maybe thousands of them. How was I supposed to choose one? How could I be sure the new one would be less crazy than Jerry? "We have three more properties to visit," his voice reminded me. Why had I agreed to go? I should have flat out told him to cancel them. Why did I have so much trouble standing up to people? I was a pushover. A wimp. I needed to work on being more assertive.

To start with, I'd interview new realtors. I was scanning the list of names and services when Elvis' "Suspicious Minds" began.

Caller ID said "Becky."

Damn. She was going to yell at me for missing the faculty meeting. After all I'd been through that afternoon with first Ty and then Jerry, I was in no mood to be scolded.

"Don't start with me." I picked up the phone swinging. "I've had possibly the most horrible afternoon in human history, and I'm not the least bit interested in what happened at that stupid meeting."

"Did you hear?" she asked.

What? She seemed not to have heard anything I'd said. "They're a waste of time. And I just don't have the patience, not after all that's happened."

"You mean you knew? Before the meeting?"

"Seriously? Of course, I knew. So did you and everyone else—"

"No, I didn't know. No one at the meeting knew. So how did you? They only just found her."

"—who's ever been to one of those—" I stopped mid-sentence. Replayed what she'd just said. *They only just found her.* "Wait, what did you say?"

"My God, Elle." Becky was crying. I hadn't heard it at first, but she sniffed, and when she went on, her voice choked. "After the meeting." She stopped, sobbing. Took a breath. "Somebody found Joyce."

Joyce? My stomach contorted. Mouth hung open. I couldn't speak, wanted to drop the phone or run, anything to escape what Becky would say next.

"In the parking lot. In her car. And, oh God, Elle. Just like Mrs. Marshall. Joyce—they cut her throat."

* * *

We met at Susan's, the way we would have anyway. Mondays, while Susan's husband took their daughters to their dance classes, we four friends usually had dinner together. That particular night we'd planned to eat at The Blue Cat, a restaurant not far from my house. But we didn't go to The Blue Cat. We sat in her kitchen, Susan drinking coffee, Jen Chablis. Becky and I not drinking at all. None of us thinking about food.

"When's he coming?" I asked.

Susan checked the stove clock. "Any time."

"WTF," Jen said. "I don't get why he wants to talk to Elle. Becky works at the school, too."

"He'll probably want to talk to both of them."

"But he said he wanted to talk to Elle," Jen persisted. "Isn't that why he's coming all the way over here?"

"Better here than at the Roundhouse."

He'd given Susan those choices? I swallowed. Decided that I would have a glass of wine after all. Went to get a glass. Listened to the others talk about me.

"Look, Elle didn't go to her faculty meeting. He'll want to know why. And he'll ask whether she saw anybody in the school or the parking lot when she left. Stuff like that."

"So why didn't she go to the meeting?" Jen addressed the question to Susan.

"How should Susan know?" I poured wine. "Why don't you ask me?"

"Elle." Susan frowned. "Do you really want to drink that? Detective Stiles should be here any second."

"Okay." Jen turned to me. "Why didn't you go to your meeting?"

"You guys always talk about me as if I'm not here."

"No, we don't," Becky said. "We don't talk about her, do we?"

"You just did it again."

"Did what?" Jen raised her eyebrows.

"Talked about me as a 'she.' If I'm standing right in the room, I should be a 'you.'"

"Your breath will smell like alcohol." Susan came over to me, reached for my glass. "You want to appear sober."

Before she could take it, I put the rim to my mouth and gulped, looking her in the eye.

"Elle, do you really want Stiles to take you downtown where he can be sure you're sober?"

"Will someone effing tell me why she didn't go to the meeting?" Jen insisted.

"I'm standing right here, Jen. Ask me."

"I just did. So why aren't you answering me?" Jen got up and refilled her glass.

"Yes, Elle, answer her," Susan snapped. She was annoyed that I was having wine. More annoyed that I'd disobeyed her.

I took another sip, just to prove she wasn't my babysitter anymore. I was my own adult person.

"For God's sake, Elle. Your friend Joyce is dead," Susan scolded.

Right. In her Toyota. With her throat slit.

"So stop avoiding the question. Tell us why you didn't go to your meeting. You need to be ready for Stiles."

"I didn't kill her."

"No one asked if you'd killed her."

I nodded. Sat. Didn't want to talk about Ty. Didn't want to think about the possibility that he'd killed Joyce and Mrs. Marshall both. Mrs. Marshall had unfairly disciplined him for years, so he'd have motive. But Joyce? She hadn't ever even been his teacher, so why would he have killed her?

Unless she'd seen him at the school after he'd come to see me and cornered him. Maybe even threatened to call the police. He might have killed her after he'd left my classroom.

But wait—maybe it wasn't Ty. It could have been Duncan Girard, preventing Joyce from spreading rumors that he was a pedophile. He'd implied that Mrs. Marshall had also accused him. Had he silenced them both?

"Elle." Susan nudged my arm. "I'm serious."

She was?

"She has no idea what you're talking about." Jen examined a fingernail. "She's pulling an effing Elle."

"No, I'm not." I had been, but wasn't anymore. "I didn't go because of Ty." I told them about his visit. About his confession of a crush.

And when their exclamations, comments, questions, and curses quieted, I told them about Jerry.

By the time Stiles arrived, all three of them were gaping at me. Which part had stunned them? Ty or Jerry? Or both?

Stiles didn't seem to mind when I finished my wine right in front of him, so I began my story again. He listened, made notes in his book. Didn't seem to think that my realtor would have reason to harm anyone at the school, focused more on Ty, listened closely as I described our visit.

When I finished, he asked if there was anything else, and I told him about the incident with Duncan Girard.

Stiles jotted more notes. Crossed his legs. Asked if I'd ever seen Joyce wearing a Phillies baseball cap.

Becky said, "God, no," and I said, "Never," at the same time. I almost laughed at the idea. Joyce would consider the cap appalling and crass. Not to mention that it would ruin her hair.

"Why do you ask?" Susan said.

Stiles leaned forward, spoke confidentially. "A Phillies cap was found on the floor of her car. Might be nothing. Probably belonged to one of her students."

"But wasn't an Eagles cap found in Mrs. Marshall's office?" I asked.

"That's right."

"So you think it's not a coincidence. You think they both belonged to the killer. That he left them there." Susan's eyes lit up, excited at the prospect of evidence.

"It's a possibility, yes. But only a possibility."

"But you're checking them for DNA, right?" Susan pressed.

Stiles met her eyes. "We're doing our job, counselor." He moved on with his questions. He asked both Becky and me how well we knew Joyce. Had she been well liked? Did she have enemies? What had her relationship with Mrs. Marshall been like? Did we know anyone who'd want to harm her? Did either of us know the significance of the carving on her face?

The what?

Becky and I exchanged glances. Susan scowled and asked what he was referring to. Jen let out an obscenity. I heard a thunk, Patsy

Olsen flew off the curb, and Mrs. Marshall appeared before me with her blood-encrusted grin.

"As you know"—Detective Stiles looked from one to the other of us—"a smile was cut onto the principal's face."

We waited. Becky's eyes filled with tears.

"And this one?" Susan asked.

"This one," he said, "had a frown."

Of course it did.

The questions stopped. Stiles left. We went to The Blue Cat an hour and a half later than our reservation. The specials were sold out, but it didn't matter; none of us was hungry anyhow.

I finally got home around ten, found a note on my front door. Mr. Johnson from Lock and Safe had come by at seven thirty. I'd missed him.

CHAPTER SIX

Only eleven of my twenty-three students came to school the next day. Seth was one of them. A lot of parents had kept their children home despite the flurry of official emails and phone calls stating that, regardless of recent tragedies, the school was secure and safe, and would remain open with a qualified team of grief counselors on hand. The administration had reasoned that, since the school building itself was not part of the crime scene, children would be best served by preventing further disruptions in their routines and proceeding with their educations in a normal fashion.

Parents had not reacted well. Phone chains had been activated and an impromptu PTA meeting organized at the high school. The police chief and members of the school board had been pressured to attend. Reporters and camera crews had crowded in, and the high school auditorium had filled to capacity.

I hadn't gone to the meeting but had seen coverage on the eleven o'clock news. Confused and panicked parents had demanded answers. What was happening at their local elementary school? Did police have any idea at all who'd killed first the principal and now a teacher? Were people at the school being targeted, one by one? What protections were being provided for their children? Should children be kept home until the killer was caught?

From what I could see on the news, police and school board members had been at a loss for answers, had tried to calm the crowd by promising police guards at the school and undercover cops in and around it. But few parents had been appeased. Many had declared that they'd keep their children home until they were certain that the school was safe. A woman whose son I'd had in class the year before told the reporter that her two boys were never coming back; she was going to homeschool them. The reporter had ended the segment by pointing out that, despite concerns, so far no children had been hurt at Logan Elementary and that school would open the next morning, on schedule.

And indeed, the next morning, school had opened right on time. Mr. Royal again had stood outside to greet the children, again had failed to have them line up by grade and classroom. This time, though, several teachers had been on hand to monitor the area, herding children into proper zones, showing them where they were to wait for the bell to ring each morning.

I'd not been one of those valiant teachers. I'd lingered at a distance, watching from the parking lot. Noting the defiant Jolly Jack's truck at the corner of the playground, the kids skipping over there to talk to Duncan. The uniformed policemen patrolling the schoolyard. The patrol car idling in the bus lane. Stan peering out from the main doorway, holding a broom. I looked for a suspicious character holding a knife. Of course I didn't see one. No one was going to attack me or anyone else with police everywhere. We were all safe.

Still, I stayed alert as I inched past the taped-off area where Joyce's car had been parked. Gradually, the shouts and laughter of children penetrated my haze, bolstered me, and carried me through the teachers' entrance to my classroom, where eleven seven-year-olds took their seats and watched me, their eyes riddled with questions and fear.

"Mrs. Harrison?"

I hadn't learned their names yet. The girl's desk was labeled "Pam."

"Yes, Pam?"

"I'm going to be on TV." She gave a proud smile.

"You are not," said a boy. His desk said "Bobby."

"Am so. A news lady talked to me—and a man with a camera."

What? "When was this, Pam? Where?"

"Just now, on the sidewalk on my way to school."

Seriously? The media were interviewing little children? Exploiting them? "What did the news lady say to you?"

"She said." Pam's chin wobbled ever so slightly. "'Are you scared to go to school?'"

"I know why," Bobby chimed in. "She thinks you're scared because first someone killed Mrs. Marshall and then they killed Mrs. Huff."

"Hold on, Bobby," I said. Pam and another Elana were crying. Maybe others. "Okay, everybody listen."

I didn't want to talk about murder with them. Instead, I told them that it was true that some bad things had happened, but that they were all safe. No one was going to hurt them. I was watching them and so were policemen. I walked around and touched each one of them on the shoulder or the head, calming them. And instead of a spelling lesson, I assigned another art project. This time, I asked them to draw their favorite places to play.

As they worked, I glanced out the window, saw a police cruiser in the parking lot. Leaves beginning to turn. Everything seemed under control. I walked around again, looking at their work. Saw pictures of playgrounds with swings and slides. A lake dotted with sailboats. A bedroom floor covered with toys. A child roller-skating on the street. And a blank paper.

Seth hadn't drawn anything. He sat at his desk whispering into the air.

"Seth?"

He kept whispering, looking down. He didn't answer me.

"Seth?" This time, I bent down, spoke into his ear.

He pulled away as if startled.

"I thought you were saying something."

"No." He shook his head. "I wasn't saying anything."

A few kids giggled. Seth turned scarlet and stared at the floor.

But clearly, he'd been whispering. He was only seven, just a little boy. Even so, maybe Seth heard voices. Maybe he wasn't well.

More likely, like a lot of kids, he had an imaginary friend.

I changed the subject. "You haven't started your picture."

He blinked at the blank paper in front of him. Reached for a crayon. Looked around. "Um. I forget," he said. "What are we supposed to draw?"

He hadn't heard the assignment. A familiar chill tickled my back. Seth had apparently wandered off in his mind and missed part of the class. It was as if he'd "pulled an Elle." Maybe he had a dissociative disorder like mine?

The thought plagued me even though he didn't whisper again that morning. On his way outside for recess, though, I stopped him. "Tell me, Seth. Who were you talking to before?"

Again, he looked at the floor. "Nobody." His voice was small, bashful.

"Because I want you to know it's okay." I waited. "Sometimes people have secret friends that no one can see except them."

He tilted his head, doubtful. "That's crazy."

Maybe. "I thought maybe you had a friend like that and that's why you were whispering."

"Me?" He took a step back, bolder now. "No, I don't have any secret friend."

"Why were you whispering, then?"

"I can't tell you." He turned to go, then turned back, scowling. "You really want to know who I was talking to, Mrs. Harrison?"

I watched him. "Yes. I do."

He took a deep breath, looked away. "My father, that's who."

His father?

"Sometimes he wants to know what's going on. Like before, I told him Mrs. Huff was killed." Seth stood next to my chair, toyed with the armrest. "You think that's crazy, don't you."

"No, I don't." And I didn't, even though his father had been dead since Seth was a baby. Fact was that if Seth was crazy, I was, too. I'd talked to my husband for a couple of years after he died.

"You don't? Honest?" He held onto my armrest, leaning back, swaying. "What if sometimes when I talk to my dad, he talks back to me? Do you think I'm crazy now?"

I took a breath. How many times after Charlie's death had I heard his voice whisper that he loved me and was still by my side? And how many times had I gotten angry with Charlie and argued with the voice of a dead man?

"No, Seth. I don't think you're crazy." Although maybe we both were.

He cocked his head, shrugged.

I folded my hands, preparing a simple explanation. I'd say that when people we love die, talking to them is a normal way to try to keep them with us. I looked up, ready to begin.

Seth was already at the door, running off to recess.

* * *

At the end of the day, Katie and her girlfriends came by to pick up Seth. The three wore identical somber expressions. Heads bent, they moved tentatively. Katie knelt and gave Seth a gentle hug, asked him how his day was. He squirmed, muttered, "Good." An auto-response.

She stood and pulled me aside, whispered that she was concerned; her brother had been shaken by the murders. "Did he seem okay in class?" she asked.

I wasn't comfortable talking to her about Seth. She was a child herself, his sibling not his parent or guardian. "How sweet of you to ask," I dodged her question. "Seth's lucky to have a sister who cares about him so much."

She lowered her voice. "And you?" She met my eyes. "How are you doing, Mrs. Harrison? These murders must be awful for you." She studied me, seemed way older than her age. Poor thing, I thought. Having to grow up so early, enduring so much tragedy, taking on so much responsibility.

Becky came in before I could answer, her eyes swollen and red, her hanky at her nose. "Oh, sorry. You're busy." She turned to go.

But Katie grabbed Seth's hand. "No, no. We're leaving. See you later, Mrs. H." She let her eyes settle on mine for a moment, letting me know she'd be thinking of me, and led her compadres away, Seth in tow.

I slumped against my desktop, drained. My legs ached from standing, my shoulder was sore, reminding me that it was still not entirely healed. And my stomach was in knots. Becky was weeping, going on about her kindergarteners. "They're just babies, but they know what's happened so they're scared, which means they're needy and cranky. At times today, I thought I'd lose it and we'd all sit in a circle and cry. Thank God for Duck Duck Goose. When you're five years old, nothing—not even murder—is going to interfere with a game of Duck Duck Goose."

We laughed sadly at that. Becky blew her nose, gazed at the bright colors of the classroom. "Mr. Royal managed to get through the day."

"Why wouldn't he?"

She looked at me. "Well, he hasn't been in a classroom for who knows how long."

I didn't know what she meant.

"He filled in for Joyce today."

Of course. Made sense.

"He says he'll stay on until they find a replacement."

I pictured him waving his arms, stammering helplessly at a classroom of second graders. "Let's hope they find one soon."

Becky giggled, agreeing. "He won't last a week. He'll be in the hospital with apoplexy."

What exactly was apoplexy? Was it a real condition? Something that would land you in the hospital? Never mind. I gathered up papers and my lesson plans, stuffed them into my bag. "Well, at least nobody got killed today. And the cops kept a low profile. I didn't see anyone who looked like they were undercover."

Neither had Becky, though she said she suspected the third-grade teacher's new aide.

"So. I'm outta here." I looked at the clock. "Want to start Happy Hour early?"

Becky frowned. "You can't do Happy Hour. You have a date."

A date? What was she talking about?

She watched me, smirking, waiting for me to remember.

But I didn't.

She finally got tired of waiting. "Ty Evans," she said.

Ty Evans? Oh God. Ty. I'd forgotten, damn. I'd agreed to meet him at Pete's for a soda. But that was before Joyce had been killed.

"I can't go. I mean—I can't." I remembered him leaning against me, breathing on my neck. I cringed.

"Elle, you can't just not show up. That's mean. Plus Ty's an ex-con—you don't want to make him mad."

"Oh, come on, Becky." Ty wouldn't hurt me. Would he? Had he already hurt Joyce and Mrs. Marshall?

"I'm just saying you need to be careful with him."

"Which is exactly why I don't want to go. Besides, with what happened to Joyce, he'll understand I'm too upset."

Becky shook her head, no.

"Anyhow. I bet he forgot all about it."

She didn't say anything, just stared at me. We both knew Ty hadn't forgotten, that he'd probably thought about nothing else.

Okay. I'd go and explain that because of Mrs. Huff's murder, I was a mess and couldn't stay. I'd be out within five minutes.

"How about I go along? I'll sit in the booth behind you and be there if you need me."

I thanked her, said she didn't need to come along.

She frowned. "Okay, but I'm going to call and check on you. When? Half an hour?"

Half an hour would be fine. If I needed an excuse to get away from Ty, Becky's phone call would provide it. I'd pretend that a friend needed help because her car had broken down or her husband had walked out or her grandmother had died. Something.

"And if you're really in trouble, say a code word."

"Trouble? He's just a kid in a soda shop."

"A kid in a soda shop who killed his father and possibly two of our closest associates."

My throat clenched. "You don't really think—"

"Elle. If you're in trouble, say the code word."

"Okay fine." What was the code word?

She shrugged. "Geronimo?"

Seriously? The only time anyone ever said "Geronimo" was when they needed a code word.

"Okay." Becky looked at her nails, thinking. "How about 'manicure'?"

Manicure? "Fine."

"Fine." Becky gave me a hug, hurried to the door. "Be careful."

I waved.

She stuck her head back into the room. "And call me the minute you get home." She blew me a kiss and was gone.

* * *

Ty appeared from nowhere as I approached the soda shop. He was suddenly next to me, matching his steps with mine. Smiling.

I opened my mouth, started to tell him that I couldn't stay. But his dimples looked so happy. I decided to wait. I'd tell him after we sat down.

"How about we take our drinks to the park?" he asked. "It's beautiful outside."

His sunny mood rankled me. No, what rankled me was that I was about to destroy it. His eyes twinkled. His steps bounced. Clearly, he'd been looking forward to seeing me. Well, what was the harm? I'd have a soda with him. One. Then I'd go.

Ty took his root beer float and I my skim milk latte to the park across the street from Pete's, less than a block from Logan Elementary. We sat on a bench, sipped.

"I'm glad you came out with me, Mrs. H." Ty grinned. "I never thought you really would."

I'd never have thought so either.

"Back in juvey, if someone told me that this would happen? That you'd even talk to me?"

"Why wouldn't I talk to you? You were my student." I tried to reinforce the boundaries of our relationship. To remind him that we were teacher/student and nothing else.

But he wasn't paying attention to what I said. He shook his head, stared at a tree. "Did I just say, 'Back in juvey'? Shit."

Silence. He set his jaw.

"That place, Mrs. H. It ruined my life. You know something? I should have never confessed. If I didn't confess, they never could have sent me there. Nobody could have proved anything." The veins in his forehead swelled, blue and pulsing.

"So why did you?" As I recalled, he hadn't confessed until weeks after the murder.

"What, confess? Because my dickhead lawyer said I'd be out in a few years at worst, that's why."

He seemed solely focused on his punishment, oblivious to the reason for it. "Ty, you killed your father."

"He deserved what he got."

"So, even after all this time, you don't regret it?"

"Regret it?" He faced me, forehead veins throbbing. Head tilted. "Really, Mrs. H? You think I did it?"

I waited a beat. "Ty. You confessed."

He looked away, pulled on his soda. Forehead veins pulsed, about to explode.

What was I doing there? I needed to leave. "Look, Ty. It's been a tough week. And now there's been another murder at school."

"So? What's that to me? Those two bitches were nothing. Especially Marshall. Marshall," he sneered. "She hated me even when I was a little kid. She tortured me. And you know what? Even back then, I could tell she got off on it."

"Ty, that's not—"

"Don't you stand up for her, Mrs. H. She used to twist my arm, pull my hair. Gave me wedgies. Bitch deserved what she got."

A man with a dog walked by. A woman pushed a toddler in a stroller.

Ty went on, not caring whether they heard. "And that other one, Mrs. Huff. She taught my sister, so I know about her. She had an attitude. She thought she was better than everybody." He smirked. "My guess is she found out different at the end." He leaned over, spat on the ground. "No, like I said, when I got out, you're the only one I cared about seeing, Mrs. H. You're the only one who ever treated me with respect." He looked into my eyes and smiled sweetly, almost bashfully.

What was I supposed to say? How could I respond? In the course of a sentence, Ty's demeanor had changed from stormy contemptuous rage to shy flirtation. He was volatile, unpredictable. He'd expressed no remorse for the murder of his father, no empathy for the victims at the school. The killings, in fact, seemed to please him. Almost to make him proud, as if he'd accomplished them himself.

Oh man. I watched him scoop ice cream out of his drink, wondered if he had any conscience at all. Was he a sociopath, a serial killer? I shouldn't have come. Needed to leave, get home, call Detective Stiles. I clutched my latte, edged away. A shiver passed through me, and I watched Ty to see what he'd do next. Would he try to take me prisoner, to live out some obsessive fantasy? If I resisted, would he hurt me? My latte was my only weapon—I could throw it into his eyes, blinding him long enough to let me run away.

"Yum." He licked vanilla foam off his lips and smiled, displaying his dimples. And, for an instant, tall, pasty Ty became a scrappy little boy with bruises.

"Thanks, Mrs. H. This is great." The little boy disappeared. Big Ty winked, looked me over. Oh God, was he trying to be seductive? "I'll tell you what, they didn't have root beer floats in juvey. No ma'am." He looked at the trees. "They didn't have trees, either."

No trees? I didn't know what to say. "How sad."

"You can't imagine. All you could see of the outside world was through a five-inch window covered with bars, and that was high up near your ceiling. If you stood on your cot, you could see a sliver of sky, a piece of a cloud. That was it."

I faced the bank of hedges across the path, imagined never seeing the sky. Never seeing greenery. After a while, I'd be desperate. And angry.

Angry enough to kill the people I blamed for my problems?

Ty sprawled on the bench beside me, his long legs jutting out, crossed at the ankle. He'd picked a blade of grass, was chewing it. The veins in his forehead were no longer protruding. He was relaxed, peaceful.

He looked like a gawky adolescent, not a killer.

But that didn't mean he wasn't one. After all, he'd killed his father, might have killed Joyce and Mrs. Marshall. Might be planning other killings. Might be just getting started. I recalled his quick mood shifts, his anger, and inched further away. Imagined making an excuse, saying that I had to leave. Or getting up and running.

"Can you?"

What? Oh dear. I'd drifted. Missed what he'd said.

"No?" I figured I had a 50 percent chance of being right.

The blade of grass twirled in his lips. He got off the bench and traced a rectangle in the dirt. "Well, this was the size. I was lucky. I had a single, no roommate because I was what they called a violent offender. But this was what I lived in. A box just big enough for a cot, a desk, and a toilet. The walls were cold concrete blocks covered with writing."

"Graffiti?"

The dimples flashed. "No, graffiti's fine art compared to those walls. This was just writing, scribbling. Stuff about girls and Jesus. All kinds of racist shit. Messages for whoever comes next. And you don't have pens or markers. No, you can't have those in your cell. So you write with a button."

A button?

"Yup. You take one off a shirt and scrape it on the concrete walls. That's how you write. Everyone does it. Hell, there's nothing else to do."

I pictured the walls, the buttons. Boys locked up, scribbling on concrete bricks.

Ty slid back onto the bench beside me and rubbed his eyes, quiet for a minute. "But you know what the worst part was? The noise."

Noise? Were people yelling? I cleared my throat, couldn't stop thinking about writing with buttons.

"It never stopped. I don't know what the hell it was. Kind of like a constant echo. Or something reverberating like we were inside a gigantic bell right after it clanged. But it was always there, just like the lights."

The lights? I swallowed. Bit my lip. I didn't want to hear more about juvey. Wanted to leave. What time was it? Becky would call any minute. I'd invent an emergency. A car accident. Or a problem with my lock box.

"See, they never turn the lights off. After a while, you lose track of whether it's day or night." He pulled the grass from his mouth, tossed it on the ground. "So now, I can't get used to real time, or darkness, or silence—silence sounds loud to me. It actually hurt my ears at first. And being outside? It's a miracle, feeling a breeze, smelling the grass, seeing stars and the moon. It's like I'm reborn." Ty looked past me, seeing something in his memory. Thinking.

A couple walked by, arm in arm. Another woman with a stroller. They seemed out of reach, part of a different world.

"I shouldn't bother you with all this, Mrs. H."

"No, it's okay." I wanted to mean it. As uneasy as I was, I felt bad for him. "It's good for you to talk about it."

"Don't get me wrong, it wasn't all bad. We had a cafeteria and a gym. School. We got to watch PG movies, and after class we could play dominoes or cards. I could stay up 'till nine thirty by the end. You weren't allowed books in your room, only the Bible, but the food wasn't bad." He smirked. "Like on Valentines Day, we got little cupcakes with hearts on them. And fried chicken—every holiday, we got fried chicken."

It sounded dismal. Hellish. A concrete box with a tiny barred window, no books, and a button to write with. Maybe he had friends?

Ty raised his eyebrows. "You don't have friends in juvey. You have gangs. You stick with your gang, which means your own race. Doesn't matter who you were on the outside. Inside, you're white or black. 'Course, nobody messed with me too much—I was 'violent,' alone in solitary. And I kept to myself."

"Sounds lonely." I looked across the park, saw dogs chasing a Frisbee. Sipped my latte.

"I guess." Ty was quiet for a moment. "You couldn't trust anyone. Even the guards. Some of them were actual sadists. Worse than the prisoners. But even they had to be careful not to go too far. Like one guard, Al. Al raped one kid too many, so the kid's gang cornered Al and rammed his head against the wall a few times. Split his skull open. Blood sprayed everywhere. We had lockdown for forty-eight hours, but we never saw Al again."

My phone rang. Thank God. I reached into my bag, saw Becky's name. "Excuse me." I answered.

"You all right?" Becky asked.

"Yes, this is she." I looked at Ty. He crossed his arms, leaned back, gazed at bushes and trees.

"Want me to come rescue you?"

"No." I paused as if to listen. "Really? Is she okay?"

"Is that a no?" Becky asked. "Because I can. Do you need a 'manicure,' Elle?"

"No. That'll be fine. I'll call you when I get there. Thanks." I ended the call, still mentally inventing an excuse. Maybe something about a friend's mother falling, breaking a hip.

But Ty kept talking as if the phone call hadn't happened. "It's a funny thing about juvey." He turned to me. "People think the guards and the guys are all in there banging each other, like it's a big orgy."

Oh my. Did I really have to hear about this? "Ty, that phone call—"

Ty cut me off with another single "Ha."

"Listen to this. When I got out, my sister picked me up at the bus. You know the first thing she said? Not 'it's good to see you,' not 'you got taller' or 'how are you?' No, what she said was, 'So, are you gay now?'"

I didn't need to hear his answer. "Ty," I began, "that phone call was my friend."

"But you know, Mrs. H? I try not to care about what other people think. I'm like a new person. I can look at the sky. The birds. The sunlight. I have no shackles. I'm wearing my own jeans and t-shirt. I can eat what I want when I want. Inside, know what we did for entertainment? We'd wet toilet paper and roll it into balls, stick the balls onto the ceiling. Ha! Now, I can do anything. Whatever I want. The world is mine."

"I'm glad you're out of there, Ty." I meant it. I put the cap back on my latte, picked up my bag.

"I've been talking too much." He eyed my bag.

"No. It's good." I'd probably have nightmares about spitballs and split skulls. But I met his eyes. "You're out now, Ty. That place, that life is behind you. Like you said, the world is yours." I paused, letting the comment sink in before trying again to leave. This time, I made no excuse, told no lie. "It's time for me to go."

Ty slurped up the last of his drink, looked up at me. "You know what, Mrs. H? First you had me, then Katie. Now, you've got Seth. You've taught the whole family." He grinned, showing his dimples. "Too bad for you, Mrs. H." He held his hand up for a high five.

I couldn't just leave his hand waiting there, so I gave it a slap. Then I stood, told him that it had been a wonderful visit, and took off in a sprint, as if escaping thunderclaps.

* * *

My ringtone began as I got into my car. Susan didn't bother with "hello."

"What's wrong with you, Elle? Do you deliberately try to get in trouble? Are you trying to get hurt?"

Dammit. Becky must have told her that I'd met with Ty. My friends were dear and caring but way too overprotective and constantly into each other's business. I closed my car door, put on my seat belt. "There was no trouble, Susan. Ty's lonely and having a tough time adjusting to life after juvey."

"None of which is your problem."

"Look, I met him in a public place. I was never alone with him."

"I don't care if you met him on national television. He's a convicted murderer and a person of interest in two other murders. You have no business hanging out with him."

Hanging out? "He needed someone to talk to." I pictured his dimples. "I was his teacher."

"But you're not his teacher now. Who knows what he has on his mind. And what about the students you have now? If you want to teach them, you'll need to stay alive."

Oh please. "Ty wouldn't hurt me."

"Mrs. Marshall and Joyce Huff might have thought the same thing."

Ouch. I started my car, tried not to think about Joyce or Mrs. Marshall, the last minutes of their lives, or whether either had known her killer. "Susan, Ty's just a kid who's been through a lot. Do you know what it's like in juvey? They hardly ever let them outside. The kids aren't even allowed books in their cells. Or writing paper—"

"You do know that those inmates aren't altar boys," Susan sputtered. "There's a reason they're in juvey. Elle, do you have any idea what Ty did to his father? He shredded him."

"You're the one who said he got a raw deal in his defense. And that he'd killed his father only after years of abuse. And that he did it to protect himself and his family."

"Yes, all that should have been taken into consideration at trial. But the fact remains that he confessed to the brutal killing of his father. Which means he has a potential for violence. Add that to his time in juvey in the company of gangs and delinquents. You have no idea how their influence has hardened him, but you do know that two murders have taken place since his release and that he hated at least one of the victims."

Up ahead, the school glowered, locked up tight. Across the parking lot, the Jolly Jack's truck started playing its song. I looked into my rearview mirror, saw it pulling away from the spot near the school. Except for my car, the parking lot was empty. Even Stan's pickup was gone. I was alone.

"I better get off the phone, Susan. I'm in the car."

We said we'd talk later, and I said I'd do my best to stay away from Ty. Then I drove out of the lot and followed the ice cream truck down the street.

At the stoplight, Duncan turned the corner, right on red. I watched his Jolly Jack's truck stop to serve a gaggle of kids, heard its persistent happy song. The light changed, and I drove on, trying not to think of Ty, the years he'd spent unable to buy an ice cream, to tell day from night, even to read a book in bed.

CHAPTER SEVEN

Somehow, the week passed without incident. On Saturday morning, Mr. Johnson didn't show up to change the locks. Maybe he was getting even for my missing our appointment on Monday. But when I'd called to reschedule the next day, he'd said he'd be by at ten a.m. Saturday. At ten thirty, I called to see where he was. Mr. Johnson answered the phone sounding sleepy, maybe hungover. He said he'd be over in twenty minutes. I said fine.

By noon, there was still no sign of Mr. Johnson.

Becky showed up, though. With scones. We were going to meet Jen at the gym, but, before we left, I got on my computer to search for another locksmith.

"Make sure there are lots of five star ratings," Becky said. "Some businesses post their own five stars to fake you out." She looked over my shoulder, pointed out Secure Locks Company.

I was reading about Secure Locks when the doorbell rang. Probably Mr. Johnson, two hours late. Well, never mind. As long as he changed my locks, it wouldn't matter. I opened the door expecting a stranger with a tool kit. Finding neither.

"Ready to go?" Jerry looked nervous.

Go?

"We have properties to see."

Oh man. He was right. Why was I forgetting everything? I hadn't even looked at my calendar. "Sorry, Jerry," I began. I wasn't

going to go. I couldn't. Wasn't in the mood to look at houses, let
alone spend time with Jerry.

Becky came up behind me. "You've got showings today?"

"You'll love these places," Jerry's voice boomed. "I preselected
them myself. And I set these appointments up starting at one, the
same time your house is being shown, so it works out perfectly."

My house? I turned to Becky, panicked. What was happening
to me? Why was I forgetting so much? I grabbed her hand.

"What?" she asked.

I had no idea what.

"Are you all right, Elle? Come sit down," she said.

But I couldn't sit down. I needed to get my mind back on track,
get organized. I left Becky with Jerry, went to my laptop, and
punched up my calendar. Sure enough, the appointments were
all there. Realtors were coming by at one with potential buyers. I
needed to focus. I took a breath. Another. Checked the time.

Ten after twelve. I had to get the house ready. I ran to the
bedroom, smoothed my comforter. Tossed my laundry into
the washer. Went to the kitchen and rinsed out my coffee cup.
Washed the tub, the bathroom sink. Scanned the living room and
dining room, checked the study.

Becky followed me around the house, whispering. "Elle? What's
the deal? Are you going house-hunting with Jerry? I thought you
fired him."

I whispered back that, yes, I'd fired him, but agreed to see these
last three places since he'd already scheduled them. But I didn't
want to, wasn't comfortable.

"How about I come with?" Becky offered. "It'll be fun."

"Really, I'll be okay," I began. But she was already on the phone
with Jen, postponing the gym until four.

We joined Jerry at the front door. When he found out Becky
was going to go with us, his eyes darted from her to me and back

and he stammered, protesting that his car was a two-seater, too small for three. I told him not to worry. Becky and I would follow him in my car.

I got my keys. As we headed out, Jerry eyed me silently, his expression a mixture of angry and bereft.

* * *

The homes were probably lovely. Becky seemed to think they were. But each time Jerry unlocked a door, I hesitated, reluctant to go in. The air inside felt too thick to penetrate, almost as if it were pushing me away.

Stop being difficult, I told myself. *You need to look at places if you want to find a new home. And you do want a new home, a fresh start.*

The first place was close to my own, in Fairmount. Green plants thrived in window boxes. The front door was arched, led into a small foyer.

"Ignore the wallpaper." Jerry stepped into the living room. "You can rip all that out and paint. But look at the detail in this place. The trim. The fireplace. And you won't find ceilings this high anywhere, not at this price."

He went on, selling. I drifted away, smelled rotting wood. Something pungent and sweet like decay. Had someone died there? I left Jerry and climbed the stairs, felt them creak.

"It really is charming." Becky followed me, chirping. "Wow. Look at that claw-footed tub."

I looked. Imagined cold water, my body submerged, a dark force holding me down. My hand clawing, fingers curling, reaching over the edge. My lungs burning, gasping for air. I blinked. The bathroom was empty, dry. Gleaming white.

"And the bedroom has built-in bookshelves!"

I didn't look at the bookshelves. I scurried down the steps to the front door, opened it, went outside. Took a deep breath.

"You haven't seen the kitchen." Jerry hurried after me.

"It's not for me."

Becky frowned, disappointed. "Really? I think it's sweet." And in the car, on the way to the next place, she scolded me. "You have to be open to change, Elle. Nothing's going to be just the way you want it. But you can make changes. Use your imagination."

My imagination, though, was the problem. It had taken over and chased me out of the first place, and it did in the second and third, as well. Everywhere we went, I imagined death or violence, violence or death. The second stop was a renovated townhouse in Old City with brand-new appliances, new floors and walls. The newness alarmed me. What were these shiny installations covering? What rot was underneath the hardwood, behind the drywall? I envisioned slime and mold, remnants of former lives. Past miseries seeping through the flooring and paneling, clutching onto whoever lived there.

Becky, of course, loved the place.

When I said I wasn't interested, Jerry became exasperated. "Fine. But you're going to love this last place."

The last place was across the park from Logan Elementary, where two of my colleagues had been murdered. As we walked up to the house, Mrs. Marshall greeted me with her bloody smile, welcoming me to the neighborhood. Jerry found the location to be an asset. "You have a view of the park, and the school in the distance. Best of all, you can walk to work." He rubbed his hands together, anticipating success.

No question, the house had appeal. It had skylights and lots of windows. The layout was open, the living room leading into the kitchen, the kitchen into the dining room. I went upstairs to the master bedroom and checked out the view.

But the view reached through the window and wrapped itself around my head. I pictured Ty out there, watching from the park, and Joyce slumped dead in her car. Mrs. Marshall blood-soaked inside the school, and up the road, Patsy Olsen crushed under a Land Rover. Somebody—Stan?—lurked in the hedges, and Duncan played a musical medley in his ice cream truck, luring children with free treats. Everything in view from the bedroom screamed murder and suspicion. I needed to get out of that house, away from that neighborhood.

But I was being ridiculous. The house had nothing to do with the murders. I blinked, shook my head, and looked out the window again, giving the view another chance. Outside, a woman chased a stroller. Kids rode bikes. At the edge of the park, a small dark-haired boy stood on a path, alone.

He looked like Seth.

But, of course, he wasn't Seth. I was imagining things.

Even so, I looked again, carefully. Decided that, no, I wasn't imagining it. The little boy was Seth. Why was he just standing alone in the park? Was he waiting for someone to pick him up? Katie or Ty?

"So? What do you think, Elle? My opinion? This is you. It's the keeper." Jerry burst into the room, carrying information sheets. "Twenty-one-hundred square feet. Perfect size. Move-in condition."

Becky joined in, agreeing that the place was roomy and light. She loved the layout, the location. The two of them went on, extolling the virtues of the house. Their voices blended, a harmonious duet.

Seth wandered over to a bench. A woman was planted there, not moving. Asleep? Her face wasn't visible, but I recognized his mother by her gaunt shape and bleached hair. Seth pulled at her a few times, but she didn't move. Passed out drunk?

"So? What do you say? Why not make an offer. Keep it low. See how they respond."

Becky and Jerry watched me, waiting.

"Listen to me, Elle. I'm going all out for you, and I know what you need. No way you're going to find another place like this. I sell homes all over Philadelphia—"

"I can't live here." I looked out the window, saw Joyce again, bloodied in her car.

"But it's everything you said you wanted—"

"And the location's perfect," Becky said.

"Tell me. Just tell me. What's the downside?" Jerry frowned.

My head ached. Why did I have to explain my decision to him? Why did I have to put it into words?

"Okay, Elle. Do me a favor. Don't rule it out. Think about it. We'll talk next week."

Becky agreed. "Good idea."

Fine. I said I'd think about it. Anything to get out of there.

"Look at that gorgeous view across the park." Jerry pointed out the window. "The trees are starting to turn. In a week, it'll be spectacular."

I glanced out the window again. Seth was still alone near his mother. He'd taken a seat, cross-legged, under a tree.

* * *

That same day, I got an offer on my house. Not asking price, but close. Too close to turn down. But how could I accept it without having a place to move into?

I spent the rest of the weekend trying to convince myself to take the place near the park. In time, the shock of the murders would fade. The location and view would become less threatening. Jerry called every three seconds, asking if I'd decided yet, reminding me that we had limited time to respond to the buyer's offer. I wandered the house, imagined leaving it. Thought of Charlie, our time there. I closed my eyes, conjured memories of his touch, his voice.

Charlie was everywhere in the house. The study was his. And every room held moments where we'd made love and plans, where we'd fought and made up, where we'd celebrated and separated. Where I'd found his lifeless body. Where I'd mourned his death.

It was time to let go. To say good-bye to Charlie. To move on.

By Monday, I'd decided to accept the offer and sell the house. On the way to school, I called Jerry, told him. He was exuberant, said we had to make an occasion out of it. Have champagne and dinner.

I said that class was starting and I had to go. He was still talking when I ended the call.

The decision to sell shook me. I moved through the day feeling detached and dazed. Had to force myself to focus on the children. But the day passed. And by the end of it, I'd accepted that I was actually going to make the change, that it was time to leave the home I'd shared with Charlie. I began to look ahead, to feel free.

Monday passed. Jerry texted me twice during the school day to ask me to dinner or at least to go look at more properties. Detective Stiles left a message for me to call him. He had more questions. Shane left a message repeating his offer of free circus classes.

In class, my students worked on subtraction and reading. We collected leaves for collages. Seth did all right, but he seemed to have trouble moving. He said he'd fallen out of a tree over the weekend, scraping and bruising his arms and knees. Several times, I saw him mumbling to himself. Or rather, to his dead father.

Katie and her friends picked him up after school. While Maggie and Trish waited in the hall, I took Katie aside, mentioned that Seth was hurting.

Katie's brows furrowed. "I know. He got pretty banged up when he fell off his bike."

His bike? Hadn't he said he'd fallen out of a tree? Why didn't their stories match?

"How are things at home, Katie?" I asked.

She looked away. "Why do you ask?"

I'd asked because I suspected she and Seth were hiding something. Just as Ty had years ago. "How's your mom doing?"

"Rose?" Katie rolled her eyes. "She's awful. Why do you ask?"

"You call your mother by her first name?"

"I don't think of Rose as my mother." Katie glanced at Seth, made sure he was busy in his cubby, out of earshot. "Or as his. I'm Seth's mother more than Rose is. I do the cooking and the cleaning. I get him up in the morning and take him to and from school." Katie's nostrils flared. "Rose is a stinkin' drunk. And I mean stinking. I can't remember the last time she had a shower. She never does anything. Since my father . . . since Ty killed Dad, she never even goes outside."

Really? "Not even to the park?" The question popped out on its own.

Katie tilted her head. "The park?"

"I saw her there the other day."

"You did? Well, I don't know. Maybe to get away from Ty. Rose is a mess, especially now that Ty's home." She stopped, looked at Maggie and Trish, watching her from the doorway. Seth came out of the cubbies with his lunchbox, eyes aimed at the floor.

"Katie, you ready?" Trish asked.

"Sure."

They said good-bye, paraded out. But at the last second, I stopped Katie, held her back. "What were you about to say? About Ty?"

She pursed her lips. "I shouldn't have said anything, Mrs. H."

"Don't worry. It's okay."

She looked up at me with startling bright eyes. "It's just Rose," she breathed. "Rose is petrified of him."

Of Ty?

She glanced out at her friends. Seth faced us, waiting. Katie turned her back to him and lowered her voice. "He's why she drinks so much. Seriously, Mrs. H, after what he did to my dad? And his temper? Now that he's back, Rose is convinced Ty's going to come after her. She thinks she's going to be next."

Before I could respond, she turned away and hurried off to meet the others. Halfway down the hall, she looked back. Made sure I was still watching.

I was. I watched until they went out the door.

Then I picked up my lesson plans, got ready to leave, thinking about what she'd said. And about Seth. He had an alcoholic mother, a brother who'd killed his father. Thank God for Katie. If not for her, no one would be looking after him. And even with her help, Seth was talking to his dead father and drawing violent blood-colored pictures. What could I do for him, other than recommend that he meet with the school psychologist? Was that enough?

Years ago, I hadn't done enough for his brother, had left him to fight his battles all alone. But now, I had a chance to help Seth. I didn't know exactly how, but this time, I was determined to do better. I headed home, ignoring the ringtone of my cell and the screen announcing yet another call from Jerry.

CHAPTER EIGHT

The new second-grade teacher began on Tuesday. Her name was Kim Lawless, and she was dark-eyed, petite, perky, peppy, and about half my age. Mr. Royal brought her by before the first bell rang, asking if I'd help her get oriented, and left us to get acquainted.

I welcomed her. Told her I was glad that she'd stepped in, that Joyce's students had been shaken by her loss and needed a permanent teacher.

Kim smiled brightly, eyes twinkling. "It's kind of daunting, trying to take her place. The students must miss her."

I told her that the kids hadn't had a chance to become attached to Joyce. She'd been killed right at the beginning of the school year.

"Good." She seemed relieved. "So, in that case, it'll be okay to make some changes."

Changes?

"I'd really like to make the room my own. For starters, I want to change the decorations. No offense to Mrs. Huff—I guess you two were friends, right? But honestly, her taste is kind of, well, bland. I want to add some life to the place."

I imagined Joyce sputtering, couldn't help but smile.

Kim looked around my classroom. "Actually, I'd like to make it more like this. Colorful and alive. Your room is so much fun."

Somewhere in eternity, Joyce let out an indignant snort. I could hear her ranting about the emotional and intellectual needs of seven-year-olds, the dangers of overstimulating them with neons and noise.

"Would you?" Kim had asked.

I'd missed the question. "Sorry?"

"I mean if it's not too much trouble. I know you have your own class to worry about."

I figured that she'd asked me to help her. But I had no idea how. Planning curricula? Decorating? I didn't know, but agreed to come by during recess.

And at recess, I crossed the hall to Kim Lawless' classroom. She was in the back, stapling colored paper to a bulletin board.

"What can I do?" I asked. I eyed the monochrome decorations. "Want help taking down these posters?"

"Fabulous, yes," she said. "You're an angel." She put down the stapler, stepped over to the desk. "But first, I have another favor to ask. Can you maybe take a look at this?" She opened up Joyce's lesson planner. "Taking the job so suddenly, I had zero time to prepare. So I hoped I could start out using her lesson plans, just, you know, until I have a chance to make my own. But her planner makes totally negative sense. It's gibberish."

Strange. "If you're stuck, you can borrow mine," I offered. "Copy it."

She looked at me, wide-eyed, and smiled sweetly. "Thanks. I don't want to put you out. If you can somehow make sense of this one, that'll be fine."

She turned the pages of the planner, found the current date. Pointed at the entries. "See?"

Indeed, the symbols weren't English. They looked like shorthand. Or Greek. Maybe Cuneiform.

I leaned over the desk and studied the first page. In the nine o'clock box was a plus sign with some numbers; at nine thirty, the stick figure of a man. A musical note was drawn in at ten o'clock. An "x" at ten thirty. A rectangle at eleven. Each time slot was filled in with a letter, symbol, or combination of both. I turned the page, found the same sorts of symbols next to the same times.

"Anything?" Kim looked over my shoulder.

Well, the musical note was clear enough, especially since I knew both second grades had music on Tuesday mornings. And the "x" was drawn in at recess time, so it must indicate a break for Joyce. Maybe the stick figure meant gym class? Or health? Or art?

"I think I'm getting some of it." I picked up the planner to show Kim what I was thinking. A slip of paper fell to the floor.

We both knelt to pick it up, but Kim got it, held it up. "Oh, and this is another mystery. Any idea what this is?"

I took it and read a list of names.

"Maybe it's a committee?"

I didn't answer. I read the names again. And again.

"Elle?"

I stared at the names. What exactly was I looking at? What was it doing in Joyce's planner? And why had I turned so icy cold?

* * *

There were seven names. I recognized all but three. All were female. Two of them belonged to murder victims. And two belonged to Becky and me.

I reasoned with myself. The fact that two of the people on the list had been murdered didn't mean anything. The list didn't necessarily belong to the killer. The seven women on it weren't necessarily his intended victims. I stared at our names. Becky's. Mine.

"What is it?" Kim asked. "I saw it before and stuffed it back into the planner in case it was important."

Actually, if it was a list of intended victims, it was vitally important. It would give the police a chance to warn, even protect, everyone on it. But beyond that, the list might provide a critical clue. The seven women named must have some connections to the killer. If those connections were found, they'd likely lead to the killer. Who would he be? Ty or Duncan? Stan?

Again, I read the seven names. Four of the women were teachers at Logan, connected to both Stan and Duncan. Ty might not have known Joyce personally, but he'd known of her through Katie. So all three men had connections to at least four of the women.

"Elle?" Kim's head was tilted at an odd angle. She squinted at me. "Are you okay?"

I clutched the piece of paper. "Sorry. Just thinking."

"It's that list, isn't it? What is it?"

I didn't know anything for sure. And I didn't want to alarm her. Kim was new and fresh. Untainted by the murders. Unaware that she might have entered a kill zone.

"Oh my," I dodged. "Recess is almost over. How about I come back at lunchtime?" I made a hasty exit, leaving Kim trying to decipher Joyce's planner. Across the hall in my room, I studied the list more closely.

It was written in pencil, hand printed in heavy letters. The paper was lined, possibly torn off a legal pad, possibly out of a notebook. I looked at my name, at Becky's. At Joyce's. The letters were not graceful, the strokes not gentle. Masculine? I wasn't sure.

I should call the police. Give the list to Detective Stiles.

But maybe I was overreacting. Objectively, the list was just some names on a piece of paper. There was no reason to believe that it had anything to do with the murders. After all, it had been in Joyce's planner, and why would Joyce have a list related to her own murder?

I reread the names.

Mrs. Marshall. Joyce Huff. Stephanie Cross.

Who was Stephanie Cross? The name was unfamiliar. Maybe the woman hit by the Range Rover? No, no—that was Penny— not Penny. Patsy. Patsy O' something. I ought to remember. The woman had been killed right next to me. Might have been killed instead of me.

Oh God.

Patsy Olsen. That was it. Definitely.

Had the killer been aiming for me the day she died, trying to check another name off his list? I read on. My name was fourth, right after Stephanie Cross. Becky's was fifth. Then came Akeesha Moses and Cherie Gallo. Two more unknowns.

My hands were unsteady, so the paper rattled as I held it. *Stop it*, I scolded myself. I had no reason to be shaking. It was probably just a coincidence that both murder victims were on the list. And the accident that killed Patsy Olsen was unrelated both to me and to the list. In fact, Becky and I and the others might have been listed for a perfectly benign reason. Maybe we'd all had items in the lost and found. Or we were all being asked to sponsor some PTA event or volunteer for a charity. Or attend a luncheon. Maybe it was a guest list. Who knew? It could be a list of nominees for Woman of the Year. There were endless possibilities, no reason to assume the names compiled a hit list.

But they might.

I needed to give it to Detective Stiles, let him decide.

The bell rang. Kids came charging into the classroom, red-faced from exertion. I stood to greet them, clasped my hands to stop the trembling, told them to take out their Think and Solve workbooks. For the moment, I shoved the list into my pants pocket. I'd call Detective Stiles after school.

* * *

But I didn't call Stiles.

I might have, except that, soon after I got home, Becky called and told me to turn on the news.

The reporter was at the scene of a murder, in the middle of his report. He was standing outside Pete's Deli, recounting how the body had been discovered behind the building by a woman walking her dogs.

"Can you believe it?" Becky asked. "It was behind Pete's. Right near the school."

I tried to listen to the reporter. He said the victim had just turned twenty-one, was a senior at Community College, studying art.

I was confused. People got killed in Philadelphia every day. Why was Becky so upset about this one? It didn't seem connected to either Mrs. Marshall or Joyce.

"Didn't you hear what they said about her?"

"No. Why, what did they say?" My heart did a two-step in anticipation.

Ty's face came onto the screen. What? Why?

"Elle. She's Ty's old girlfriend."

My mouth opened but would make no sound.

The reporter was reviewing Ty's history. The screen showed a younger Ty with his now dead father, and then as a young teen with his arm around a girl, presumably the murder victim. A voice explained that Ty had been convicted of killing his father and that he'd been released only weeks ago, just before Stephanie's murder.

It wasn't yet known if Ty had been in touch with Stephanie, but police were looking into it. A clip of the dead girl's mother began.

"Stephanie was a joy. A beautiful joy." Her hair was uncombed, her eyes dazed. She talked on.

"So what do you think, Elle?"

I thought my blood had stopped circulating.

Becky had theories. "Maybe he called her and she wanted nothing to do with him. What if he'd been obsessing about her the whole time he was away, and then he found out she'd moved on? That might have made him mad enough—"

"So you think Ty's going around killing anyone he's mad at?"

"Well, who else could it be? It's a pretty big coincidence that this girl got killed right after he got out. Just like Mrs. Marshall."

Gooseflesh rippled up my arms. Becky was right. I turned off the television, didn't want to watch a reporter exploit a mother's grief. Was Ty really the killer? I recalled him slurping up an ice cream float, savoring trees and fresh air. Was that guy—a kid with bad skin and dimples—really a savage murderer?

"Think about it," Becky said. "So far, there are three dead women. All of them had their throats slit, and all of them had connections to Ty. Mrs. Marshall was his childhood nemesis. Joyce taught his sister, Katie—"

"That's no reason for him to want to kill her. Joyce adored Katie."

"Still, it's a connection." Becky was on a roll, didn't stop to think. "And now, his old girlfriend Stephanie Cross. What are the chances?"

"Wait, who?" The gooseflesh spread from my arms onto my neck and back. "What did you say her name was?" I pulled the piece of paper out of my pocket. Reread the list. Before Becky repeated it, I found the name. It was right before mine: Stephanie Cross.

* * *

That night, Susan met us at London Grill on Fairmount. We sat at a quiet table in the back. The waiter brought us glasses and a bottle of Pinot.

"This is it." I gave her the list, picked up the bottle and poured. Didn't stop to taste it, just filled the glasses.

Susan looked it over. "This was in Joyce's planner?"

I nodded. Took a sip.

"And you kept it? Why didn't you give it to the police?"

I explained that I hadn't been sure it was significant until after Stephanie Cross had been killed.

Susan leaned forward. "Damn, Elle. Do you have any idea what this is? Or who wrote it?"

No, not a clue.

"I mean you must realize how significant this list might be. Your names are on it along with the names of two murder victims—and you found it in the possession of one of those victims. Stiles needs to see this." She shoved her hair behind her ear as she turned to Becky. "You knew about this, too?"

Becky sat up straight, shook her head, no. She hadn't known a thing about it. And she wasn't happy about that. "Why didn't you tell me, Elle? I had a right to know if my name is on some killer's list—"

"But we don't know that's what it is. I didn't want to worry you—"

"You should have at least mentioned it. Don't argue, either. You know I'm right."

I didn't know, but I apologized and squeezed Becky's hand.

She nodded. Apparently, I was forgiven.

Susan took a long drink, pushed her hair back again. "So let's get this straight." She read the list of women's names and reviewed the connections between Ty and five of the seven. And she reminded us that three of those five had been killed since Ty's release.

"It could have been four killed," Becky said. "Elle was almost run over by that car."

I heard the familiar thunk. Patsy Olsen flew onto the asphalt. Susan and Becky were talking, watching me. I swallowed wine.

"I'll take care of it." Susan finished her drink. "I'll put in a call to Detective Stiles and, as your attorney, I'll give him the list. Meantime, the two of you be careful."

"How?" Becky's eyes widened. "What are we supposed to do? Carry guns? Wear armor?"

Susan folded her hands, looked us each in the eye. "For one thing, be alone as little as possible. I want you both to stay at my house until this is cleared up. You can share the guest room."

Becky and I exchanged glances. Really? Did Susan think the danger was big enough that we should pack up and leave our homes? Becky was already answering that she couldn't impose, couldn't leave her cat. I shook my head, no, thinking of Susan's three demanding daughters, their constant turmoil and bickering. When they were home, I found it difficult even to drop in at Susan's for coffee. Staying overnight was unthinkable.

"Well, think about it. At least think about staying somewhere other than home. But whatever else you do, stay away from Ty." Her eyes bored into me when she said that.

"It's not like I hang out with him." I shifted in my seat.

"Have you heard from him since your date?" Becky asked.

"It wasn't a date," I snapped. "And no, I haven't."

"Well, stay away from him," Susan commanded. "And, while you're at it, stay away from his mother, too."

"His mother?"

"Yes. Rose Evans has as many connections to the victims as Ty has."

Again, Becky and I looked at each other.

"Rose Evans? You seriously think she's dangerous?" The idea seemed ludicrous. Rose was a ninety-five-pound drunk. According to Katie, she was rarely awake long enough to leave the house.

"Anyway, why should we worry about her? Ty's the one who was convicted of murder." Becky's skin was still flushed. Red blotches had erupted all over her neck.

Susan leaned forward, lowered her voice. "What I'm about to say is just between us, okay?"

Okay.

"We all know that Ty confessed. His confession closed his father's murder case."

So? We knew that.

"But until he confessed, he wasn't even a suspect. Guess who the main suspect was? His mother. Rose Evans was an abused wife and a heavy drinker. The night of the murder, she had fresh bruises and a gash on her head. She was at home with the victim and the knife that killed him. In other words, she had motive, means, and opportunity to kill her husband."

Becky and I sat silent. Rose? It made sense. She might have done it.

Except that Ty had confessed. So, apparently, she hadn't done it.

"But if they had such a strong case against Rose, how could they accept Ty's confession?" Becky didn't understand.

"His confession rang true. Ty knew all the details of the crime. And besides, he had as much motive, means, and opportunity as his mother did."

Nobody spoke for a moment. Becky sipped wine; I refilled Susan's glass, then my own.

Susan stared at the bottle. "I wasn't handling the case, but I was in the loop. And honestly, I thought the confession was horseshit.

I thought Ty was a skinny, abused teenager who was covering for his mother."

"But he confessed to murder, Susan. It's serious, not like he covered up for a shoplifting charge." I didn't get it.

"Think about it, Elle. If Rose had been convicted of killing her husband, even if she got manslaughter instead of murder, she'd go away for a long time, if not for life. Ty, his baby brother, and younger sister would be without any parents at all, and they'd end up in foster care."

My stomach fluttered, realizing what Susan was getting at. "So you think Ty confessed for the sake of the other kids."

"It crossed my mind back then that his mother must have pressured him to take the fall. By confessing as a juvenile, at most he'd serve five or six years. He'd be out by age twenty or twenty-one and still have his whole life ahead of him, and his mom would get to stay home raising the little ones. The family would be safe and intact. So yes, I thought it likely that Ty went away for his family's sake."

Wow. Poor Ty. I could imagine him doing that, sucking it up, playing tough guy, a silent hero. But if Susan believed he'd been innocent back then, why did she suspect him of these recent killings?

She answered without my asking. "My thinking has changed." She toyed with her wineglass. "Knowing the family better, I doubt Ty was covering for his mother. Rose Evans is a neglectful self-destructive drunk. Not the kind of parent anyone would want to leave his younger siblings with. Certainly not at the price of spending years in jail."

I didn't agree. "Rose might not have been perfect, but she was the better of the two parents. She wasn't drinking as much back then. And she was the only mother Ty knew. I can see him taking the blame for her." I pictured Rose shrieking at Mrs. Marshall, defending Ty. Maybe she and Ty had been close back then, and maybe Ty had imagined that, free of his father's abuse, she would stop drinking and straighten up, taking care of the younger kids.

But I remembered something he'd said: "My own mother's afraid of me. She wants me out of the house."

If Rose had committed the murder and Ty had covered for her, why would she be afraid of him? Wouldn't she welcome him home and spend her life trying to thank him?

The waiter came by, asked if we'd like another bottle.

I said, "Fine," at the same time Susan said, "No."

I said, "I guess not then," just as she said, "Okay, sure."

Becky finally said, "No thanks," and asked for the check.

He went to get it. For a moment we were quiet.

"Bottom line," Susan said, "we don't know what happened. It might have been either of them, so stay away from them both, okay?" She emptied her glass. "And move into my guest room."

Becky huddled in her seat. I put my hand on her arm. "We'll be okay, Becky," I said.

"Sure we will." She swallowed the last of her wine. "As long as we stay bolted inside Susan's guest room."

More silence. Susan's idea about Rose bothered me. It didn't fit—and as I emptied my glass, I realized what it was.

"Rose might have killed her husband," I said. "She had plenty of motive. But what motive would she have to kill the women on the list? And why would she start now?"

"Who knows? Maybe she started now because Ty's out." Again, Susan pushed her hair off her face. "Maybe now his release triggered something in her, and she's going after the women who've been important in his life. Or maybe they're a sick kind of team, acting together."

That theory made no sense to me.

"Susan's right. Maybe it's both of them," Becky said. "Maybe Rose killed her husband, and Ty covered for her. And then being in juvey turned him into a hard-core criminal so now he's killing people and she's covering for him. Tit for tat."

No. She wanted him out of the house. According to Katie, Rose was afraid Ty would kill her in her sleep.

I thought of little Seth, living in a house of murderers. Well, at least he had Katie.

"Ty's always been mean," Becky went on. "Even as a little kindergartener, he was always in fights, hurting other kids."

Fine. So he'd been a bad boy. That didn't make him a brutal killer. Or prove that he was planning to kill all the women whose names were on that list. After all, what did he have against Becky? Or me? Hadn't he told me that I was the only one who'd ever been nice to him?

My ringtone and Becky's started at the same time. Becky looked at her phone and gasped. "It's Jen. What should I say? She'll think we planned to get together without her. You know how she gets."

Susan said something, but I didn't hear. I was answering my own phone, taking a call from a number I didn't recognize. Listening to high-pitched giggling, then silence at the other end.

* * *

That night, Susan's warnings reverberated in my mind. I bolted the door, locked the windows. Opened a bottle of Syrah and sat in the kitchen with knives at my fingertips. Thought about Joyce, Mrs. Marshall, and Stephanie Cross. Had they recognized their killer? Was it the same person who'd pushed Patsy Olsen off the curb? Had they had time to realize they were dying?

What would it be like, having just seconds to think your last thoughts? Would you think at all—or would shock and reflex block out thoughts? Would you feel pain? My ringtone began.

Becky was calling, checking to see if I was all right, telling me she'd gotten home safely. "Do you think Susan's right? Does someone want to kill us?" Her voice was higher, thinner than usual.

I said I thought we should be cautious.

"I called Carlo," she said. "He's going to spend the night."

Carlo was an ex-boyfriend who was still in love with her. She'd thrown him out for being too possessive. I doubted that having him spend the night was a good idea.

"He'll be on the sofa, Elle. He knows the deal."

Okay, at least Becky would be safe. Carlo was a solid guy. No one would mess with him.

"But what about you, Elle? Are you going to be okay?"

I assured her that I was fine, locked up tight.

I assured myself the same thing. Taking my wine with me, I went through the house, turned off lights. Stopped at the living room. Something wasn't right. A chill rattled me as I realized what it was. The lamp on the end table was twisted. The cord faced the room, not the wall.

I never would have moved the lamp that way.

And that wasn't all. The vase on the coffee table had been moved to the mantle.

For a moment, I stood still, doubting my own eyes. Trying to convince myself that nothing was out of place. Then, wine splashing, I ran back to the kitchen and exchanged my glass for a butcher knife. I started through the house, room by room. Someone had been there, moving my stuff. Probably Jerry again. But whoever he was, if he was still in the house, he'd be sorry.

Knife in hand, I moved down the hallway, punching numbers into my phone, making a call. Jerry picked up and began talking.

"Elle? Did you get my emails? Have you signed the documents? What about that property? Have you thought any more about it? Because I'll tell you this: it's not going to be avail—"

"Were you here?" I barked. "Did you come into my house again, Jerry?"

"What? Please. Not that again, Elle."

I repeated my question, hoped that he'd say, yes, it had been him.

"No. Elle. I haven't been there. So what about the house?"

"Don't lie, Jerry. I know you've used the lock box key. I know you've come in before—"

"I came in, yes, when I had a reason to. I told you. I came to improve your staging, but now the house is sold. Why would I come in?"

"You tell me."

"I wouldn't. I'd have no reason to. You act like I'm your boyfriend, the way you harp at me." His voice was a whine.

"You swear it wasn't you?"

"Oh my God, Elle. Look, I know you're upset, what with your friends being killed, but remember, I'm a busy man. I have dozens of clients who want my time and attention—and by the way, their properties are worth ten or fifteen times more than yours. But even so, I do more for you than I do for any of them. Don't ask me why. Okay, I admit it's because I like you. But I've about had it with your crazy games of cat and mouse, hot and cold, inviting and accusing. So just tell me—did you sign the document I sent?"

I took a breath. No, I hadn't signed it. I hadn't even seen it. I'd been out all day working.

"Well, sign it, will you please?" He went on, suggesting we look at more properties, but I warned him not to come in without permission ever again and said I had to go. I clicked off before he could say anything.

I stood in the hallway, gripping the knife, peering down the hall, up the staircase. The house felt empty, and I doubted that the intruder was still there. Still, I finished my search, going through every room, closet, and cabinet. I looked under the bed, behind the sofas. Found no one.

My phone rang a few times. Jen called, miffed about not being included earlier. "It doesn't matter that it was a legal matter. I still could have sat with you and had some wine."

Susan called to see how I was. "I'm seeing Stiles in the morning. Once he's seen the list, you should expect a call."

Sometime after midnight, with every light in the house turned on, with my butcher knife and wine bottle, I went to bed. When the sun came up, I was still awake.

CHAPTER NINE

I was bleary eyed the next day. Twenty-three seven-year-olds had no sympathy. They bounced into class, full of energy.

"Mrs. Hawwison?" Emily couldn't say her *r*'s. "Look what I bwought for 'Show and Tell.'" She held up a stuffed hippo.

I'd forgotten. I'd asked the children to bring in something to talk about with the class.

"Mrs. Harrison," Millicent said. "Guess what? We're getting a puppy!"

"So?" Bobby said. "Our dog had puppies and we got five."

"I'm getting a new baby."

Kids talked at once, outdoing each other. I clapped my hands for attention, asked who'd brought items for "Show and Tell." About twenty hands went up.

Seth's wasn't one of them. He folded his hands in front of him, whispering. Talking to his father?

I told the class that anyone who hadn't brought anything could still take a turn and tell us about a special memory or possession. I looked at Seth to let him know I hoped he'd participate.

That's when I noticed his bruises.

Casually, asking Emily to begin, I walked over to his desk to get a better look.

As Emily and her hippo made their way to the front of the room, I checked out Seth's wounds. They were worse than they'd been when he'd fallen "out of a tree" or "off a bike." His arms were ringed with bruises near the wrists and above one elbow. His lip was puffy, and his cheek was blue and swollen under his eye.

I didn't say anything right away but, at recess, I held him back and asked what had happened.

He told me he'd fallen off his bike.

"What happened?" I asked.

"I was trying to do a trick but I flipped." His eyes aimed at the floor.

I asked him straight out. "Seth, did someone hurt you?"

He didn't look at me, just shook his head slowly, no.

He was lying, probably too scared to tell the truth. But clearly, rings of hand-shaped bruises hadn't come from falling off a bike. I tousled his hair and sent him to recess, then headed to Mr. Royal's office. According to protocol, I had to inform him first, even though I knew my assertion would fluster him, and he'd try to make it go away. He wouldn't be able to, though. I wouldn't let him.

Like his brother, Ty, before him, Seth was being abused. I'd let Ty down, but this time I was going to do something to stop it, starting with making a call to the Department of Human Services.

* * *

Early on Thursday morning, hours before the start of school, under dark clouds and intermittent rain, social workers showed up at Rose Evans' home to remove Seth and Katie. Seth was temporarily placed with a foster family in the same school district. Katie was able to move to her friend's house because Maggie's mother somehow intervened, arranging for Katie to stay with them.

I later heard that, while the children were moving out, Rose exploded. Ty and a neighbor had to physically restrain her. She'd raged all day, calling lawyers and officials until she was too drunk to speak.

On Friday morning, when I got to school, she was waiting.

"Bitch! I'll kill you!" She stood across the parking lot, bellowing as I got out of my car. She yelled more, but she was far away, and I couldn't understand her words.

Few other cars were around. Clearly her yelling was intended for me. But why? Unless she'd found out that I was the one who'd called DHS. But she couldn't have. That information was confidential, never to be released.

Rose shouted something, put her head down, and charged.

Fortunately, in her inebriated condition, she wasn't particularly coordinated. While she teetered toward me through last night's rain puddles, I unlocked my car and got back inside. By the time she rammed my door, I was safe in the driver's seat. She stood outside my window, ranting, pounding the glass.

"You had no right," she shouted. "What made you think you had the right?" She slammed the window.

I gaped at her.

"Oh, don't play innocent." She bent over, her voice slamming the window, her face up against the glass.

I saw the mole on her chin, the stray coarse hairs on her withered upper lip. Her flaring nostrils. Her spit on the pane. I looked away.

"I know it was you. Don't pretend it wasn't. You think Seth didn't tell his mommy that you made him go to the principal's office and tell you both how he got hurt? And when he told you, what did you do? Did you believe him that he had an accident? No, you went and told lies about me, and you had him taken away.

Guess what, you fucking bitch know-it-all, kids get hurt. They get hurt all by themselves every single fucking day. A bruise doesn't mean their mother's hurting them. But you don't know—how could you? You don't have any kids. You're just a fucking dried-up childless authority who doesn't know any-goddamn-thing."

That comment stung. I'd never intended to be childless at forty. She was right. I didn't know what it was like to have kids. For a moment, I had second thoughts. Maybe I shouldn't have reported the violence so fast. Maybe I'd jumped to conclusions, deciding that Seth was in immediate danger without enough actual evidence.

Rose had quieted and backed away. At first, I thought she was leaving. When she body-slammed the door, I wasn't expecting it, smacked my chest into the steering wheel.

"I'm a single fucking mother." She kicked the car. "A widow." Another kick. "I'm struggling." Slam. "To do my best for my kids." Bam with both fists on my hood. "Those kids—they're everything to me. Everything." A kick, another. "Seth and Katie are all I have." She stopped, bent over, and looked in the window again. "You bitch, breaking up my family, what I've got left of it." She growled, low and menacing. "I'll tell you what. If my husband was alive, you wouldn't dare interfere with us. He'd rip your fucking face off. Come out here and face me, you coward, you freaking coward bitch. I know it was you." She backed away again and rammed the side of the car.

Okay, I'd had enough. The initial shock had worn off enough for me to realize that I had options other than sitting frozen. While Rose kept kicking my car and screaming at me, I turned the key in the ignition and leaned on the horn as I backed out of the parking spot.

Children lined up, waiting for the school doors to open, turned their heads toward the blaring horn. Officer Salerno, on duty at the front door, looked our way and headed over to see what was happening, Stan right behind him. Hal Sorenson and Dolores Sanchez, two upper-grade teachers who had just parked in the lot, heard the horn and gaped at Rose as she continued to kick my door and punch my hood even as I backed up.

"Hey—what're you doing?" Hal called to Rose. "Hold on there."

I kept honking and moving back on wet asphalt. Rose ran alongside my car, pounding and shouting, ignoring Hal. Telling me what she'd do to me if I had the balls to get out and face her. Officer Salerno and Stan converged on her from one direction, Hal and Dolores from the other. Still, she wouldn't stop until a pair of handcuffs restrained her movement, and even with the cuffs, she kicked and cursed all the way to the patrol car. More cars arrived in the lot. Teachers focused on finding parking spaces, didn't notice us.

"You okay?" Hal asked through my window. He tried to open the door for me, but it was still locked. I didn't unlock it. Didn't move.

"That was crazy," Dolores said. "Who is she? She looks familiar."

I nodded, didn't answer. Didn't explain who the woman was or why she hated me so vehemently. I sat at the wheel, nodding when they asked if I was okay, shaking my head no when they asked if I needed help.

Stan stood in front of the car, eyeing it, saying nothing. After a few minutes, Officer Salerno came back. The four of them conferred. Finally, Dolores and Hal set off through rows of Toyotas, Kias, Jeeps, and Chevys toward the school. Stan straggled behind them.

I sat, recovering from Rose's rage. Her words echoed in my head, peppered my body like machine-gun fire, ratatatting my chest, my belly. Being the target of so much rage seemed to have paralyzed me. When I saw that Rose had been loaded into the back of a police car, I took a few breaths before unlocking the door. Another few before opening it.

Officer Salerno helped me out of the car. He had questions. Was I all right? Did I know Rose Evans or why she'd want to hurt me? What exactly had happened? Had she injured me or just my car?

My car. I stepped away and looked behind me. The driver's door and hood were pockmarked with scuffs and dents. I thought of Seth, his small battered body. Had Rose kicked and punched him, too?

Officer Salerno kept asking questions, trying to take a statement. My answers were abrupt, unfocused. I didn't have time to talk. School was about to start. I told him that I was uninjured. That, yes, I knew Rose Evans. That she was the mother of a student.

Mr. Royal fluttered over, interrupting the interview, repeating, "Oh, goodness," and, "Goodness me," shaking his finger my way as if I were to blame for triggering Rose's temper. As if he'd warned me this might happen.

Officer Salerno tried to keep me on track. Asked again if I knew why Mrs. Evans was so angry. Mr. Royal eyed me, waiting to see what I'd say. I said that her son had been taken to foster care, and she blamed me. Mr. Royal stared into the heavens.

"Why would she blame you?" Officer Salerno wanted to know. "The Commonwealth doesn't take children from their parents without a good reason."

I met Mr. Royal's eyes, said nothing. He pulled at his mustache, his face beet-red.

"Elle! Thank God!" Becky rushed over, oblivious to the puddles she splashed through, grabbed my hand. "They're saying somebody attacked you—you know what I thought. I nearly fainted. But here you are and you're okay. Tell me what happened."

"Ma'am." Officer Salerno tried to quiet her. "Please step back."

But Becky wasn't going anywhere. She hung onto me. "Oh my God. It was Rose Evans, wasn't it? That's why she's over there in the police car."

She didn't give me time to answer.

Her face turned white. "So this is it."

What?

"Ma'am." Salerno tried to step between us. "I mean it. Move away."

"It's her. It's Rose Evans. Ty's mother—don't you see?"

"Ma'am. You're interfering with a police investigation." Salerno put his hand on Becky's upper arm and firmly moved her back and away.

"See what?"

Becky stood on tiptoe, walking backwards, talking to me over Salerno's shoulder as if they were waltzing. "Rose wrote the list. And your name was next—"

She was right. Elle Harrison had been listed right after Stephanie Cross. So what was Becky saying? That Rose Evans had made the list of victims? That she'd killed Mrs. Marshall, Joyce, and Stephanie Cross? That she'd planned to kill me because my name was next?

Rose Evans? Skinny and usually half-drunk, could she be a murderer?

I hugged myself, recalled the hatred blazing in Rose's eyes, felt the impact of her fists slamming the roof of my car. Heard her hiss. "Bitch, you cold, unfeeling bitch."

If she'd been able to, I had no doubt that she'd have killed me. But did she hate everyone on the list that much? And the timing didn't make sense. The list of names had been written long before Seth and Katie had been taken from her home. Why would Rose have hated me before her son had gone into foster care?

After dancing a few yards, Officer Salerno deposited Becky behind a blue Volkswagen, came back to me, and resumed his questions. I was more articulate now, able to explain more clearly who Rose Evans was, how I was connected to her. Meantime, a small throng of teachers gathered around. They strained to listen, whispering and gawking until the bell rang and they scurried off to their classes. Becky lingered by the Volkswagen, mouthing words and making hand signals I couldn't understand. I waved her away so she wouldn't be late.

When she finally left, it was reluctantly. "Recess," she called. "Your room."

There were more questions. I answered them quickly, summarizing for Officer Salerno what had happened. Rose had been waiting for me. Had attacked without warning. Behind him, the children—my second graders—filed into the school building.

Salerno saw no reason to hurry. "According to your friend, this attack was more than just an isolated incident. What did she mean? What do you know about that?"

I shook my head, watched the children. Who would greet my class? Had word filtered to them that Mrs. Harrison had been attacked? "Nothing. Becky was just upset."

"Really? Because two other women who work at Logan Elementary are dead, and now you've been attacked. Was your friend indicating that these incidents are related?"

I told him I doubted it. After all, the other women had been stabbed, not beaten up. And Mrs. Evans hadn't had a knife.

He smirked. "Why does the public assume a killer always uses the same weapon?"

The public? Was I "the public"? Did everyone in "the public" all think the same things? And were we wrong?

"In fact, sometimes some serial killers do use the same method. But not all killers have such a definite pattern. Usually, if a person wants to kill you, trust me, they'll use whatever's around."

I nodded. Saw Rose's fists land on my windshield, heard the thunk. Saw a woman smacked by a Land Rover. The weapon didn't have to be a knife. It could be a hand. A car. Whatever was around.

The thunk kept repeating. But I couldn't let on. I thanked Salerno for helping me, assured him I was fine, turned down his offer to walk me to my classroom. I hurried, looked back at my wounded car. Puddles on the asphalt gleamed, reflecting the morning sunlight. Beyond them, the Jolly Jack's truck parked at the far end of the parking lot. Duncan Girard stood behind it. He lifted an arm and waved. How long had he been standing there, watching? I had the feeling that, though he hadn't come to my assistance, he'd been there for a while, that he'd watched the whole scene. And that it had given him a hearty laugh.

* * *

Somehow, I made it through the day, talking to Becky at recess and lunch, convincing her that we couldn't be sure that the killer was Rose Evans. Paying attention to Seth without drawing attention to him. Making sure he was all right, not completely traumatized by his move. By the time I got home, my whole body ached. All I wanted was a glass of wine and a bubble bath.

I should have known better. When I was parking my car, I saw Ty on my front steps, waiting.

"Why, Mrs. H? Why did you do it?" His teeth were clenched. So were his fists.

"How are you, Ty?" I had no desire to take on another angry member of the Evans family. I kept walking, tried not to look alarmed.

"I trusted you. How could you do that to me? To my family?" He came down the steps, steaming.

He charged me just as his mother had, and I considered turning around and dashing back to my car as I had that morning. But I didn't. My keys were in my hands. I separated them, positioned one so I could jam it into his face, even an eye if he seriously meant to hurt me.

"You made a big mistake, Mrs. H, ripping my family apart."

"I didn't do anything to your family."

"Really? Are you going to say it wasn't you? You're going to lie to my face?" He was over six feet tall and looked down at me, his face distorted with rage. "Did you think Seth wouldn't tell us you and the principal looked at his scrapes? That you took him to the nurse's office, made him take his shirt off, and asked him all kinds of questions about how he got hurt? Well, guess what? He did tell us. He told us you didn't believe him when he said he got hurt when he fell, and he was right. Because like a day later, social workers show up and take him away. So don't pretend it wasn't you. Don't fucking lie to me." His breath flew into my face. It was fiery.

Don't act frightened, I told myself. But I took a step back. Another. "Calm down." I spoke to myself as much as to him. I took a breath.

"Calm down?" He unlocked a fist and slapped himself on the forehead. "You destroy my family and then, when I confront you about it, all you can do is tell me to calm down? What the fuck, Mrs. H? Who are you? Really, I mean that. Because I thought you were someone I could count on. Someone I could trust."

"You can trust me, Ty. But you can't ambush me on the street."

"My mother's in fucking jail because of you. And my little brother? God knows where my brother is."

"Seth is safe. He's with people who will care for him so he won't come to school with bruises all over his body."

"Bullshit. Nobody hurt Seth."

"Then why would the authorities take him to foster care, Ty? The state doesn't just randomly take kids from their homes."

His eyes narrowed. The veins in his forehead protruded. His voice softened to a hiss. "So you admit it was you then? You called to report my mother."

I reminded myself that I was the teacher; he the pupil. I saw him as a boy being dragged by the shirt collar into the principal's office, his nose bloody and knees scuffed. "Sometimes it's necessary to intervene, Ty. Seth had clearly been beaten. There were hand marks on him. He had a black eye, bruises all over the place."

"Did you ask him what happened? Did it ever occur to you, before you 'intervened,' to check out his story? How did you decide my mother was hurting him?"

"I didn't." I had no proof.

"Then why's she in jail?"

He didn't know? I wasn't going to tell him how she'd come after me. How it had taken four people including a cop to stop her. No, I wasn't going into that. Instead, I shot out a reply without thinking. "If your mother didn't hurt Seth, then who did? You?"

He recoiled as if I'd punched him. Again, I saw the little boy scrapping with other kids, pretending to be tough.

"Look, Ty," I tried to reason with him. "I didn't accuse anyone. But as a teacher, I'm required by law to report any—"

"Mrs. H, you really think that I'd hurt Seth?" He stared at me, wounded. His eyes filling up.

"No, of course not. I was just pointing out that he was being harmed in your mother's home."

"How could you think that?" The tears burst, spilled down his face. "Why did I ever trust you? You're just like everybody else, you don't care. You pretend to, but you don't."

"Ty—"

"No, don't talk. Just the fuck don't talk. Listen for once. I did everything I could—everything to keep my family together. That's why I did what I did. It's why I went to fuckin' juvey. For my family. To make sure Katie and Seth could grow up at home and be okay. But now, thanks to you, everything I've done is useless. All for nothing. I went away for all that time, I gave up college and ruined my future. For nothing. Because of you, what I did doesn't matter. My family's gone anyfuckinghow."

He stopped, pinched the bridge of his nose to stop the tears. I waited a beat.

"I'm sorry, Ty." I kept my voice low. "I'm really sorry but I had no choice."

He sniffed. Turned away.

"Look, I know you did what you did to your father in order to protect your family from him. I know that you sacrificed yourself and your future to keep your mom, brother, and sister safe."

He didn't say anything, stared at the line of cars parked along the street.

"But the fact remains that, even with your father gone, someone's been hurting Seth. And someone should examine Katie to make sure she hasn't been hurt, too."

Ty's mouth opened and he faced me with a look of disbelief. "You're amazing, Mrs. H. Just amazing. You don't get it. Nobody's hurting them but you with your suspicions. And, honestly, after all I've done to keep them together, do you seriously think I'm going to sit by and watch you pull them apart?" The forehead veins throbbed. His eyes blazed.

Whoa. "Are you threatening me, Ty?" My voice was a thread. I clutched my keys, ready to strike.

Ty looked down at me with smoldering eyes. "No, Mrs. H. I'm not threatening you. But I swear, you'll be sorry."

Before I could respond, he wheeled around and strode away, leaving me in front of my house, my keys digging into the flesh of my palms.

* * *

My hands were shaking when I took Susan's call. She sounded harried. "What the hell happened today, Elle? Are you all right?"

I plopped onto my sofa, not sure where to start.

"Becky called to say Rose Evans was arrested for attacking you. I checked, and Rose is at the Roundhouse, waiting for a hearing—in fact, she might have already had it. So she'll probably be out on bail any time."

"On bail?" They weren't going to keep her locked up? I looked at the front door, pictured her kicking and banging it in.

"Maybe not. They might let her out on her own recognizance."

What? "You mean they might just let her go?"

"Maybe. Rose has a clean record, and she's not a flight risk."

"Susan, she tried to kill me." I couldn't believe they'd just, poof, let her out of jail. I kept staring at the door, expecting it to come crashing down.

"Don't worry, Elle. Given her charges, I'd expect she'll have to post a hefty bail. And the judge will probably warn her to stay the hell away from you." I pictured Susan pushing her hair behind her ear, thinking. "Okay, look, I'll find out about bail and her release status, when her arraignment is, exactly what the charges are. How's that."

"Thanks." Why would they let her go? She'd no doubt come after me again. And I had nothing to defend myself with—the house was stark and decluttered. No candlesticks or ice picks. No fireplace poker or tongs. Maybe the porcelain vase on the mantel? I could throw it, hit her head. But wait. I was worrying needlessly. Rose wasn't going to burst into my living room. In fact, it wasn't even my living room anymore. Someone had made an offer to buy it, and I'd told Jerry to accept it. The house was as good as sold. I pictured Charlie in the wingback chair, legs crossed, frowning. "You're really doing it? Selling our house? Moving? Leaving me here alone? How can you, Elf?"

Stop it, I told myself. *Your mind is wandering. Pay attention.*

Susan was repeating my name, waiting for me to answer her.

"Sorry." I didn't explain. Didn't need to. Susan knew me well.

She repeated her question. She wanted me to tell her what had happened, why Rose was so furious. I told her about Seth's bruises and welts. The Department of Human Services complaint that Mr. Royal and I had filed.

"But those complaints are confidential," Susan said. "There's no way that Rose or any parent can find out who contacted—"

"Seth told her I'd asked about his bruises and had the principal and school nurse take a look at them." I felt the impact of Rose's fists slamming my window, her legs ramming my door. The car rocking with impact. I picked up an embroidered throw pillow, hugged it to my chest.

"Okay, so you reported abuse. And then?"

"And then, DHA got some kind of emergency order to remove Seth and Katie from the home. They got them out the very next day."

"Who's Katie?"

"Seth's sister."

"Was she hurt, too?"

"I don't know. They took both minors."

"Okay." Her voice sounded uncertain.

"We had no choice, Susan. You should have seen that little boy's chest. He had red welts on his ribs. And a bruise under his eye." I shook my head, chasing away the images. Noticed a thin coat of dust on the coffee table. But so what? The house was sold. I didn't need to keep it pristine for showings anymore. I could let dust build up to the ceiling.

"—and after all, he has a violent history. And the abuse started right after he got out of juvey, didn't it? Sounds like he's the one hurting Seth."

Was she talking about Ty? No, I couldn't imagine Ty harming little Seth.

Then again, I wouldn't have imagined him killing his father. Or showing up at my home, threatening me.

Besides, we couldn't be sure when the abuse started. It might have begun years ago without anyone noticing. Or over the summer, long before Ty came home.

Or not. Despite my doubts, Ty might be responsible. Maybe that was why Rose was afraid of him, why she wanted him out of her house. I saw him at my doorstep, anger pulsing in his forehead. Why was I trying to deny it? Ty was a killer who'd spent years locked up with other violent youths. He might well have been hurting his brother. I sat up, replaced the pillow against the sofa cushion. Took a breath.

"Now. About the list."

The list? For the briefest moment, I didn't recall what list Susan was talking about.

"Becky thinks Rose wrote it."

Oh, that list. The list of seven names, the first three belonging to murder victims. The fourth belonging to me.

"So pack a bag," Susan said. "You're staying at my house."

What? God, no. With her three banshee daughters and a passive-aggressive husband? "No, Susan. Really—"

"Just for a few days."

"No." I said it more emphatically than I'd intended. "I mean I don't want to intrude—"

"Elle, don't argue. You shouldn't stay alone, not now, with that psycho Ty out there and Rose out on bail. Even if they have nothing to do with the murders, your name is on that list. And so is Becky's. We have room for you both. If you don't want to share the guest room, Lisa and Julie will double up and you can have Lisa's room."

"I don't know." I wasn't sure which was worse. Spending the night at Susan's house of chaos or facing a knife-wielding murderer.

Susan waited. I pictured her at her desk, surrounded by files and case notes. A voice in the background interrupted, sounded urgent. Susan said she had to go, her clients had arrived. "See you later. Just bring Becky and come. I'll bake banana bread."

I agreed to talk to Becky about it, but said I didn't want to disrupt her family and besides, I'd be fine at home. Even though I hadn't had the locks changed yet, I would double bolt the doors. I was talking about the bolts when I realized that Susan had already clicked off, that I was talking to dead air.

* * *

I was on my way to Charlie's study, to get a bottle of Syrah from the rack on top of the bar when the doorbell rang. I figured it was Becky, coming by to urge me to stay at Susan's. I was so sure that the person on my doorstep was Becky that I almost opened the door, but at the last moment, I realized that it might be Rose, so I put the bottle and glass on the foyer table and checked the peephole.

It wasn't Rose. Wasn't Becky either. Not even Ty. No, the person at my door was Jerry.

"Elle." His voice boomed through the door frame. "It's me. Open up."

I didn't move, didn't say anything. Didn't want to deal with Jerry.

"Come on, Elle. It's important. I know you're home."

He did? How?

"We need to talk."

Jerry was persistent. If I didn't answer, he'd keep yelling. Wouldn't go away. "Jerry," I called, "it's not a good time. Is this about the house? I'll email the forms to you tonight." I hadn't signed them yet, had to get on it.

"It's not about the forms, Elle. It's something else."

Damn. Was the buyer backing out? I opened the door. Jerry looked dapper, as usual, his hair slicked back, his suit expensive. He held a bouquet of red roses in one hand, a bottle of Syrah in the other.

"Hi there." He smiled.

I swallowed. "Jerry, like I said—"

"These are for you." He held out the flowers, stepped forward toward the door.

I didn't take the roses. Jerry had no business buying them.

"Look, Elle, I know how you feel. I get it. But look, we suc-ceeded. We got it done, sold your house. We need to celebrate. Plus I don't want you to have hard feelings about me. Can't we sit down while you sign the papers online, drink some wine, and make peace? I want to part on good terms, that's all."

My neck was strained, looking up at him. He looked like a huge puppy with large sorry eyes and slumped shoulders. Still, I didn't want him to come in. Didn't want his flowers or his wine either.

"That's sweet of you, Jerry. But really, I'm going out—"

"Really? You've got a date? Who's the guy?"

I hesitated too long. Didn't answer.

"Come on, Elle. This is me. You don't need to pretend. I know you're not seeing anybody."

"It's not your business."

"Besides, I won't stay long. Just one drink." He stepped for-ward, brushing past me to enter the house. "Let's sign your papers and toast your sale, and I'll be out of here."

"Jerry, no." I put up a hand, blocking him.

He stopped, pouting, feigning surprise and pain.

"I told you this isn't a good time."

He nodded, bit his lip. "Okay. Fine then. I guess I'll go." He held out the wine and roses. "Here. Take these. I bought them for you."

An awkward moment passed before I accepted them. "Look, this was sweet of you. But you should have called first."

"Why? What's the point? You don't take my calls."

It was true. I'd been avoiding him. I felt my face redden.

"Fact is, a divorced woman your age should be grateful for the interest of someone like me." He didn't smile. "You could do a lot worse."

What? Had he been drinking? "Time to go, Jerry."

"You sure? Because frankly I'm tired of your I'm-too-good-for-you attitude. I've been patient, but I'm going to be honest with you, Elle. This is your last chance."

My last chance? That was it. Jerry had crossed a line. I dropped the flowers onto the foyer floor, grabbed the door, and showed him out.

"Really? That's how you're going to play it? Fine. I'll see you around, Elle. At settlement. Be sure to send the papers."

I pointed to the street.

He sauntered past, spun around on the front stoop, and tried again. "Just one drink?"

I didn't answer, just shut the door.

"Well," he shouted from the porch, "even if you don't share it with me, promise you'll drink the wine. I want you to relax and enjoy. My treat."

"Bye, Jerry."

"Promise?"

What the hell? "Fine. I promise."

When I was sure he was gone, I threw the roses in the trash, almost threw out the wine, too. Instead, I opened it. The cork came out easily, and I poured a glass, pretty much gulping it down. Jerry, Ty, Rose, Seth. Duncan. Stan. Patsy Olsen, Stephanie Cross, Joyce and Mrs. Marshall. Faces and voices swam in my head. I poured another glass, took it and the bottle to the living room. Jerry's gift was unwelcome, but there was no point in wasting a good bottle of Syrah.

CHAPTER TEN

Rain pounded the windowpanes. I moaned and started to roll over. My muscles screamed in protest. No part of me wanted to move. I didn't argue, lay still with my eyes closed. Didn't move or think, didn't exactly sleep. Just lay in bed, aware only of rain.

The first time I heard my ringtone, I let it go. It sounded dim and far away, and my arms were too heavy to reach for it. But it rang again. And again, who knows how many times before I finally forced my eyes open, my head off the pillow, my torso off the sheets to look for the phone. Where the hell was it?

The ringtone stopped before I could locate the source. But there I was, sitting up, awareness creeping into the slog of my mind. The rain—hadn't it just been raining? It had subsided, had diminished to a gentle drizzle. The nightstand clock said 9:14.

And I was naked.

Naked?

I looked down again, making sure. Yes, indeed, I had not a stitch on. No nightgown. No t-shirt. No comfy sweatpants. Nothing. A puzzling shiver of disgust skittered down my back, and I pulled the sheet up over my chest, covering myself, looking around the room, at the bathroom door, into the closet, as if hiding myself from unseen eyes.

But of course no one was there. I was alone.

I leaned back against the pillows, confusion setting in. Why was I naked? Had I taken a shower late at night and fallen asleep before putting on a t-shirt? I didn't know, couldn't remember. But I never slept naked. Never. Not since Charlie. So why had I decided to last night?

And why was I so repulsed? Nudity didn't normally bother me, but now my body felt nasty. I needed to wash, get clean. I forced myself out of bed, into the bathroom, into the tub. I turned on steamy water and soaped up, scrubbing away angry images of the day before. Rose Evans. Ty. And someone else? I couldn't remember. I rinsed and soaped again, straining my memory until the water cooled.

My phone rang again. I let it go. Started over, running hot water until I was burning, and scrubbing and washing until my flesh was raw. Then I repeated the process, scrubbing, soaking, reheating the water. And still, I didn't feel clean.

The phone continued to blare my ringtone. "We're caught in a trap. I can't walk out . . ." At some point, it occurred to me that the call might be important. Otherwise, why would someone keep calling? I ought to find my phone and answer. But not yet. I wasn't clean yet.

Eventually, as it rang, I dragged myself out of the tub, grabbed a towel, and followed the ringtone to the stairway. The ringtone stopped, but I found my phone on the foyer floor along with my toothbrush, t-shirt, and sweatpants, the clothes I would have worn to bed.

Why would I have shed my clothes and dropped them in the foyer with my phone and toothbrush?

An image flashed—a man, silhouetted in the doorway. I tried to see his face, but the figure vanished. The phone began again. I pounced, grabbing it without even looking at the screen.

"Elle? Thank God." Becky's voice. Frantic. "We were going to call the police."

"Becky." I closed my eyes, basked in the familiar, normal sound of her voice.

"Are you all right?"

"It's the strangest thing." I wasn't sure how to describe what had happened. I wrapped the towel around myself. I was dripping onto the hardwood floor, making water stains.

"What's going on, Elle? Have you looked at the clock? Do you know what time it is?"

Yes, I did. I tried to remember. Nine something?

"Where are you? Are you sick? Why didn't you call in?"

"What day is it?"

"What's wrong with you? It's Monday. And it's almost ten."

Monday? "Oh God. I forgot!" I wheeled around, dizzy but mortified, and bounded up the steps, holding my toothbrush and sweatpants. My class—how could I have messed up so badly? I needed to get dressed, get to school.

"You forgot? Seriously?" Her tone shifted from worried to furious. "How could you forget to go to work? Elle, what's wrong with you?"

Good question. What was wrong with me? What had happened to the weekend? Fear rumbled in my belly, providing an answer: my dissociative disorder. It must have finally taken control of my mind, making me miss not just a stretch of conversation, but an entire weekend. Maybe next time, I'd slip away for good. I pictured a hospital, a straitjacket. Becky and Jen bringing flowers once a week.

Stop, I told myself. *Get going*. I tried to hurry, but felt like I was swimming through pudding. Or was it Jello? What difference did it make? Why was I wasting time thinking about swimming in desserts? I raced to my closet, yanked a pair of black pants off a hanger, a cream-colored blouse. "I'm coming in now." I jabbed an uncooperative leg into the pants, missed the leg hole, realized I hadn't put on underwear. Pulled my leg out, ran to the dresser.

Becky was talking. Repeating herself. "Haven't you heard anything I've said? I'm telling you not to come in."

"No, it's okay. I'm okay. I'm on my way. I'll be there in fifteen. Have my class write stories using their spelling words—"

"Elle, dammit, stop jabbering and listen!"

Was I jabbering? I stopped, listened.

"There's a substitute. Mr. Royal had to get someone at the last minute and he's ticked off, so it's better if you play sick and stay home. But what the hell happened? Why didn't you answer your phone all weekend? Jen and I called maybe a hundred times. Susan called, too, which is incredible of her given what you said to her."

What? "I didn't say anything to Susan. I haven't talked to her." I sat on the bed, trying to sort my thoughts. Nothing made sense. Sleeping nude, not going to work, not hearing the phone for two days, not remembering a whole couple of days. My head felt light as if it had floated off my body, disconnecting me from my life.

"Elle, I was standing right next to her when she called you Friday night. I know you talked to her."

I did? I tried to remember, couldn't. "What did I say?"

"You know very well what you said."

"Becky, I don't remember saying anything to Susan."

"Really?" She didn't believe me. "Why not? Did you hit the wine again?"

Again? What? "No. I mean, I don't remember. Just tell me what I said."

Her voice was cautious, unconvinced. "We were supposed to stay at Susan's Friday night. Do you at least remember that?"

Now that she said it, yes. I remembered Susan insisting that we sleep over. Taking out underwear and a t-shirt, starting to pack a bag.

"But you didn't show up, didn't even call. About eleven, we got worried. Susan called to see where you were and you blasted her. Tell me you don't remember that."

I told her I didn't remember that.

"What you said about her kids? Elle, she was almost in tears. I agree that they're spoiled and rude, but even so, your language was uncalled for."

Oh God, what had I said? I let go of the cream-colored shirt and black pants, let them slide to the floor, ran a hand through my hair. Noticed my overnight bag in the corner of the room. Had I taken it out to pack for Susan's?

I didn't remember packing. Didn't remember lambasting Susan's daughters. My neck tingled, and I touched it, vaguely expecting to find slime.

Becky was still scolding me. ". . . would have come to check on you, but Susan figured you'd been drinking and needed to sleep it off and chill on your own for the weekend. But then this morning, you didn't show up at school, and we all went nuts."

I sank onto the floor beside my clothes, wiped away a tear. "Becky, listen. I don't know what happened, but something's wrong with me. I don't remember anything that happened since Friday night. I had no idea it was Monday. I don't know what happened to the weekend. This morning, I almost couldn't wake up." The man in the doorway glimmered in my mind, disappeared. My chest tightened.

"Sounds like a hangover."

Boom. I remembered a bottle of Syrah. Jerry giving it to me.

My doorbell rang.

"Becky, someone's here." I held the towel up, watched the bedroom door.

"It's Susan and Jen. I told them you didn't come to work and Susan freaked. They're prepared to find you murdered."

Murdered?

I stopped breathing. Mrs. Marshall grinned at me with her carved, bloody smile. Joyce slumped over her steering wheel with her throat slashed. Stephanie Cross lay lifeless—and now, my friends expected to find me dead.

Of course they did. I was next on the list.

I turned, looked at my pillows, the rumpled sheets. Recalled the murkiness of waking up, the heaviness of my limbs. My inability to move or think or remember. But my friends were downstairs, ringing the bell, frantic. I got off the phone, struggled to pull on a pair of jeans and a t-shirt. Every movement took concentration, as if my body parts weren't quite my own. I started down the stairs, careful to measure each step. What was wrong with me? Why had I slept so deeply and so late? How had I lost two whole days? Why had I been naked, felt so unclean? Why had I been so awful to Susan on the phone? Why couldn't I remember? Was it really because of my dissociation disorder? Or was it something else?

"WTF, Elle?" Jen shouted. "Open the eff up!" She banged on the door.

I heard Susan's voice. A key turned in the lock. They were coming in, expecting to find my body.

Near the bottom of the staircase, I saw my sweatpants and toothbrush on the floor. Fragmented thoughts pulled together, formed a simple explanation for the state I was in: I'd been drugged—or maybe poisoned.

But how? Someone would have had to come in and kept me drugged or poisoned. For the whole weekend.

That shadowy figure of a man—maybe he wasn't a nightmare, but an actual memory. And if he was, then I was lucky that I'd merely overslept. Probably, I hadn't been meant to wake up at all.

* * *

They rushed into the house fussing.

"Are you all right?" Susan raised an eyebrow, eyed me head to toe.

"JFC, Elle," Jen said. "You scared the shit out of us. Why didn't you pick up your damned phone?"

It went on like that for a while until they realized I wasn't answering any of their questions.

"What's wrong with her?" Jen asked.

"She's not right," Susan agreed.

"No," I agreed. "I'm not." I smeared tears across my cheeks, told them I couldn't remember anything about the weekend. Not talking on the phone. Only vaguely eating or going to the bathroom. Nothing concrete until that morning when I hadn't been able to get up.

"Should we take her to the hospital?" Jen looked at me, talked to Susan.

Susan walked into the living room, returned with an empty wineglass and Syrah bottle. "She might just have a hangover."

"I don't have a hangover." I'd had hangovers before. This was not the same. And I wasn't a binge drinker, hadn't ever lost a weekend to a bottle. I turned, went to the kitchen, my body feeling foreign and robotic. They followed, Susan carrying the bottle and glass.

I sat at the table, trying to remember drinking the Syrah. Replaying events. Jerry had been at the door, holding a bottle of wine. Had been angry when I'd told him to leave.

"How many bottles did you drink?" Susan pressed her hangover theory.

"I don't remember. I might have had a glass or two." Actually, I didn't remember drinking at all.

"This bottle's almost empty." She sounded like a lawyer, cross-examining me. She checked the recycling bin in the pantry, began counting the empties. Stopped at five.

"OMG, she hasn't even made coffee." Jen opened the refrigerator, looking for a can of coffee beans. Noticed a bunch of roses in the trash. "Whoa. Where'd these come from?"

Susan looked at the roses, turned to me and squinted. "Elle? Why are there roses in your trash?"

"I'll make coffee." I didn't want to talk about the roses. I stood, got the coffee out of the freezer, poured beans into the grinder. Had to concentrate on each step. Measuring the water, putting ground beans into the filter. Things I normally did on automatic took intense effort. Susan and Jen watched me and whispered, seemed far away.

"Her speech seems okay," I heard Susan say. "And she's moving her arms and legs. I don't think it's a stroke."

"So WTF is it? We've seen her hungover before, and she's never been like this."

The coffee was brewing. They sat across the table from me, studying me.

"Maybe she pulled a gigantic Elle?" Jen suggested.

Oh dear. That was what I'd feared, too.

"You think she'd check out for a whole weekend?" Susan frowned, pushed her hair behind her ear. "She's never done that before."

"I know, but what else—"

"And she only pulls an Elle when she's shocked or stressed out."

"Duh, Susan. You don't think she's stressed out by these murders? She found that first body—the principal. And what about that woman who was hit by the car—she was right there."

"Right. But when she pulls an Elle, she never misses more than a minute or two. Even when Charlie got killed."

I was standing right there, but they didn't think to ask me about my symptoms. Susan was right, though. Until now, my dissociative episodes had only lasted for only a few moments. But I worried that they'd increase in duration and frequency, and that someday, I'd drift into my own mental world never to return.

"It wasn't an Elle," I said.

They both looked at me as if surprised to find me there.

"This wasn't me pulling an Elle," I repeated. "Look, when I have an episode—when I 'pull an Elle'—I remember it. I go away into my thoughts for a little bit, but afterwards, I know where I've gone. I might revisit a specific moment of the past or imagine the future. But whatever, if you asked me about it later, I could describe it in vivid detail."

"And this time?" Susan asked.

"This time," I said, "I don't remember anything. Not a minute since Friday night."

They exchanged looks. Didn't they believe me?

The coffee was ready. Susan got out mugs and poured.

Jen scrounged for something to eat. Found frozen bagels, popped them into the microwave.

I closed my eyes, straining to remember. Saw Rose attacking my car, Ty coming over, threatening me. And Jerry at the door with roses and wine.

"I remember Friday night—Jerry brought the roses as a peace offering."

"Jerry?" Jen's eyebrows raised. "And you let him in?"

"I made him leave."

Again, I saw the dim figure of a man in the dark.

I looked at the almost empty bottle. I must have opened the wine. Must have poured a glass. And then?

Nothing.

Or no, not nothing. I shuddered, rubbed my neck. Saw the man again, a blurred shape coming toward me. Hovering over me. But I was paralyzed, unable even to scream.

Susan was taking jam from the fridge. Jen was cutting warm bagels, saying that she couldn't believe I'd thrown out such pretty flowers. It was a real shame. It wasn't their fault they'd come from Jerry.

"I've been raped."

The first time I said it, they didn't seem to hear. So I repeated it, louder. And then, realizing how true it felt, I said it once again.

They both blinked at me. Two faces, identical expressions.

Then the questions started. "When?" "Where?" "Are you all right?" "Who raped you?" "Was it Jerry?" "Was it Ty?" "What happened, tell us from the start."

I had no answers. Just a vague memory of a shadowy man.

I told them about waking up naked. About feeling drugged and unable to move. Didn't mention feeling filthy.

"Let's go. We'll take you for a rape test." Susan stood, picked up her purse.

I shook my head, felt my face heat up.

"Don't be embarrassed, Elle. If you've been raped, it'll help catch the creep who raped you."

Except that it wouldn't. "I took a bath."

"You what?"

"Before you got here."

"Good Lord, Elle, why would you do that?" Susan pushed hair behind her ear. "Never mind. The test might still work. You'd have to clean yourself really thoroughly to get rid of everything."

I met her eyes.

"Really? You seriously—"

"I was extremely thorough."

They looked at each other, then back at me.

"I douched."

"You douched."

I nodded. "Several times."

Again, Susan and Jen exchanged looks. Didn't they believe that I'd been raped?

"But, Elle. Surely you knew you were washing away evidence—"

"No. See, I didn't remember what happened. I just felt like I had to wash."

Silence. They watched me.

"Okay, maybe there are other signs." Jen began examining my arms and neck. Looking for bruises? "Take off your pants. Let's see your thighs."

I'd already seen my thighs. "There's nothing."

Jen sighed and sat down. Susan crossed her arms and frowned. Their faces expressed doubt.

"Oh God," I breathed. "What if I'm pregnant? Or what if he gave me an STD?"

"What time of month is it?" Jen asked.

Good point. I was due to get a period in a couple of days. So it was unlikely that I'd have conceived. But I'd still need to get tested for STDs, damn it. But maybe it was okay. Because maybe he'd worn a condom. In fact, he probably did wear one. After all, no modern-day rapist would risk leaving a semen sample, not when his DNA might lead the police right to him. Not when he didn't know I'd douche it all away. Still, I should get a test. I would. Soon.

Susan was talking. I'd missed the beginning. "And besides, you've been through a tremendous amount of stress, Elle." She put the jar of jam down and sat beside me. Her eyes looked sorry. Or maybe disappointed. She took my hand, and I understood.

"You don't believe me."

Susan pursed her lips. Jen broke off a piece of bagel, popped it into her mouth.

"Here's what we believe. We believe that you're not yourself. And that something has happened to you. But rape? Elle, there's no sign of a break-in. No sign that anyone but you was here last night. No marks on your body or sign of a struggle. And you've washed away any semen—"

"Here's what I think," Jen interrupted, munching. "I think she had way the hell too much to drink and then took sleeping pills because of all her stress and ended up pulling one giant-sized eff-ing Elle."

Sleeping pills? "I didn't take sleeping pills."

"How do you know? You said you don't effing remember anything."

I glared at her but didn't answer. Her comment offended me. She was right that I didn't effing remember anything, but I knew I wouldn't have taken pills even if I'd had any.

Susan looked at her watch. "Damn. I have to get back. Now that I know you're all right, I've got to take care of actual paying clients. Can you stay with her, Jen?"

"Me?"

"It's all right." I gathered coffee mugs. "I'm fine now. I don't need anyone to stay."

"You aren't fine," Susan said.

"You look like hell," Jen added.

"I'll go back to bed. I'll be fine if I sleep." I didn't mean that. No way was I going back to bed. Not to those sheets. I pictured the man. This time he was at the bathroom door, watching me on the toilet. Oh God. And then I saw him again, carrying a tray to the bed. No, not a tray, a box. Was he bringing me pizza? Water—making me drink it? Was that how he'd kept me drugged, by putting something in the water? Damn, why couldn't I remember? And why didn't they believe me? My friends should have been helping me remember details so I could identify the rapist. They should have been soothing me, reassuring me. Instead, they were acting like I'd simply and irresponsibly drunk myself into a stupor of hallucinations. Crazy Elle. Undependable Elle. Neurotic Elle. Whatever else they thought of me, at that moment, I was indignant Elle, and I wanted both of them to leave.

"How about this?" Jen said. "I have tennis at noon. I can stay with her until eleven thirty."

That was only an hour. "I don't need you to stay, Jen. Go." I stood.

"You sure?" She grabbed her bag, not arguing. "Because I'm here if you need me."

I forced a smile, didn't let on how hurt I was. Didn't confront them about not believing me.

Susan was on her feet, studying me. "You should see a doctor. Why not call your shrink?"

My shrink? Not my internist? Not my gynecologist?

I stiffened, thanked them for coming, apologized for worrying them, and walked them to the door. They meant well. They cared about me. But neither of them believed me.

When they left, I locked the door and stood in the foyer, searching my mind, desperate to locate memories. My skin tingled, either from my repeated baths or from fear. Fury roiled in my belly, and I felt entirely alone.

* * *

Minutes later, I called the police, asked for Detective Stiles. Even though he was in homicide, I knew him. I could tell him about the rape. He'd listen.

The operator put me on hold. Maybe Stiles was in the field or at a meeting. Maybe I should call back later.

No. I'd hold on. I would report what had happened to me, wouldn't be a silent victim.

I waited. Watched cars pass out my window, splattering puddles from the earlier rain. Thought about what I'd say to Stiles. I'd tell him that a man had come in during the night.

Stiles would ask if I'd known the man. I'd say I wasn't sure. He'd ask me to describe him. I'd say I couldn't. I'd explain that I must have been drugged because I remembered only his silhouette, his shadowy form. He'd ask what exactly happened. I'd say I couldn't remember details, but that he must have kept me drugged until Monday morning when I'd awakened naked and stiff. And feeling violated.

"That's it?" he'd say. He'd pause patiently. Then he'd suggest a rape test.

I'd explain about my bath.

I'd hear him shift in his chair. He'd ask what exactly had led me to believe I'd been raped.

I'd try to explain.

I'd say that there were several suspects. Jerry had brought me wine and roses and had been furious when I'd rejected him and made him leave. And Ty had come by steaming mad, blaming me because his brother and sister were in foster care and his mom was in jail. And Duncan Girard had intimated that he'd get back at Joyce and me because Joyce had flat out accused him of pedophilia. And Stan—well, Stan was just creepy. I'd explain that Mrs. Marshall, Joyce Huff, and Ty's old girlfriend Stephanie Cross had already been killed, not to mention Patsy Olsen who'd been dressed like me, and that my name was next on the list that Kim Lawless had found in Joyce's planner. Also, who knew who could have gotten into my house because I still hadn't replaced the locks, and someone could have copied the lock box key, which I'd remove now because my house had been sold even though, oh God, I didn't know where I was going to move because nothing else felt like home because even though Charlie was dead, I still missed him after more than two years, even though he'd been a lying cheat.

Maybe I'd cry.

Lord, I sounded crazy even to myself. Susan and Jen were right. Rape or no rape, I should call my shrink.

Out the window, the sidewalks were nearly dry. A man passed by with his Corgi. A woman pushed a stroller, maybe taking her curly-haired toddler to the park. Sunlight speckled the street, filtered through colored leaves.

I was still on hold when I decided that Stiles wouldn't believe me any more than Susan and Jen had. Maybe they were right that no one had gotten into my house. Maybe I'd pulled a monumental

Elle and imagined the shadowy man lowering himself onto me. Maybe I was slipping into dissociation, completely losing touch. I pushed END, set the phone down, and wandered the house, running my hands along wainscoting and furniture, concentrating on tangibles like wood and fabric, trying to swallow my fear.

At around noon, it occurred to me that if my attacker were real, he might come back. I might have to defend myself. I got my bag and went shopping. Held a few guns before deciding against getting one. Bought some mace instead. Stood taller with it in my bag.

On the way back, I drove past Logan Elementary. The Jolly Jack's truck was parked at the end of the schoolyard. Duncan Girard was on the curb, laughing and selling ice cream to some boys. Was he built like the shadowy man? I kept my eyes on him, pictured him skulking through my house, into the bedroom. Looked up just in time to avoid hitting a parked car.

Duncan Girard. Was he the man who'd spent the weekend drugging and raping me? I heard him threaten, "I'm warning you. If you spread rumors about me—"

But Joyce interrupted, shaking her head, no. "Don't be silly, Elle. Duncan Girard wouldn't rape you. He only likes children."

Joyce didn't know that, though, not for sure. She'd had no proof. And besides, rape wasn't about sex; it was about power. I'd read that somewhere or heard it on television. Either way, it sounded true. And anyway, I had no proof that I'd been raped, much less that Duncan Girard or any other man had even been in my house during the night.

I went home. That afternoon, Pete from Safe and Lock showed up at two. The front door lock was changed by two thirty. Pete assured me that his lock was strong and durable. He gave me a spare key. Despite how woozy I was, I went to the hardware store on Fairmount Avenue and had copies made for Becky, Susan, and Jen. Then, I went home and stayed there, doors locked and bolted.

I avoided people, ignoring calls from Jerry and unknown numbers, answering the phone only if it was Becky, Jen, or Susan, and only to convince them that I was fine. But in truth, I was a mess. I was certain I'd been drugged and raped but had no evidence and no credibility even with my closest friends. Two of my colleagues had been murdered, and my name and Becky's were on a list of potential victims. Ty Evans and his psycho mother both had come after me. Jerry was hounding me. Plus my house wasn't mine anymore. I had to move out and leave my memories behind, but everywhere I looked, I saw Charlie and heard his long-dead voice declaring love.

I even answered him sometimes, asking why, if he loved me so much, he hadn't chased away the rapist.

I was out of control, so I hid inside, talking to a ghost, reviewing events, letting my mind ricochet to exhaustion.

Dinner was frozen pizza at around ten. Then I changed my sheets and put on fresh flannel pajamas. When I went to bed, sometime after midnight, I slept with one hand on my mace.

CHAPTER ELEVEN

I slept through to the next morning. On Tuesday, I got up early, went to school, and stopped in Mr. Royal's office to apologize for not calling or showing up the day before. I told him I'd been so sick that the alarm hadn't awakened me, that it must have been a twenty-four-hour flu.

His response was flustered. "Glad you're better. Don't let it happen again." He shuffled papers, glancing at me. "Any more repercussions from that Evans situation?"

I didn't mention Ty's visit to my home. "Not that I'm aware of. But I haven't seen Seth yet."

He harrumphed. "See that you keep me informed. We don't need parents attacking teachers on school property."

Would it have been okay if Rose had attacked me off school property? "There was no way to predict Mrs. Evans' behavior."

"Maybe not. But she posted bail and she's been released. So be sure you keep your distance."

I was supposed to keep *my* distance?

"Anyway, you'd better run along. The bell's about to ring. After yesterday's snafu, you want to be there for your class."

I clenched my jaw. Decided not to reply. Went to my classroom to find a pile of get well cards on my desk. The substitute had told the children to make them, but each one was heartfelt and sincere. Pictures of flowers, dogs, cats, and sunshine. Wishes for my health. I gathered them together, held them against my chest. Blinked away a tear.

When the class filed in, I thanked them with a choked voice. Then we had sharing time, where each student could tell something that happened the day before. When it was Seth's turn, he didn't notice. He was mumbling to his invisible friend.

"Seth?" I called his name a second time.

He looked startled. Some kids giggled. "Seth talks to himself," someone said. More giggling.

I scowled at the gigglers, quieting them. "Do you have something to share, Seth?" I asked.

Seth's eyes darted back and forth, then down. He shook his head.

We moved on to Bryan and then to Bethany. Seth went back to his murmured conversation. It continued through arithmetic. It continued even when other children told him to be quiet and tattled on him, complaining, "Mrs. Harrison, Seth's whispering out loud. I can't think."

I knew Seth was having a hard time, having been taken from his home and moved to a foster family. I didn't want to add pressure by telling him to be quiet. Instead, I told the children to concentrate on their own work, never mind about other students. But at recess, I asked Seth to stop and talk to me before he went out. He was so focused on his whispered conversation that he didn't hear me the first time. I had to repeat myself twice more.

* * *

He stood beside my desk looking healthier than he had just days before. His bruises looked fainter, his hair freshly washed.

I asked how he was. He said good.

I asked about the house where he was staying. He said it was good, too. A couple of other kids lived there. The house was big. The mom baked every day—blueberry muffins, chocolate cake. He had to make his bed, though. He picked at a fingernail while he talked. His hands were clean. He smelled like soap.

I changed the subject. "Seth," I said. "You haven't been paying attention in class. You've been whispering."

He shrugged, looked at the wall.

"Why were you whispering?"

He shrugged. "I already told you."

"Tell me again?"

"I was talking with my dad." He shifted his weight, squirmed in his chair.

Seth needed more than foster care. He needed a therapist. "What were you talking about?"

"I don't know. Nothing."

I waited.

Seth scratched his leg. "Just my dad was talking about my brother."

About Ty? It made sense. Poor little Seth must be struggling to figure out what had happened, why his brother had killed his father.

"I guess your dad's pretty mad at Ty," I said.

"Uh-uh." He rubbed his nose, couldn't stay still. "Why would he be mad?"

Seriously? Was it possible Seth didn't know that Ty had killed their dad? Maybe the family had protected their youngest from the truth.

"I don't know."

I backpedaled. "What was your dad saying about Ty?"

Seth's eyebrows furrowed. He looked at his feet, crossed his arms. "I'm not sure I should tell you."

"I don't think your dad would mind. After all, I'm your teacher."

"Yeah, but you're like everybody else. You think Ty killed my dad, don't you?" He faced me, watched my eyes.

So he did know about the murder. And about Ty's guilt. Seth watched me, deciding how much to trust me. I had to be honest with him. "Ty told the police that he killed your dad, Seth. That's why he was sent away." That sounded harsh. But at least I hadn't told him that his father and imaginary friend had been an abuser. I stumbled. "But no matter what Ty did, I don't think he meant to do anything wrong."

"He didn't."

He didn't? "Didn't what?"

"Ty didn't do anything wrong." He was emphatic.

Okay. Seth was clearly twisting reality so that he could cope. I wasn't going to argue and disrupt his way of handling the truth. Instead, I was going to ask him to tell his dad that they shouldn't talk during school. It distracted other students and interfered with Seth's ability to pay attention. But I didn't have a chance.

"Mrs. Harrison." Seth leaned close, his voice hushed and confidential. "Ty didn't kill my dad."

I didn't know what to say. It wasn't my place to set him straight or insist that he accept the facts.

"Everybody says he did, but he didn't." He watched me with solemn eyes.

I measured my words, hoping he'd open up. "Seth, if everybody says he did, why do you think he didn't?"

"Because."

Why was I pressing him? Seth had been a baby when the murder had occurred. He didn't know that Ty was innocent. He simply wanted him to be.

"Because," he started again, "my dad told me. That's how I know." He said it plainly, the same way he'd mentioned his foster mother's chocolate cake. "He told me Ty didn't do anything."

A shiver tickled my neck. Little Seth had created his own fantasy world where his brother wasn't a killer and his dad was still around to talk. He looked out the window and slid off his chair, ready to go out and play, his attention span depleted.

With gooseflesh on my arms, I sent him out to recess and sat thinking about him. Seth was overwhelmed by real life and coped by escaping into his mind. Imagine that. Seth wasn't the only one who coped that way. I might as well have been describing myself.

* * *

At the end of the day, Seth dawdled. The rest of the class filed out to the bus circle, but he lingered still in the cubbies, organizing his backpack.

I was about to hurry him when Katie showed up with Trish and Maggie.

"Katie?" I was surprised to see her.

"Hi, Mrs. H. Seth ready?"

She'd come for Seth, just as she had before he'd been placed in temporary foster care. I wasn't sure what to do. Was it okay to release him to her?

"The place he's staying is right near Maggie's house, where I'm staying." Katie beamed her shiny smile. She turned to her friends. "Tell Mrs. H how convenient it is."

Maggie nodded. "My mom even knows Mrs. Laurence."

"That's whose house Seth is staying at," Katie explained.

"We don't mind taking him there," Trish said. "Mrs. Laurence always has after-school treats laid out."

"She said she's glad we can walk him back."

She did? Shouldn't I have received a note? I wasn't sure, didn't know if there were rules. Under the terms of his temporary placement, was Seth even allowed to see his sister? How did I know that the girls would take him straight home?

Then again, how did I know where any student went once he left school? I couldn't know where Seth would go or with whom.

"Seth?" Katie called. "Where is the little dweeb?"

I knew where he was. I saw him peeking out from the cubbies, not making a sound. Was he playing some hide-and-seek game? Why wouldn't he come out?

"So." I hoped I wasn't going to upset her. "How are you doing, not staying at home?"

"Are you kidding? I'm doing great." Katie giggled. "It's like Maggie and I have a sleepover every night. Popcorn and Netflix." She beamed, squeezed Maggie's hand.

"I wish you could stay at my house." Trish pouted.

"You'll stay with us tomorrow night, Trish. Don't be jealous." Katie gave her a hug, and her sleeve crept a few inches up, revealing a patch of thin red lines. Ink? Had she been drawing on her arm?

"There he is!" Trish spotted Seth and darted into the cubbies to get him. Seth ducked away, ran out to the classroom, around the desks. Trish, joined by Maggie and Katie, chased him around work spaces, through the reading corner, laughing and calling his name.

"Okay, hold it." I moved toward them. "Girls. Stop."

But the girls didn't stop. "Come on, Seth." Katie laughed. "Come to Katie."

Trish came up behind him, Maggie from the side. He scooted, raced through the aisle between stations. Katie cut him off by jumping over a chair.

"Katie!" I shouted, rushing toward Seth. "Stop. I mean it."

She ignored me, reached out to grab him. But Seth burst away, sprinting my way. Breathless and wide-eyed, he took cover behind me. I reached around, my hands on his shoulders, protecting him.

The three girls stopped chasing, caught their breath, and gathered around us. They saw the fury on my face.

"What was that?" I glowered.

"What?" Katie's eyebrows raised.

"We're just goofing."

"Goofing? By ganging up on him?"

"Ganging up?" Katie looked baffled.

"We weren't ganging up on him," Maggie said. "We'd never—"

"We were just playing," Trish agreed.

"You were inappropriate, girls." I sounded like a schoolteacher. Like Joyce. "You're in my classroom, not a playground. I expect better of you."

"Sorry, Mrs. H." Three voices apologized.

"But he likes us to chase him, don't you, Seth?" Katie smiled. She stooped and reached her arms out for him. "Come here, little bro. Show Mrs. H it was just a game."

Seth hesitated, then slowly went to her. Katie embraced him, tousled his hair, called him a little squirt. Stood. "Sorry if we upset you, Mrs. H. We must have looked like maniacs."

"Are you okay, Seth?" I knelt to ask him. "Do you want to go home with them?"

His eyes were large and solemn, but he nodded, yes.

Later, I realized I should have asked him that privately, not in front of his sister and her friends. But at the time, my only thoughts were of Katie. When she reached her arms for him, her sleeves had risen up her arms again, exposing not ink, but rows of thin incisions cut into her arms.

* * *

Katie was cutting herself. No doubt about it. The cuts were of varying lengths, not exactly parallel in a cluster along her arm. No wonder she wore long sleeves, even in warm weather.

I went to my desk, Googled "cutting" to refresh my memory about its causes. "For some kids," a doctor wrote, "cutting is a way to control their emotional pain."

I held my breath. Was Katie hurting herself in order to take control of her pain? It made sense. What with her brutal father getting killed, Ty coming back from prison, her mother drinking, her little brother depending on her, and, now, her family being ripped apart, she was probably in a heap of emotional pain, even if she pretended that life was a great big pajama party.

I scanned the rest of the article. Read that self-injury was a defense against what was going on in the cutters' families and lives. That cutting not only subdued their emotional pain; it even caused a kind of high.

And that cutters often had a history of sexual, physical, or verbal abuse.

I stopped, read that part again.

Seth had had bruises all over his body. Did Katie have them, too? Had Rose been beating both kids?

But how? Katie was a cheerleader, physically toned. I couldn't imagine pint-sized Rose getting the best of her in a physical struggle. And Katie wasn't shy. If she were being abused, she wouldn't just endure it. She'd tell someone. Her friends or her teachers. Wouldn't she?

I rubbed my eyes, read on. Self-injury wasn't always a sign of abuse or emotional pain. It could also be a symptom of psychiatric conditions like borderline personality disorder, anxiety disorder, bipolar disorder, schizophrenia. I doubted that any of that applied to Katie.

Then again, as I logged off the computer, I kept seeing the demonic look on Katie's face while she'd chased Seth around the room. Could she have an undiagnosed mental disorder? No, a bizarre facial expression didn't mean she was mentally ill. She and Seth were siblings. Siblings played rough. They got wild, even mean. It was normal. The fact was that Katie was an incredibly well-adjusted kid from an incredibly messed-up family. She was cutting herself not because of some underlying mental illness, but because of overwhelming emotional pain.

Pain, for example, caused by DHS officials barging into her house at sunrise, waking her family, making her and her little brother pack their things and go with them. Pain caused by being ripped away from her mother and brothers, being forced to leave the only home she'd ever known. That kind of pain?

Oh God. I leaned back, covered my face. What had I done? If I hadn't insisted that Mr. Royal call DHS, Katie would still be at home. Maybe she wouldn't be as troubled, wouldn't be coping by cutting herself. In trying to help Seth, had I caused even more severe problems for his family, making their lives even worse?

I told myself that Seth, not his entire family, was my student. His well-being and ability to thrive were my concern. I couldn't be responsible for the repercussions of protecting him.

And yet, as I turned off the classroom lights and walked down the hall to meet Becky, I couldn't dispel the image of Katie, pressing a razor into her skin.

* * *

On the way to Becky's room, though, I was distracted by shouts from the opposite direction.

"Get out of my way. Let me see him!"

There was no mistaking the voice. Rose Evans was back. I hurried to the main office, saw her in the waiting area, cornered like a stray dog by Mr. Royal and Stan.

"You can't keep me here," Rose bellowed. "You have no right." When she saw me, she bellowed, "There she is, the damned bitch—go get Seth. I demand to see my son!"

"I demand you lower your voice." Mr. Royal stood tall, his hands on his hips.

"Seth left a while ago." I joined them in the corner of the lobby, directed my comment to Mr. Royal, not to Rose. "His sister picked him up."

Rose blanched. "No, you're lying. Katie didn't pick him up. They separated them."

"Mrs. Evans, my understanding is that the Department of Human Services separated the children from you, not from each other."

"But he's staying someplace else—not with Katie. So why did she take him?"

I didn't explain it. Didn't want to converse with her. I looked at Mr. Royal.

"The police are on the way," he told me.

"Yes, they are. This asshole called the cops." Rose was indignant. "And guess what. They'll set you all straight. I have every right to be here. This is public property, and I'm a citizen—"

"Citizen or not, Mrs. Evans, you know very well that you aren't allowed on school property because of your pattern of intolerable behavior. I explained it to you. The judge explained it to you. And so did your lawyer."

"Tell him, Missy. Tell him to let me see my son. I need to see him and know he's okay."

Even several feet away, I smelled Rose's stale booze breath. Half drunk, she hadn't grasped the fact that school had ended for the day an hour ago, that Seth had gone. I repeated the information, more slowly. "He's not here, Mrs. Evans. Katie came for him."

She blinked at me, then at Mr. Royal, then at Stan. "Who's this guy?" she asked. "Why's he looking at me like that?"

I glanced at Stan. He hunkered over his broom with his usual vague expression, eyes aimed at the floor.

Mr. Royal turned to me. "Can you stay with her a minute and make sure she doesn't take off? Officer Salerno's out patrolling the grounds. He should be back any second. I've already called in the complaint, so you won't have to stick around long."

How could he ask me to stay with her? My car was still dented from our last encounter.

"Stan here will make sure she behaves, but I've got a committee meeting." He glanced at the wall clock. Didn't wait for an answer. "Thanks so very, Mrs. Harrison. Much appreciated." He scooted away.

I looked down the hall toward Becky's classroom. She must be wondering what was keeping me. I took out my cell and called to explain. She didn't pick up, must have stepped out. Meantime, Stan ushered Rose to a bench against a lobby wall. I sat on an adjacent bench a few feet away, beside the American flag.

We waited. I watched the double doors, wished for cops to appear.

"Why is everyone so awful to me? You have no idea how hard my life is." Rose shook her head, gazed across the lobby. "It's hell. Pure hell."

I looked up at Stan. Backlit by the door and windows, he appeared in silhouette. Oh my God. I froze. Recalled the shadowy figure looming over me in the night. Could it have been Stan? Had Stan raped me? I opened my mouth but didn't know what to say. Should I just ask him? Would he finally look at me? Would he answer? I squinted, shutting out the glare surrounding him. Saw his emotionless face, his glossy, unreadable eyes. He didn't return my gaze, wouldn't meet my eyes. Was that out of habit or of guilt? Was he afraid I'd recognize him?

Rose went on whimpering and complaining. But I kept watching Stan, looking for subtle differences in his behavior, not sure what they would be. How would a rapist act around his victim? A smug smile? A smarmy smirk? A guilty blush? A threatening leer? Stan did none of that. His face, as usual, was expressionless. He stood at his post like a human guard dog, eyes averted. I told myself that my rapist hadn't been Stan. The sunlight framing him had simply made him look like my shadow man. But my stomach twisted, and my heart banged a warning. After all, what did I know about Stan? I'd worked at Logan for seven years, and he'd been there all that time. Yet, I knew nothing about him. Not whether or not he was married or single. Not if he had kids. Not where he lived. Not if he was a fan of the Eagles or liked cheesesteaks. All I knew was that he was the guy to call when a kid threw up. He emptied trash bins, washed floors and blackboards. He did odd jobs.

Like rape?

I squirmed. Stan stepped a few steps to the left, out of the light. His shoulders were stooped. His arms long and thin. Maybe he wasn't my rapist after all. Not that I remembered details of my rapist's physique. I looked at the clock. It was after four. I should call Becky again. Where the hell were the cops?

The double doors opened and Officer Salerno came in, spotted us in the corner of the lobby, and came over. He recognized Rose.

"I didn't think we'd see you back here so soon, Mrs. Evans." He took a cop's stance, legs apart, arms crossed.

"Why not? My son's here."

Stan nodded at the officer and wandered away. I watched him until he turned to enter a classroom. Told myself that he was harmless, that his shape wasn't what I remembered.

Now that the policeman was there, I could leave, too. I picked up my bag and stood.

"Where you going, Mrs. H?" Rose stopped me. "What's your hurry? Can't wait to get away from me, can you. Like I'm garbage. You're just like all of them, acting like I'm the one who killed somebody. Well, guess what? I had nothing, nothing, nothing to do with it. Not one goddamn thing. It was Ty, all Ty. I know what people say—that I made him take the fall—"

"Mrs. Evans," I interrupted. "I have to go." I looked at the officer; he nodded a good-bye.

"But they're wrong. I had no part in any killing." Rose went on as if I hadn't said anything. "It was Ty and Ty alone. If not for him, my husband would be alive today. He'd be earning a good living, paying our bills. My kids and I would be together. We'd be fine. Except for Ty."

Just walk away, I told myself. *Go down the hall and meet Becky.* I turned and began walking. Rose kept talking to me.

"But now Ty's back, and things are worse than ever, Mrs. H. You know that no one thought about taking my kids from me, not until Ty came home."

I stopped walking. Played back her words: no one thought about taking her kids away until after Ty had come home. She was right. What if Ty, not Rose, had caused Seth's injuries? Rose might be innocent of child abuse. Katie and Seth might need protection not from her, but from Ty. I pictured him outside my house, the coldness in his eyes. He'd promised that I'd be sorry for breaking up his family, but was the intervention by the Department of Human Services really what had angered him? Or had Ty exploded because he no longer had power over his siblings—because his human punching bags had been removed?

"Now, Ty's back and all of a sudden, they say my house isn't safe for my kids. They blame me, but Mrs. H, you know I'd never hurt my kids. Katie and Seth would be home where they belong if not for Ty."

I looked across the lobby at the main office. How often had Mrs. Marshall dragged Ty there, scolding him for fighting? Ty had been a bully as a little boy. Maybe he was a bully still.

Behind me, the double doors swung open. Two uniformed cops strutted in. One addressed the officer on duty. "Eddie, how's it going?" The other recognized Rose. "Mrs. Evans. We meet again."

Rose didn't acknowledge them. She turned my way, got to her feet. "Ty's my son, but he's mean to the bone. Always has been. I can't sleep when he's around. For all I know, he'll come with an axe and kill me just like he killed his daddy."

While the officers cuffed her, I started for Becky's room.

"I have every right to be here," Rose insisted. "This is public property." She didn't give in. I heard her asserting her citizen's rights until the double doors shut behind them.

* * *

The hall was empty, the floors scuffed from a day of heavy traffic. The air stuffy with smells of peanut butter, apple juice, and sweaty kids. I hurried, knowing that Becky would be waiting. We had plans to visit places for next month's outing.

Jen wanted us to go back to the circus school for our free lesson, but I wasn't eager and my shoulder wasn't ready to take on the trapeze. Becky and I were going to look for a tamer activity, one that took place closer to the ground. She'd arranged for us to visit a spa, a comedy improv school, and a bar where they provided materials and you took a painting lesson while drinking.

None of the activities excited me. I was tired. No, I was worse than tired. I was lifeless. I hadn't pulled an Elle, but I'd separated from myself, from my surroundings, going through the motions of teaching without feeling present. I felt wounded. Violated. I'd heard myself presenting new spelling words, explaining how to add numbers with double digits. I'd guided children at the computers, at the art and writing station. I'd answered questions, paid attention to Seth. But the whole day, I'd been far inside myself. Or outside myself. Someplace else.

I'd promised Becky that I'd go, but I wanted to go home, take another bath, get into bed and hide. I passed Joyce's old classroom, lights off for the day. And my own dark room. The school was silent except for the hollow clack of my footsteps and the buzz of fluorescent lights that glowed an eerie shade of green. Except for Stan, Becky and I were probably the last ones there. I looked behind me, quickened my pace. Ran the last few steps to Becky's kindergarten room. The door was already closed.

"Becky?" I threw it open, dashed inside.

And saw Stan.

Stan? Shoulders slumped, he stood beside Becky's desk, a wall of children's watercolor paintings behind him. He didn't turn to look at me.

My stomach clenched. "Where is she?" But I knew, even as I asked, that she was on the floor behind her desk. Stan was looking at her.

I ran, shoving Stan out of the way, kneeling, taking her hands.

"Becky? Becky?" I couldn't manage to say anything else.

Her hands were still warm. I touched her face. Tried to remember first aid. You had to check things in order: bleeding, heartbeat, and breathing. Or, damn. Was it heartbeat, breathing, and bleeding? I couldn't think. Kept repeating Becky's name. Put my hand to her throat to feel for a pulse, but remembered that if she were breathing, then for sure she'd have a pulse, so I put my finger under her nose, and yes, felt small bursts of warm moist air. Thank God. Becky was alive.

"What happened?" I turned to Stan.

"I came in to clean." He watched her legs. "She was on the floor."

I looked her over. Remembered that I shouldn't move her in case she had a broken neck. A broken neck? I saw no blood. Had she fainted? What did you do for someone who'd fainted? I couldn't remember.

"Get a blanket," I told Stan.

He didn't move. But Becky did. She moaned and stirred, opened her eyes, winced. Reached for her head. Moaned again.

I said her name again. Her gaze followed my voice, landed on me.

"Elle?" She tried to sit up.

"No, don't get up yet," I told her. "Lie down."

She ignored me, sat up. Saw Stan's legs. Looked up at his face. And screamed.

* * *

Still on the floor, Becky skittered like a crab, scooting away from Stan.

"What?" Stan asked her. "I came in to mop, that's all." He nodded toward the bucket near the door.

Becky cowered. I put an arm around her. "What happened?"

Her hand went to her ear. "He bashed me on the head."

"Me?" Stan pointed to himself.

"Stan?" I asked.

"No way." Stan shook his head. "Uh-uh, no, sir."

Becky didn't argue. "What time is it? Was I unconscious?" She rubbed the side of her head, wincing. Gently, I touched the spot she'd rubbed. A bump was already swelling behind her ear.

"No, ma'am, no, sir. It wasn't me." Stan backed away, shaking his head. "I didn't do anything to you or to anybody. I'm just here to do my job."

Becky and I eyed him.

He took another step back. "How come you're looking that way at me? You know me. I'm Stan. I do my work and I mind my business. That's all. I don't hurt people. Why would I?"

"How should I know why?" Becky glared. "Maybe because of the list. Because I was next after Elle."

Stan's eyebrows furrowed. "What list?"

"My name was after Elle's," Becky repeated.

I kept an arm around Becky, watched the exchange. Could Stan have written the list? Could he have killed Joyce and Mrs. Marshall?

"I came in to clean." Stan kept backing away. "To clean. That's all. But now I'm going to go look for the guy who did this."

I got my phone out. "I think we should all stay here."

"What are you doing?" Stan's eyes widened. "Who are you calling?"

"Who do you think?"

"I think the police."

He was almost right. Actually, I was calling 911, reporting an assault, requesting an ambulance.

Then we waited. I held Becky's hand, wouldn't let go of it. She could have been killed. Oh my God. Who could have done this to her? Why Becky? She was the kindest, warmest, most loving and generous person I knew.

"I think I'm all right." Becky took her hand from mine, tried to stand. "Really. I just want to go home."

"Don't even try." I tugged her arm, made her sit, and reclaimed her hand.

After a few minutes, Stan said he'd better go find Officer Salerno. I told him to stay with us. Somehow, I'd become the one in charge of the others, controlling the scene.

We waited. I hung onto Becky's hand, couldn't bear to let it go. Becky could have been killed. Oh God. Killed? Becky had been my best friend for over thirty years. She'd been my maid of honor, had helped me through all the troubles with Charlie, through the aftermath of his murder. And before that, she'd been by my side through my mother's illness and death. Hell, when we'd been teenagers, before my second date with Bobby Baumann, Becky had taught me to dance, even to kiss. I remembered how she'd demonstrated by kissing my cupped hand, heard her directions about parting my lips and making them soft. Lord, if anything happened to Becky, I'd be lost. I wondered if, over the years, I'd been as good a friend to her as she'd been to me. I hoped so. I couldn't think about how close I'd come to losing her. So I chattered, making small talk, keeping Becky engaged until Officer Salerno finally showed up, having received a call from dispatch about the incident. He stood beside Becky, asked her what had happened, looked around the room for signs of the attacker, and left us when he got a call to go meet the ambulance and guide the EMTs to the kindergarten.

From then on, it was chaos. A jumble of police and EMTs scrambling through the kindergarten. I had to move out of the way so EMTs could examine Becky, checking her vital signs, her wound. My hand felt cold without Becky's, and I rubbed it, trying to get it warm. Uniformed police asked Stan and me questions. I tried to answer, but my mind was on Becky. On what had almost happened.

"Elle?" Becky called. "They're ready to take me."

EMTs with matching blue shirts were helping her onto a stretcher.

"You'll call and cancel our appointments?" she asked.

Our appointments? Oh, yes. I nodded. Of course I would. "I'll follow the ambulance. I'll meet you at the hospital."

She looked small and lost. I hurried to squeeze her hand once more before they wheeled her away. I watched them lift her into the ambulance, went back to her desk to get my bag.

"You can join her, but first let's have a chat."

I wheeled around, hadn't noticed Detective Stiles across the room in the book corner. He sat on a kindergartener-sized chair with Stan who sat cross-legged on a pillow. When had Stiles come in? Had I called him? I thought back, remembered taking out my phone, but not making the call.

Stan and Stiles stood. Stiles shook Stan's hand and said he appreciated his help and his time. And Stan walked out, carrying his bucket and his mop.

* * *

I watched Stan walk away, free. Apparently Stiles didn't suspect him of knocking Becky out.

But if Stan hadn't, who had?

"Mrs. Harrison." Stiles motioned for me to join him on a tiny chair. When I hesitated, he offered to move somewhere more comfortable.

I told him I'd stand.

He said, no. He wanted me to relax.

For a few awkward moments, where we would talk became the topic of our talk.

We ended up at Becky's desk, with Stiles perched on her blotter, me in her chair.

And, then, endless seconds passed while he didn't say anything. He just watched me. I felt heat where his gaze landed. What was he doing? Why was he wasting time? I couldn't just sit there. I needed to get to the hospital to be with Becky.

"I thought you wanted to talk to me," I finally said.

"I do."

"Okay. So?"

He crossed his arms. The man would have been dashingly, disarmingly handsome except for that jagged scar that crossed one cheek. "What do you think happened here?"

Seriously? Wasn't it clear what had happened? "Someone smacked Becky on the head."

"And why would someone do that?" He fiddled with an apple-shaped paper weight. Tossed it hand to hand.

"You know why. Because she was next on the list."

He met my eyes, still played with the glass apple.

"Susan gave you the list, didn't she?"

He didn't confirm, didn't deny it. Just watched me.

"So now, the first three women are dead, and Becky's name was next after mine."

"After yours." He tilted his head. "So this incident is a deviation from the list. Because, so far, nothing's happened to you."

"No. It has—somebody attacked me."

"Really?" His face looked doubtful and he set the apple down. "When was that? When Rose Evans came after you? Or are you referring to the day you saw a woman get hit by a car?"

"No." I shook my head. "The night before last. Someone broke into my house and assaulted me."

His eyes shifted slightly. An eyebrow rose. "I haven't seen that report."

My face heated up.

"Who did you speak to?"

I looked away. The opposite wall was covered with collages of colored leaves. "I didn't call the police." I hugged myself. What could I say?

"Why not?" He leaned forward, eyes intensely on mine, waiting for me to go on. "What happened, Mrs. Harrison? Tell me."

And so I did. I folded my hands, looked straight at him and said that I had very little memory of the actual attack. Then I told him about Jerry's increasingly aggressive behavior, his Friday evening visit with a gift of possibly drugged wine. About my missing, memoryless weekend. About waking up Monday morning unable to move or remember anything but an ominous shadow, about feeling overwhelmingly contaminated, needing to bathe. About being certain that I'd been raped.

When I finished, my hands weren't just folded. They were clenched. I stared at them, expecting Stiles to doubt, even to mock me.

He did neither. His tone changed, became gentle, and he asked if I wanted to see a doctor or talk to a rape counselor. I said no, but my eyes filled. Stiles believed me. He even asked for Jerry's contact information.

But I wasn't finished. I went on, told him I wasn't sure the rapist was Jerry, that there were other possibilities. I didn't mention Stan because I'd just seen Stiles shaking his hand like an old buddy. But I told him that Duncan Girard had been so afraid that Joyce or I would sully his reputation that he'd threatened us.

Stiles made a note. Asked if there was anything else.

There was. I looked across the room at the small tables and chairs, saw little Ty with his scraped knees and bruises. I blinked the boy away, picked up the glass apple that Stiles had set on the desk. It was still warm from his hands. I told Stiles that Ty had shown up at my house, furious, almost violent. Not only that, I told him that Ty was directly connected to two of the murder victims.

"Good work. You should be a detective." Stiles smiled. Rather, the unscarred half of his face smiled. "Actually, Ty's connected to all three victims. Joyce Huff never taught him, but she taught his sister, Katie. Katie was one of her favorites."

I didn't see how Joyce teaching Katie connected Joyce to Ty. Certainly it didn't give Ty a motive to kill her. But none of that mattered. What mattered was that Stiles had believed me. He'd offered me rape counseling and taken Jerry's contact information. He'd taken me at my word when my own closest friends had doubted me and assumed I'd dreamed or imagined the rape by pulling a gigantic weekend-long Elle.

Then again, I hadn't told Stiles about my dissociation disorder. Hadn't confessed that I sometimes slipped away mentally and might have experienced the entire attack only in my mind.

"We're well aware of Ty Evans and his record," he assured me. "He's a person of interest. And you're right. It seems clear that someone is meticulously harming the women on that list."

Again, Stiles believed me. About the rape. About the list. He would question Jerry. And Ty, and even Duncan Girard. He said that Stan had been cleared. His alibi had checked out. My shoulders relaxed. Tension eased in my back, arms, neck. My hand loosened around the glass apple. Stiles was in charge. Investigating the murders. Protecting those who hadn't yet been attacked. For the first time in days, I felt light. Air rushed into my lungs.

But he was still talking.

". . . so you might still be at risk."

What? I'd missed something.

"Sorry?"

"The first three women." He cleared his throat, started again. "The first three were attacked brutally, in a consistent fashion. Knives were involved."

Again, my airways tightened.

"Whereas the attacks on you and your friend haven't followed that pattern. There were no stab wounds. No blatant displays of the corpses because, thankfully, there were no corpses. You're both still very much alive."

The room had become cold. How? The windows were all closed.

"So it's not just the last two women on the list we're concerned about, Mrs. Harrison. It's four. You and your friend, as well."

I bit my lip. "But then why were we attacked?"

He paused. "It's quite likely that your rape and today's assault on your friend are unrelated to the murders." His voice was still gentle, as if he were talking to a child. "It's doubtful that they were committed by the killer."

I repeated his words in my head, tried to understand. "So the killer hasn't struck at me or Becky yet?"

Stiles said nothing.

"And the attacks on us—what are you saying? That they're only a coincidence?"

He blinked a few times, then nodded. "For lack of a better word. Probably."

I heard his voice vaguely, telling me to stay with a friend if I could, to be alone as little as possible. To take precautions, keep him informed of any suspicious contacts. By the time his voice stopped, I was icy cold. I couldn't sit there another minute. Had to get to the hospital to check on Becky.

Stiles reached for my hand to help me up. I stood, heard a crash, reflexively jumped into his arms. Looked down to see the shattered glass apple. For a heartbeat or two, I stayed where I was, safe in the arms of a strong, handsome man. I wanted to stay there. But I felt Stiles' discomfort and thought of Charlie. Took a breath and let go. Stooped to clean up the mess.

"No," Stiles said. "Don't bother. Stan will take care of it."

Again, he offered me his hand.

* * *

I raced to my car and took off for the hospital. Sped through a stop sign in my hurry to get to Becky. Kept hearing Detective Stiles say that the assault on Becky and my rape had nothing to do with the list or the murders. He seemed sure, but how could he be?

I stopped for a red light. Drummed my fingers on the steering wheel. Considered that Stiles might have been wrong about Becky. The killer might have intended to follow his pattern and cut her but had been interrupted when Stan showed up.

Except, no. Becky's name came after mine on the list. If the killer followed his pattern, I'd have been murdered first.

So was Stiles right? I blew through another stop sign, heard a honking horn. If not the killer, then who'd slugged Becky? And who'd raped me? Why couldn't I remember anything but the vaguest hovering shadow of a man, a slimy touch, stale hot breath? My throat clenched and a wave of angry sorrow rose in my chest. Charlie sat in his study, holding a glass of Syrah, winking. Damn. If he hadn't died, he'd have been home with me that night and no one would have dared to rape me. And I wouldn't have been selling the house, wouldn't have had to deal with Jerry.

Jerry?

I cringed at the thought of him. Saw him standing uninvited at my door, holding wine and roses, and the cringe expanded. My chest burned, stomach twisted with loathing. And right then, I knew. My whole body knew—my bones, my teeth, my breasts, my scalp. It had been Jerry.

Oh God oh God oh God. Jerry. He must have drugged the wine, waited for me to drink it, and come back later to rape me. My skin contracted at the thought. My lips twisted in a revolted grimace. Ugh. The pig, the creep, the repulsive lowlife dirtbag. I wanted to call Stiles, but realized I had no proof. Not a trace, nothing.

Still, I was sure.

So now what? How could I sit with him at settlement? How could I be in the same room, the same building with him? And how could I even be thinking of Jerry when Becky was in the hospital with her head bashed? I saw her again, lying unconscious on the floor. Hot rage seared my veins. I stepped on the gas, changed lanes, zigzagged through traffic.

My phone made a gong sound. Someone was texting me.

Caller ID said Becky. Even though I was driving, I opened it, anxious to find out how she was. The text said that she'd been

released. She was fine except for a mild concussion, and she'd be
staying at Susan's to rest.

Good. I'd go over there in a while and make sure she was all
right.

I turned around, headed my car toward home. But my hands
were shaking. Images swirled. Jerry, his shadow, his shape. Becky,
motionless on the floor. I told myself that she and I were both
going to be fine. I turned on the radio, listened to some country
station. Tried to pretend my life was normal like the world outside
my windshield. A driver in the next car was talking on his phone.
A woman walked a Doberman. A guy pranced around with a leaf
blower. Everyone seemed at ease as if breathing didn't hurt, as if
their mouths weren't dry.

But I wasn't like them. I'd been raped by my real estate agent.
Plus my best friend had been assaulted. And some sick bastard
was planning to hunt us down and carve us up. Mrs. Marshall
smiled at me from the sidewalk, from the passenger seat in the
car beside me. From the hood of my car. She and her bloody grin
crawled toward me, dripping blood on my windshield. She wasn't
really there, I knew that. She was only my imagination. Even so,
I sped up, swerved, then braked hard, trying to escape her image.
A horn blared and brakes screeched. My car lurched as the tires
scraped the curb. I slammed on the brakes. Turned off the engine.
Tried to stop shaking.

Someone was pounding on my window. For a nanosecond, I
thought it was Rose Evans.

"Are you all right?"

I didn't know the man. He was stocky, had thick black hair. I
nodded, yes. I was fine. I opened my window.

"You cut right in front of me. I almost rammed right into you."

I nodded. "Sorry." What else could I say?

"You turned right from the left lane. You didn't even look where you were going." He leaned over and shouted into my face. His nose was speckled with big black pores. "Don't you know how to drive?"

"I bet she's drunk," a round woman behind him suggested. Was she his wife? She was short, wore her hair cropped short.

"No," I said. I didn't want them to call the police. "I'm not drunk."

They sputtered, staring at me.

I needed to stop shaking, to find words. "Sorry." It was all I could think of.

"You shouldn't be on the road." The man turned to the woman. "You ready?"

They got into their car and drove off. When they were out of sight, I started my car, edged away from the curb. Tears blurred my vision all the way home.

* * *

When I got home, I locked my new door lock, took my phone from my bag, ran upstairs to my bed, and climbed under the covers. I lay there absorbing the tenderness of down pillows, the protection of a comforter. When my breathing was calm and my pulse slowed, I called Susan to find out how Becky was. Susan was in the middle of making dinner and lecturing one of her daughters about the consequences of leaving food in her bedroom. Pots clanged and Susan chided, but I gleaned from broken sentences that Becky had a headache and didn't remember being attacked.

"Do you want vermin?" Susan scolded. "In your room? Because that's who you're inviting, Julie. Rats. Voles. Mice."

In the background, Julie yelled, "Mom. Relax. It was only some popcorn."

"Sorry, Elle. Julie's not happy with just having a dog. She apparently wants other pets."

"Lisa left a bag of cookies in her room. You didn't say anything to her!"

"Liar! I did not!" Lisa shouted.

"Lisa has nothing to do with this. I'm talking to you about what you did." Water ran. Julie answered back that Susan always picked on her, never on Lisa.

"Susan?" I tried to get her attention.

Lisa chimed in. "Me? What did I do?"

Paper, maybe plastic wrapping rattled. Julie whined. Susan told her to stop, and then finally addressed me. "Elle, listen. I can't talk now. But I've heard from Stiles so we should talk. Come for dinner and stay the night."

"Mom—Julie cursed!"

"Quiet, both of you!" Susan shouted. "Becky can't be around loud voices. Here. Hold on, Elle."

Hold on? I heard cloth rustling, movement. A door opening.

"Elle?" It was Becky. She sounded sleepy.

"Are you all right?" I saw her lying on the floor, not moving.

"My head feels like a bowling ball."

Yikes.

"They told me I can't work for a week, maybe longer. I can't even read or watch television. What am I supposed to do?"

I thought about it. Take long baths? Binge eat? Lie in bed under a comforter?

"So did they arrest Stan?" She thought he had to be the one who'd hit her. The last thing she remembered was standing at the bulletin board, hanging leaf collages. And then she was lying on the floor, looking up at Stan.

"Stan said he found you."

"Of course he did. Was he going to say that he knocked me out?"

She had a point. But Stiles hadn't suspected him. "Stiles doesn't think it was Stan."

"Stiles?" Becky's voice rose in pitch, became soprano. "Why is Stiles involved? Isn't he homicide?"

Oh damn. I'd worried her, hadn't meant to. "He came because it's another attack at the school. He thought it might be related to the other cases."

She paused. "I think it's Stan. He's always been so creepy strange. I think he tried to kill me."

"Becky." I tried to sound soothing. "Listen. Stiles doesn't think Stan or anyone else tried to kill you. He doesn't even think what happened to you was connected to the killings."

"Not related? Is he serious?" Her voice was too high, too tight. I thought it might snap. "Then how does he explain what happened? Oh God. My head."

I pictured her face pinched with pain, her hand covering her forehead. "Sorry. I didn't mean to upset you." I waited a beat. "Look, you're perfectly safe at Susan's. And you need to rest, not get riled. Nothing bad is going to happen." I went on talking in nursery rhyme rhythm, until I couldn't stand it anymore.

"Thanks, Elle." Her voice was back at alto. She sounded calm.

When we hung up, I turned onto my side. Thought I should stay the night at Susan's. Thought about her scrapping daughters.

Reconsidered and thought about staying home. But Stiles had warned that Becky and I should take precautions, be alone as little as possible.

I got up. Put my overnight bag on the bed, tossed in a t-shirt, a pair of sweatpants. Had déjà vu, remembering that I'd been packing for Susan's the night of the rape. Stopped packing. Sat. Remembered that I'd told Jen I'd call her back.

Jen had already talked to Susan and knew all about Becky. "You shouldn't stay alone, Elle. Shit, come stay here with me and Norm."

I thanked her, said I was going to Susan's. Jen said that I was an effing moron to stay with Susan's monster offspring and that her invitation would remain open in case I came to my effing senses.

The truth was that I would have rather stayed with Jen but didn't have the energy to trek out to the suburbs to her house. I didn't have the energy to go anywhere, wanted to stay home in my own space. Even though that space wouldn't be mine much longer. I went into the hall, down the stairs. Walked through the living room, the dining room, the kitchen. Pictured myself there with Charlie, cooking dinner. Charlie pouring wine. Dicing onion or eggplant. Coming up behind me while I stood at the sink, wrapping his arms around my waist, startling me so I'd splash water all over the counter. Turning me around for a kiss.

Charlie. I smiled. We'd liked the same wine. I went to the bar in his study, opened a fresh bottle. Poured a glass. Imagined him in his leather easy chair, feet up on the hassock, drinking with me. Toasting our life together. I imagined his smile. His arms reaching out for me. His kiss, warm on my neck.

Damn, why was I remembering these sweet moments? Why wasn't I remembering the woman I'd caught him with in the shower? The money he'd stolen from my inheritance? His slippery charming manipulative lies and other reasons I'd filed for divorce? Why, after all this time, did I still picture him everywhere, in every room of this house? Was it the house? Had it somehow absorbed the moments that had passed within its walls? Did Charlie's energy remain there despite his death?

No, ridiculous. Besides, it didn't matter. I was done with the house and with Charlie. Saying good-bye, moving out. I chugged my wine and stomped out of the study, marched upstairs to finish packing. A sweater, a bra. Black slacks.

And stopped.

Somebody was scratching. Trying to use a key at the front door. Not aware that I'd changed the locks?

I listened, heard nothing for a while. Tossed underwear into the case.

And there it was again. Louder, more distinct. Coming from downstairs.

Someone was fiddling with the new lock, trying to get into the house. I stepped into the hallway, looked down the stairs. My bag was down there with my mace. And my phone—I'd had it with me in the study. Had I left it there? Damn. Who was out there? The rapist? The killer? Either way, if I hurried, I'd have time to go downstairs, get my phone and my mace. And a carving knife.

Go, I told myself. *Move.* I took a deep breath and, eyes on the front door, raced down the stairs to my bag, rutted around for my mace, dashed into the kitchen, and grabbed a large serious knife. Kept going, ran to the study. The sun was setting, and the furniture cast long, ominous shadows on the bar. But I found my phone and grabbed it, began to punch in 911, but my hands were full with the mace and the knife, and I fumbled, dropped the phone.

Knelt to pick it up and the knife slipped from my grip. My hands jerked unsteadily, but finally I got to my feet, fingers tight around the knife handle, arms juggling the mace and the phone. I shoved the mace under my arm and was repositioning the phone, trying to dial 911 when the doorbell rang.

CHAPTER TWELVE

I held still. The person who'd been scratching at my lock must have given up on breaking in. Was he hoping I'd open the door and welcome him? I froze, remembering the silhouetted man in my bedroom. Had it really been Jerry? I should call the police. Tell them that someone was ringing my doorbell and it was probably a rapist or serial killer.

That sounded nuts.

I held onto the knife, the mace, and the phone, trying to convince myself that a serial killer wouldn't announce his presence by ringing the bell. That the person at my front door was probably a fund-raiser, collecting for clean air or green electric power. Or a delivery man? Maybe someone had sent me a package.

Unless the killer was disguised as a fund-raiser or delivery man.

The bell rang again. I couldn't remain frozen in Charlie's study. Wasn't going to let someone stand on own my front porch and terrorize me. No. I'd had enough. If this dude wanted to kill me, I might as well fight back. I got up, tucked the mace under my arm, the knife in one hand, phone in the other, and I started down the darkening hall toward the door. But wait. Shouldn't I switch the phone with the mace? If someone lunged inside attacking me, what good would it do to hold onto the phone? I rearranged. Put the phone under my arm, the mace in one hand and the knife in the other, and ventured to the front door, where I silently peeked out the peephole.

At first, all I saw was the empty porch. The edge of someone's head and shoulders slid into view. Whoever was out there had moved to the side of the porch, out of range from the peephole.

I clutched my weapons and watched, preparing to pull the door open and charge at him, taking him by surprise, spraying him in the eyes and holding the knife to his throat. Before he could grasp what had happened, I'd call the police.

I visualized it. Held my finger on the spray button. And stood at the door, watching through the peephole. My heart slammed my rib cage, my stomach contorted.

The guy reached an arm out, but I didn't anticipate the bell and when it rang, I was jostled, almost dropped the knife. Why would he ring the bell three times, especially after trying to break in? Had breaking in been his Plan A, but having failed, was he moving on to Plan B?

My breathing was shallow, my palms clammy. I couldn't just stand there, waiting for him to come up with Plan C. On the count of three, I would open the door with mace ready. But first I checked the peephole one more time.

Damn. I didn't bother to count.

"Go to hell, Jerry!" I shouted.

"Open up, Elle."

"How dare you come over here after what you did! Get off my porch or I'll call the cops!"

"We have to talk. Just for a minute."

"I mean it. I'm dialing 911." I wasn't, but he couldn't know that.

"I swear. It's important."

"Talk through the door." I clutched the knife and the mace.

"Elle, you want the whole neighborhood to hear your business?"

Fine. I grabbed the knob with the hand that held the knife, turned and pulled the door open, ready to spray the mace and thrust the knife. "What do you want to tell me?"

"What the hell, Elle?"

I hesitated for the briefest moment, just long enough for him to reach out and slap the can of mace out of my hand and grab hold of the arm that held the knife. My phone slipped from under my arm, onto the porch. I stood helpless, face-to-face with Jerry, his face distorted by rage.

* * *

"You locked me out!" Jerry thundered. He gripped my wrists tightly, strangling them. "The key from the lock box doesn't work. You changed the locks. When, yesterday? Because my key didn't work yesterday, either. How do you expect me to get in?"

"The house is sold, Jerry." I squawked, sounded hoarse. "There's no need for you to come in anymore." I tugged my arm.

"I'm the realtor," he roared. "I decide when there's no need to come in. Until settlement, I need access to this house. At all times."

Was he crazy? "Let go of me." Jerry had transformed. He'd become the shadow man. I couldn't breathe, but tried to sound unafraid, authoritative.

"What are you doing, coming at me with a knife? And what's that? Pepper spray? Are you insane?"

"I heard someone trying to break in." I twisted my wrists, trying to get free. "Jerry, let go—you're hurting me."

"No one was breaking in, Elle. I was legitimately trying to get inside."

Legitimately? I glanced around him, hoping to call out to a passing neighbor, even a passing stranger. Saw no one. Why wasn't a single soul out on the street? Usually, at this time, people were still coming home from work. Walking their dogs.

I took a breath. My wrists burned, but I told myself not to show pain or fear. "Jerry, let go of me. Now."

"Why are you so difficult, Elle?" His voice became less loud, almost a whine. "I've been devoted to you. I've spent extra time on your house—even though, by the way, your place won't bring me anywhere near as high a commission as the other properties I represent. I've got a dozen multimillion-dollar houses listed out on the Main Line. I'm so busy I don't have time to take a piss. But never mind, I took time out for you and your piddling little property. I treated you like a queen. I offered to take you for drinks. Out to dinner. Do you know how much I'm worth, Elle? Do you have any idea how much I made last year alone? Believe me, most women would jump at the chance—"

"Oh shut up, Jerry. Just shut up and take your hands off me," I hissed.

He stopped rambling and glared at me. "First, drop that knife."

I considered it for a moment. I didn't want to drop it but saw the futility of continuing the impasse. So I let it go, heard it land on the porch. Planned to duck down and scoop up the knife the second I was free.

But after I'd released the knife, Jerry didn't let me go.

"Inside." He pushed me through the doorway, into the house.

I stumbled backwards, resisting. Reliving the shadow in the night, wet breath on my neck.

"No!" I kicked him, lost my balance, fell back and dangled by my arms in his grasp, kicking at him as hard as I could. "Let go!"

"Stop the game playing, Elle." He backed me through the foyer, dragged me into the living room. I recognized his smell, his breath. "We're way past that."

"Get away from me." Was he planning to rape me again? While I was awake? This time I'd claw his face off, poke his eyes out.

He pinned me on the living room floor. Again, I saw the dark shadow—Jerry's shadow—lowering itself over me. Adrenalin pumped through my veins.

"Let go, Jerry," I growled. "I swear. If you don't take your hands off me—"

"What? What will you do, Elle?" Jerry smiled. His teeth were wet, his lips fat, his breath thick. He held me down, pulled my arms up over my head, and grasped both wrists with one hand. "Come on. Why are you being so belligerent?"

"You think I don't know what you did? You drugged me, Jerry. You put something in that wine."

"Really?" He leaned onto me, slid his hand under my shirt, inside my bra. "How could I have drugged that wine?" His whisper was low and obscene. "The bottle was sealed. What do you think I did, inject drugs through the cork?"

I was gasping, twisting. Trying to pry my arms free.

"That's absurd. Where would I even get a needle? Well, unless I happened to take one from a doctor's office. By the way, did you know I was the realtor for that new walk-in clinic on Belmont Avenue?" He laughed, pleased with himself. "My only worry was that you'd notice the damage to the cork. Tell me, did you? Was there anything suspicious about it?"

I wrested a leg out from under him. He rolled onto me and my body recognized his crushing suffocating overpowering weight. I squirmed, tried to turn. Couldn't.

"Stop fighting." He squeezed my breast hard, held on. Watched my face. I tried not to show pain.

"Get off me, Jerry," I snarled. "You disgust me."

He nuzzled my neck. "You weren't disgusted last weekend. In fact, you couldn't get enough. It's better when you let go, Elle."

"Fuck you," I grunted.

"Dear sweet Elle. I was betting that you couldn't wait to open a good bottle of Syrah."

His hands were all over me, creeping like rabid snakes.

"Oh, by the way. It was silly to change the locks. A smart realtor always has an alternate way into a property in case something goes wrong with the lock box. If you hadn't opened the door, I'd have come in anyway, through your basement window."

The basement window? Had he broken it? Unlocked it? Damn. I shut my mouth and turned my head to avoid his tongue. His saliva slimed my cheek.

"Stop pretending you don't enjoy this. You know you want it."

Oh God. What I wanted was to crawl out of my skin. I yanked my arms, wiggled, and twisted. Couldn't get free. Physically, he outweighed and outmuscled me. I'd need to use my brain. Make him want to leave. But how?

His fingers were on my waistband, digging inside my pants.

"I talked to the police."

His hand paused. He lifted his head to look at me. Shook his head. "No, you didn't."

"I reported you to Detective Stiles. I told him you raped me."

Jerry's hand retreated. "You what? Why would you say that? I've never raped anyone—I can get any woman I want. Women are all over me."

Really? I twisted my wrists to get free.

"Come on, Elle. You're joking with me, right?"

I squinted at him. "You thought I was too drugged to remember what you did. You were wrong. And you better not have given me an STD—"

"No way. I always wear protection. If you really remembered, you'd know that."

So he admitted having sex with me. "You make me sick."

His face changed. Jerry looked wounded. His hand came off my body, moved to his head. Scratched. "I don't get you, Elle. You've led me on for months. You've given me signals. You've teased and flirted, but then, whenever I got close, you'd back up and play hard-to-get. Now I make a move and you go to the police about me? Are you kidding?"

"They're testing that wine bottle, Jerry." I made that up. The bottle was long gone, picked up by the recycling truck.

"Fucking hell, Elle. It wasn't like that. I went to a lot of trouble. I did all that just so you'd finally relax and let yourself go—it was for your own good."

So he was outright admitting it? He'd drugged and raped me. Spit flew from my mouth, hit him on the chin. He didn't wipe it off, but his eyes bulged and he pulled me to my feet, yanked me around so I'd face him, put his nose right against mine.

"You know what you are, Elle? A fucking tease. An ungrateful fucking bitch. Forget it. You've finally pushed me to the limit. I'm done." He tossed my wrists at the air and began to turn away but did a double take. His eyes widened.

At least I think they did. And I think I saw a jolt of blazing white light.

When I opened my eyes again, I was lying on the foyer floor. My whole face ached.

And a man was sitting beside me, staring. Holding my hand.

* * *

I pulled my hand away. "No—don't touch me!" I leaned on my elbows, skittered backwards. Bumped into the table in my foyer, the one I dump my mail onto.

"It's okay, Mrs. H."

"No. Just go away."

His brows furrowed. "It's okay. It's just me, Ty."

Ty? I blinked, registered the pain under my left eye. We were in my foyer. On the floor. Nothing made sense.

"What are you doing here? How did you get in?" I scanned the area. My phone lay at the bottom of the stairs. How did it get there?

"Your door was wide open." Ty spoke urgently. "I was passing by and saw it, so I came to see if you were all right."

My door was open? Why? I closed my eyes, saw Jerry. Jerry had been there. He'd grabbed my arms, held me down. He'd been vile, unapologetic about drugging and raping me. What had he said? I was a flirt and a tease? As if his attack were my own fault.

I had to get my phone, call Stiles. I sat up, but my head reeled and, dizzy, I flopped backward. Ty caught my head before it slammed against the floor.

"Honest, Mrs. H. What with everything that's, you know, been happening, I got worried when your door was open. I looked in to make sure you were all right and there you were, lying so still I thought you were dead."

I closed my eyes, held my face. "Did you call anyone?"

"Call? You mean like the cops?" He paused. I heard him take a breath. "No."

Of course Ty wouldn't call the police. He'd be afraid they'd arrest him. And they probably would have.

"I mean I would have if you didn't wake up. I was about to, I swear. Besides, I've only been here like a minute."

"I was alone?" I pictured Jerry, driving off all smug and cocky. "Nobody else was here?"

"You mean like the person who knocked you out?"

Yes, exactly like that person. Like Jerry. The son of a bitch had coldcocked me.

"No, Mrs. H. I didn't see anybody."

It didn't matter. I knew exactly who'd punched me. I would call Stiles and tell him to arrest Jerry for assault and rape. I opened my eyes. Focused.

Ty was watching the door. Blinking rapidly. I was grateful that he'd found me. Needed to thank him. Except, no. Something was wrong about him finding me. I tried to figure out what it was. Of course. The problem that, in order to find me, he had to be at my house.

"What are you doing here, Ty?"

"I already told you, Mrs. H." He spoke slowly and clearly, as if he thought I had a brain injury.

"No. You told me my door was open. Not why you'd come to here."

"I was just passing."

He was lying, wouldn't even meet my eyes. "Bullshit." I sat up again, slower this time. My skull and the bones in my cheek pulsed electric pain. I needed ice. "Tell me the truth. Why are you here?"

"Honest. I was worried about you, that's all. I came by to check on you."

I didn't say anything, just looked at him.

"You don't believe me. Okay, what do you think I came here for?"

"I don't know." I pressed my hand on the sore spot beneath my eye. Found a hot puffy bulge. "Why don't you just tell me?"

"You don't trust me, do you? Even now after I found you and stayed with you. Instead of thanking me, you act like I'm a criminal. Fine, Mrs. H. I'm done. I won't check on you ever again." He got to his feet. "But you know what? Whatever happens to you from now on isn't my fault. I tried to help, but all I got for it was doubt and suspicion. You're the same as everybody else. So now, I don't give a shit. You're on your own." He stomped out of the house, slamming the front door.

* * *

I felt bad when he left, as if I'd done something wrong but couldn't figure out what it was. Ty's outburst seemed random, unprovoked like a toddler's tantrum. I'd asked him why he'd come to my house, and boom, he'd exploded. And now, I was alone with a throbbing head.

My phone was by the steps. I'd call the police. I'd call Susan. I tried to stand, but my balance was off. So I crawled. Crawling felt awkward, uncoordinated. Was it an arm and a leg together? Opposite sides or the same side? Or was it one limb at a time? I tried them all, wobbled, made little progress. Pain surged in my shoulder when I leaned on the side that had been dislocated. But I was making progress, moving across the foyer. My can of mace lay halfway down the hall on its side. It must have rolled there. But what about my knife? Where was my knife? I stopped, looked around. Didn't see it.

Maybe Jerry took it? Not that he needed it, having decked me. Why had he done that? Was he insane? How did he think he'd get away with it? This wasn't like the rape. This time, I'd been awake. He must have known that I'd call the police and report him. A few yards from my phone, I had to stop to catch my breath. The bone under my eye was probably broken. That whole side of my face and head raged. My nostrils flared. Jerry was going to pay. Jerry was going to jail.

But first, I needed to get to my phone. I continued crawling, counting seconds until I'd put my hands on it. One, two.

Someone giggled.

I stopped. Looked up. Listened.

Maybe I'd imagined it? No. I'd heard it. A clear definite giggle. Coming from—the coat closet?

I swiveled to face the closet. The door wasn't quite closed. Had I left it that way? Was someone in there? I looked from the closet to my phone, compared the distances. If someone was in there, was he watching me, getting ready to pounce before I could make a call?

But who could be in there? Jerry was gone. And Ty.

Rose Evans?

The thought of her pushed me forward, and I scooted to my phone, grabbed it, my finger poised to punch in 911. I looked at the screen, let out a wail.

The phone had been smashed. Its face crushed. Like mine.

Behind me, I heard a shuffle. The faintest of movements, like a pillow being fluffed.

First a giggle, now this. Was it Jerry? Had he come back while I was unconscious, destroyed my phone so I couldn't report him? Was he watching me?

Or was it the killer, here to murder the next person on the list?

My mace was far away, too far. I spun around and faced the closet door.

"I know you're there." I used my schoolteacher voice. "You might as well come out."

I was ready to confront Jerry. Or Rose. And if Stan or Duncan Girard had come out, I wouldn't have been surprised. But when the door swung open, I couldn't accept what I was seeing. Katie, Maggie, and Trish tumbled out of the closet, giggling, and covered with blood.

* * *

They pointed at me, choking with laughter.

"Mrs. H." Katie was breathless from laughing. "You should see yourself. Your cheek—you look so ridiculous."

"The look on her face when she saw her phone." Maggie leaned back, guffawing. She had a baseball bat in her hands. So Maggie had smashed my phone? Why?

And oh dear. Had she also batted my head?

Trish sat on her knees chortling. Clutching my knife.

It looked bloody.

I edged toward the door. But Trish leapt to her feet, darted around me. Stood in my way. For a moment, I felt faint, as if my heart had stopped beating. What were these girls doing in my house? Why were they laughing instead of helping me? Were they on drugs? And whose blood was on them? Mine? I glanced at my shirt, touched my face and head. No. I wasn't bleeding. Then whose?

"She looks so confused." Trish pointed at me and laughed.

"Okay, I'll explain. Your basement window was unlocked, Mrs. H." Katie chuckled.

"What were you doing at my basement window?"

"Point is, anyone could get in."

"You haven't answered me, Katie. How would you know about my window? What are you doing here?" I held my head, started toward the door again. Trish still blocked my way.

"Why shouldn't we visit you?" Trish asked. "You seem to like it when Katie's brother comes by."

"Your freakin' brother, Katie." Maggie shook her head. "He almost saw us."

"I know." Katie's eyes popped. "That would have been, oh my God, amazing. What would he have done?"

"Forget him—what would *we* have done?"

"We could have *Ty*ed him up."

"No—we could have made Ty die."

Oh God. They were making puns about hurting Ty? They rocked with laughter when nothing was funny. Had to be stoned. But why was Trish holding a knife and Maggie a bat? What were they planning to do? I watched Katie, tried to make her meet my eyes and face me. Her features seemed blurred and runny. Was something wrong with my sight? Was my skull cracked, my brain bleeding? Was I dying? I wobbled, needed to call for help, get to a hospital.

"Okay, girls." I spoke calmly through their laughter. "Party's over. You need to leave." Forget getting help. I wanted to lie down. To sleep.

"What did she say?"

"Who?"

"Her." Maggie pointed at me. "She said something."

"I said"—I made my voice sturdier, fearless—"you all need to leave."

"She wants us to go." Maggie feigned a pout. "Mrs. H doesn't like us anymore."

"Okay. Let's be fair. We'll take a vote," Katie said. "All in favor of us leaving?"

Trish shook her head. Maggie was silent.

"Okay. All for staying?"

All three said, "Aye."

"Sorry, Mrs. H," Katie said. "Majority rules."

"What do you want, girls?" I felt like I was swaying. Or the room was. I reminded myself that the girls were good kids, that I'd known them since they'd been second graders. That they would never actually hurt me or anyone else. That they were just high on something, playing a stupid game. That they would be embarrassed and apologetic as hell when they sobered up.

Even so, Trish stood at the front door, preventing me from leaving.

The others closed in, formed a ring around me.

"Back away," I scolded.

"Uh-uh-uh, Mrs. H," Katie said.

"Seriously. I'm expecting company any minute." I lied. But maybe not. Maybe Susan would call and worry when I didn't answer. Maybe she'd come by with Becky. Or maybe she'd call Detective Stiles and he'd come check on me personally.

The girls were whispering, laughing.

"If that's who she's expecting, she's going to be disappointed."

"Oh my God, remember when he saw us!" Trish's eyes were teary with laughter. "I thought he'd piss himself."

Who were they talking about? Ty? No, not Ty. Jerry. Jerry might have seen them after he'd slugged me. He'd probably bumped into them as he ran out of the house. That made sense—hadn't Ty said he'd found the door open? Jerry must have left it that way.

Unless the girls had opened it.

Katie chuckled. "He was definitely surprised."

"Well, so were we."

"You're right." Katie's smile faded. Her brows furrowed. "Yes, we were surprised."

"Yeah. So? It worked out."

"Because we were lucky. Guys, we can't count on luck. We have a plan and need to stick to it. No more surprises. We've had too many already."

"What are you talking about?" Trish frowned. "Oh, the thing in the kindergarten?"

Wait, was she talking about Becky?

"I had no choice, Katie," Maggie said. "She'd have seen you with Seth. Besides, I only knocked her out."

I turned, studying one face after another, reeling. Trying to understand what I was hearing. Maggie had assaulted Becky? I couldn't believe it. No. It didn't make sense. And she did it because Becky would have seen Katie with her little brother? What?

"... that other time." Trish was still talking. "You didn't think. You took off and rammed her."

What?

"Pow. Zoom." Maggie laughed, mimicking a rocket launch. "That girl flew."

Right next to me, Patsy Olsen took off from the curb, landed with her customary thunk. My stomach lurched, and I saw her crushed body. No, they couldn't be talking about Patsy Olsen— their conversation just reminded me of her. Besides, witnesses said she'd been shoved by a guy with long hair.

My eyes settled on Katie. She had long hair. And an athletic build. A small bust. Had she been mistaken for a guy?

Damn. I couldn't believe it. These girls—was it possible that they'd attacked Becky for some minor nonsensical reason? Accidentally killed Patsy Olsen in a misguided impulsive prank? Susan had talked about the adolescent brain, how it wasn't fully developed, couldn't foresee consequences, couldn't control its urges. Oh my God. These girls had gone haywire. And now they were trying to involve me in their mischief. My fists clenched. They needed to stop.

". . . not my fault she looked just like Mrs. H. But fine. My bad. My mistake. But this guy—we were making things up as we went. We had no plan at all. He was a deviation."

"A what?"

"You didn't even know him, Katie. You shouldn't call him names."

"Very funny. From now on, let's just stick to the list, okay?"

The list?

Wait. As in the serial killer's list?

No, what was I thinking? These girls were in bad trouble, but they weren't involved with the serial killer. They were just unruly misguided teenagers.

Except that these unruly misguided teenagers had forced their way into my home with weapons. They'd surrounded and menaced me. Katie stepped forward, put her hands on my shoulders, and pushed. I resisted.

"Katie. Stop. Think about what you're doing."

Katie smiled. "This is going to be great."

The others took hold of my arms and walked me backwards down the hall to Charlie's study. My throat tightened so I almost couldn't breathe. I was still dizzy and stumbled. Trish and Maggie caught me and dragged me until I regained my footing.

"What do you think you're doing?" I used my schoolteacher tone, but my voice was weak. "Girls. Stop." I took a breath, forced myself to speak louder. "This behavior is unacceptable."

"Tsk-tsk." Katie grinned. "Did you hear that, Maggie? Our behavior is unacceptable."

They chuckled, mimicked me. Kept grinning at each other and, as we entered the study, began humming. Maggie and her bat were to my left. Trish and my carving knife to my right. Katie, facing me, reached into her pocket and took out a knife of her own, serrated and stubby. All three began moving around me in a kind of dance.

"You didn't really care about that guy, did you, Mrs. H?" Trish asked.

What guy? I tried to look at her, turned my head too fast. Mistake. The room whirled and pain erupted in the side of my face. They circled me, talking.

"We didn't plan on him, see," Trish said. "He wasn't on the list."

The list again.

"But there he was."

They couldn't mean the killer's list. Must have some list of their own.

"And plus we wondered if it would be different with a guy."

Oh God. An image flashed. Jerry's mouth opening, eyebrows rising—and a burst of white light. Had Jerry hit me? Or had he seen a girl sneak up behind me, about to swing a bat?

The girls orbited me, slowly, as if playing ring-around-the-rosy. Their arms were bare, and I noticed identical patterns of thin red scabs and scars. They were all cutters. Did they cut themselves together? How else could their wounds match? I tried to remember what I'd read about cutting, about why people did it, but I couldn't think while they circled me. I stood in disbelief, watching them. Maggie held a baseball bat, and the others each held knives.

* * *

The weapons were raised, ready to strike.

"Spin and spin, go round and round," they sang to the tune of "Ring Around the Rosy."

"What are you doing?" I rotated, watching them, saw Charlie reclining in his easy chair. *Not now,* I told myself. *This is not the time to pull an Elle and imagine Charlie.*

"Round and round. Whirl and dance."

"Girls, stop!" I tried to sound authoritative. I turned, saw Charlie again. Blinked.

He wasn't my imagination.

And he wasn't Charlie.

"Spin and spin, go round and round. Time to have a chance."

Maggie stood in front of me and swung the bat, aiming at my head. I ducked just in time, felt it sweep my hair. The others laughed. Started the song again, circling me. Chanting like small children.

"Girls, my God! What have you done?" I shouted. "Is he dead?"

The answer was obvious. Jerry's blood had drenched his shirt and pooled onto my hardwood floor. "You killed him? For God's sake, what the hell are you doing?"

". . . to have a chance."

Trish faced me this time. Her eyes gleamed as she raised her arm. Her knife swooped, and I dodged, jumping back and away, but not far enough, not fast enough. Her blade sliced my sleeve, grazing my arm above my elbow. I looked down, saw a tear in my t-shirt, felt a scrape on my skin.

The girls were screaming and hooting.

"First blood goes to Trish! It's Maggie zero, Trish one."

"You're zero, too, Katie," Maggie reminded her. "At least I took a shot."

They began circling me again, singing, while across the room, Jerry sat in Charlie's easy chair, watching with dead eyes.

* * *

I don't know how long the craziness continued. I got better at dodging, but the game went on. After that first scratch on my arm, I got another on my calf. A couple more on my arm. Only one was deep, a gash on my thigh that spilled blood down my left leg. Even with that, I faced them as they lunged or swung at me as if they were piercing a bull in the ring. I tried to stop them. I scolded them, told them that they were better than this crazy violence, that, if they'd stop, I'd personally see that they got help. That, if they'd stop, I'd make sure their consequences were minor. I promised all kinds of things—various and substantial amounts of money, even my car. Nothing I said brought a response, so I stopped talking to them, concentrated solely on evading their strikes.

How long would it take them to kill me? Who would render the final blow? The pain in my arms and legs so far was sharp and thin, like a hundred piercing needles, but it wasn't overpowering. Most of the time, my body moved as if it sensed where the blows would fall or the blades fly just in time to dart away. Or almost away. But even as I darted and dodged, I disconnected from the moment. The scene didn't feel real, couldn't be happening. Or at least, it had to be happening somewhere else, to someone else. I'd jump away, watching a woman surrounded by a frenzied ring of girls jump away or crouch or bend or twist or arch to avoid a swinging bat and swiping blades. I saw her get bashed and sliced, but her wounds didn't affect me. They were merely information that clicked cleanly, unemotionally through my mind. For example, I observed that the woman's blood was trickling not gushing, which meant that, so far, except for her thigh, her cuts were superficial. Nothing deep. Then again, the girls were just warming up, playing cat and mouse. Taking their time. Preparing for the kill. They skipped around her, mocking her for her slow reflexes, clumsy movements. Pathetic tears.

My tears? Was I crying?

How come I didn't even know whether I was crying? *Pay attention*, I scolded myself. *You're crying, yes. And more importantly, you're bleeding. Stop drifting and think, damn it. Figure out how you're going to get away.*

Right.

I smeared a bloodied hand across my eyes, wiping tears, noticing that the tempo of the singsong had picked up. The circle was spinning faster, faster, almost at a run. In a few seconds, at the end of the verse, they would screech to a stop to let whoever faced me take another swing. And sooner or later, that swing would kill me. How was I supposed to get away? I was trapped. If I tried to break through the circle, all three would pounce, stabbing and pounding me.

Maybe I should run anyway. Maybe a fierce fatal attack would be preferable to this sick game. At least death would come faster. I considered it. Pictured the girls' hands dripping blood, their knives penetrating my chest again and again. Would they carve a smile like Mrs. Marshall's on my dead face? A frown like Joyce's?

The bat slammed the back of my wounded thigh, and I went down to cheers and applause. I'd drifted, lost track of the attacks. I wished I could drift away again. Mentally just leave. Pull one last colossal Elle. I thought of Becky, Jen, and Susan. Of my twenty-three sweet students. I'd never see any of them again. And Charlie. Would he be waiting for me on the other side? Was there another side? I hoped so. I thought of Charlie, only of Charlie, and the chance to start over with him.

Until the singing stopped again. I was still on the floor, writhing and clutching my thigh. Katie faced me with her knife raised. Her eyes blazed, skin glowed, and she smiled. I knew, looking at her, that I was about to die. Katie was going to plunge her blade into my chest or neck. She was hesitating, anticipating the kill, salivating, panting.

I lay back, waiting. And when she knelt, holding the knife over my throat, I reached up and with all my might, sucker smacked her arm.

She hadn't expected it. She lost her balance, teetered. She didn't lose hold of the knife, but while she was recovering, I managed to sit up and grab the wrist of her knife-bearing arm with both of my bloody hands, and, while she punched me with her free hand, I thrust all my weight at her, pushing her, twisting her arm, pushing it back.

"Help me, you idiots," she yelled. "Don't just stand there!"

Katie started to stand up but slipped on my blood and toppled onto her side. I still had her wrist when Maggie raised the bat over my head. I rolled fast, right on top of Katie, who was kicking and swinging at me. The bat came down, but not onto me.

Katie screamed. "Owww! Damn it, Maggie, oh God, you fucking broke my hand." Her body coiled around her smashed fingers. Cursing and moaning, she withdrew her hand from the knife. Preparing my wounded body to run, I reached for it.

"Don't even try." Trish's blade was an inch from my eyeball. She told me not to move, said that, if I did, she'd plunge the thing through my eye all the way into my brain.

I opted not to move. I held still, barely breathing while Katie moaned and Maggie apologized to her. The room blurred and spun. Dimly, I heard footsteps in the hallway.

No. I was imagining them, inventing them. Drifting again, wishing for a rescue.

Rescue? Fat chance. Jerry sat in the easy chair, mocking me. *Nobody's rescuing you and it's your own fault. If you hadn't rejected me, we'd have been together and we'd have fought them off. But no. Because of you, we're both dead.*

I blinked at him. What an asshole.

Trish nudged me. "Get up," she said.

"Wait—shh!" Katie held up her uninjured hand. "Listen."

They were soft and slow, but, definitely, there were footsteps in the hallway. We froze, silent. All eyes on the door. Waiting. I prayed for Detective Stiles. Or any cop, really. Any kind of good guy with a gun.

The footsteps stopped outside the door. Which swung open.

And Ty walked in.

CHAPTER THIRTEEN

He stopped a few feet in, looking around.

"Ty." Katie bit her lip, forced a smile. "Hey."

Trish and Maggie exchanged mini-glances.

"Hi."

Hi? He stood there, mouth open, doing nothing. Wasn't he going to help me? My heart did a somersault.

"So what are you freaks doing?" Ty's voice was flat, not the least bit appalled.

Of course it wasn't. Violence was nothing to Ty.

"Nothing," Katie said. She cradled her injured hand. "Just hanging out."

Ty didn't say anything. He strolled across the room, eyeing Jerry. Maggie and Trish watched Katie. Her brother, her call.

"He tried to molest Maggie," Katie said. "Him and Mrs. H. The two of them lured us here so they could take advantage of us."

Ty stood in front of the body. Put his hands in his pockets. Rocked back and forth.

"Ty? Say something."

He didn't.

"What are you even doing here, busting in like this?" Katie scowled at him.

"Didn't bust in. Front door was open again. And, Mrs. H, for your information, I know I closed it when I left. You really shouldn't leave it open—it's dangerous. Unless, did you guys open it?" Ty directed the question to Katie and her friends but still faced Jerry, didn't turn around. "You know? I've seen this guy before. He was stalking you, wasn't he, Mrs. H? I've seen him hanging around."

He didn't seem surprised or upset that Jerry's throat had been slashed. Or that blood was everywhere. On Jerry. On me. On the rug and the hardwood floor.

"So I guess he won't be bothering you anymore."

"Ty," Katie persisted. "How come you're here?"

He spun around. "Me? You know perfectly well why, Katie. You know that Mrs. H and I have a long-standing close relationship. I already told you that she's the only one who was glad to see me when I got out. Mrs. H and I are tight. But we had a little disagreement before, and I felt bad about it. So I came back to talk things out. That's what I'm doing here, okay?"

He took a few steps toward her. Maggie gripped the bat. Trish held her knife to my face. I looked for Katie's knife, saw it still unclaimed on the floor. I leaned ever so slightly closer to it. Trish grabbed my shoulder and squeezed.

"Don't even try," she whispered.

"Now it's your turn." Ty scanned their faces, met their eyes one by one. "Tell me what's happening here. The truth."

Katie shrugged. "Just a game."

"A game. With a dead guy and blood everywhere." He moved closer. "What's with your hand?"

She tried to smile, winced. "Game's kind of rough. Like fight club."

Ty nodded, as if it was cool. As if he got it. Probably he'd played bloody games all the time in juvey. Sometimes even games where kids got killed.

Ty went to Katie, bent over, and reached for her hand. "Let me see."

She extended it cautiously. "Careful. I think I broke—"

Her mouth opened to release a silent howl as Ty grabbed her hand, squeezed and twisted it.

"Ty!" she moaned.

Maggie held the bat up, ready to swing, and Trish jabbed the knife up to my face.

"Ty, let go," she said. "Or I'll cut her nose off."

Something warm and wet trickled down my cheek.

"Fuck you, Trish." Ty spoke over Katie's wails. "You three suck, you know that? You think I can't figure out what's going down here? You lie to my face? Everybody thinks that Katie, she's so sweet. How did a perfect girl like Katie come out of that fucked-up family?" He gave her hand a final squeeze and, as she yowled, let it go.

Katie moaned and lay back, hugging her hand, tears streaming.

"Put your fucking toys away, you two." Ty waved an arm, didn't bother looking at Trish or Maggie. "Either one of you comes at me, I'll frickin' break your neck so fast you won't know you're dead for a full half minute." He paused, turned to Trish. "I said: put it away!"

Trish put the knife down. Maggie dropped the bat.

I let out a breath.

"You three think I'm stupid? I can't figure out what you're doing? Well, you're the ones who are stupid. Because it's obvious. You killed that guy over there. You'd have killed Mrs. H if I hadn't stopped by."

He paused, sat down beside me. "You all right, Mrs. H?" He looked me over, one leg, the other. Same with my arms.

I looked with him. Saw my wounds, my severed clothing. My smeared and dripping blood. The gash on my left thigh. My arms and hands trickled blood from seven spots that I could see. No doubt there were a few more on my back.

"You guys are upping your game." Ty made Maggie fetch nap-kins from behind the bar, tape from Charlie's desk. He talked while he bandaged the wound on my thigh.

"Shut up, Ty," Katie sneered.

"I know what you've done," he continued. "Just not why you've done it."

"You don't know anything."

"I know that you killed the Marshall and Mrs. Huff."

Silence.

"And Stephanie."

Air seemed to be sucked from the room. The three girls held their breath, Trish and Maggie watched Katie. Katie shook her head. Signaling them to be quiet?

Ty tightened the tape around my thigh. Pain surged, the room spun, and my skull still throbbed, but I didn't make even a whimper.

"I get what you've done. The only thing I don't understand"—Ty reached for Katie's knife, picked at the tip—"is why."

* * *

Katie watched Ty play with the knife. Her face had contorted. Her lips stretched back in a grimace, her eyes glowered, beaming dark-ness. She didn't look like herself anymore. Wasn't even a little bit pretty. When had she changed? When had all of them changed? My thigh pulsed; the tape was too tight. When I moved, I both-ered cuts on my legs or arms, so I didn't move.

The silence tightened and stretched, became taut. If nobody broke it, it would soon shatter on its own. Trish and Maggie were bug-eyed, staring at Katie, waiting for a signal or a command? Ty sat motionless watching the point of the knife.

Silence. I watched blood leak through the pile of napkins pressed onto my thigh. Wondered vaguely if I would actually bleed to death before anyone spoke.

There was no transition. Ty never stood up. One second, Ty was seated beside me; the next, he was springing through the air, landing in front of Katie, bending over, pressing his face into hers, holding the knife to her belly. She didn't have time to react, not even to look startled.

"Who the fuck are you, Katie?" Ty whispered these words, his mouth not an inch from hers. But though his voice was low, he uttered them so fiercely that her body bounced backward, the glasses on the bar shook, my bones rattled. The entire room shifted.

"You think what you're doing is some kind of game?" His eyes bulged, his nostrils puffed. His hand tightened around the knife.

Ever so slightly, Katie's chin quivered. "Please, Ty." She blinked. Tears spilled. Her features reformed, became pretty again.

He stared at her eyes, breathed onto her face. Finally straightened up, held the knife loosely at his side. "You have to stop. You know that, don't you?" His voice was stern but no longer a shout.

Katie nodded, released more tears. Seeing this, the other girls began crying, too.

I thought of my smashed phone. Would anyone notice if I eased out of the room? I tried to stand, felt a warm spurt from my thigh. Maybe I could crawl? My shoulder hurt. My arms, too. And my head. I was tired. My eyes wanted to close. Maybe I'd wait and rest a minute. I leaned back against the legs of the coffee table.

". . . first, tell me why," Ty insisted.

I'd missed something. Was I fading?

Katie wiped her eyes. Sniffed. "What difference does it make why?"

"Answer me."

"Why should I?" Her attitude changed again. The tears vanished. Katie stood, defiant. "What are you going to do, stab me? Kill me like you killed Daddy?"

Ty stiffened. "What?"

"Oh, poor Ty. You don't get it, do you? Why would anyone but you kill your old girlfriend? Or the principal who you accused of ruining your life? Or the teacher you had a crush on but spurned you?"

He watched her, eyebrows rising.

"Think about it, Ty. Who links all the victims? Nobody but you."

"But I don't have a grudge against Mrs. H. Or any of them—I hardly knew Mrs. Huff."

"Oh, Mrs. Huff. Right. We added her because—"

"We just felt like it." Trish grinned.

They felt like it?

"She pissed us off," Maggie explained. "We come to get Seth, and she hushes us. Can you believe it? She tells us we're talking too loud in the hall?"

"And fuck her. We weren't even loud. School was already out."

"'Young ladies!'" Maggie imitated Joyce. "'Quiet! This is a school not a barnyard!'"

"Remember hiding near her car? It was like we were in a spy movie."

"Shut up, you guys," Katie cut them off. "Point is, it doesn't matter how well you knew her. We left evidence to tie Mrs. Huff to the others. Which means, to you."

"Bullshit," Ty said.

"Seen your Phillies cap lately, Ty?"

"How about your Eagles hat?"

"You fuckers—" His hands closed around the knife.

"Because hats like yours were found with the bodies."

"Plus there's a list of names—" Maggie began, but Katie cut her off. "No, nothing. That doesn't matter."

"What list of names?" Ty frowned.

Katie pouted, glaring at Maggie. "Fine. I'll tell you. It's a list of names of murder victims who connect to only one person. Which would happen to be you."

Ty licked his lips. Nodded. Didn't react.

"Okay, what about this guy here?" He pointed to Jerry. "He doesn't connect to me. I don't even know him. Why would I kill him?"

"You don't need a reason. You're a serial killer. Look, Ty. It's not that complicated. You've already confessed to Daddy's murder. They'll assume you liked killing so much that you continued to do it, and they'll send you away. But this time you'll go away for good."

Ty took a step back, digesting her words.

"Why would you frame him, Katie? He's your brother." My voice was a croak.

Katie glanced at me and laughed. Turned to Maggie. "Did you hear that? She sounds like a drowning pig."

In an eye blink, Ty's arm swung, slapped her face.

Katie sneered at him. "You'll pay for these murders more than you paid for Daddy's."

"Come off it, Katie." Ty shook his hand, relieving the sting of the slap. "You know damn well why I confessed."

"Let me think. Hmm. Oh—because you did it?"

"Shit no. You know I did it so Mom wouldn't go to jail."

"Oh, please."

"Look, I was a kid. If I confessed, they'd put me in juvey and spring me after a few years. But if Mom got convicted, she'd go away for life. And then what would happen to you and Seth? You were just a little kid and Seth was a baby. I couldn't let them stick you and the baby in foster care. Besides, it wasn't like Mom was dangerous. She wouldn't go killing anyone else. She only killed Dad because he was beating the shit out of us."

Katie stared at him wide-eyed and silent. Then she burst out laughing.

"What?"

"Nothing." Another bout of laughter and snorting. "Sorry. I'm sorry. It's just . . . you said you didn't do it."

"That's right."

"Seriously."

"Yes."

"You confessed to protect Mom?" She was still grinning.

"Yes." Ty steeled his shoulders. "I swear, Katie. I thought you knew. I confessed for the sake of our family: same reason Mom killed him."

"Wow, this guy Ty's a real-life hero, Katie." Trish feigned a swoon.

"What a guy," Maggie sighed.

"Shut up," Katie told them. She shook her head. "All this time, you've believed Mom killed Dad? It's funny. It's really funny."

Everyone watched her. Her laughter had subsided, but she chuckled to herself.

"Why is it funny?" Ty asked.

"Because it means you didn't have a clue. And all this time, I thought you knew the truth. That's why I've been setting you up as a sicko serial killer. So you'd get sent to jail where you can't tell anybody anything, and even if you do, no one will believe you."

"What are you talking about?" Ty looked from one girl to another. He looked at me. "Does anyone know what she's talking about?"

Katie stepped over to him, reached up with her good hand and stroked his hair.

Ty started to back away, but the other two girls moved swiftly, surrounding him as they'd surrounded me earlier. He raised the knife, but Maggie and Trish each had knives at his throat. Katie took his wrist, pried the knife from his hand, held it against his chin, then tucked it into her waistband. Strolled over to the bar. Saw the bottle I'd left open there, sniffed it. Put it down. While Maggie and Trish held onto Ty, she surveyed the wine rack. Selected a fresh bottle. Picked up the corkscrew and began to open it.

"Relax, Ty. You're going away for a long, long time. Might as well enjoy a glass of wine with your sister."

"You're sick, Katie."

"You think?" She popped the cork.

Ty wrenched his body to get free, but he was lanky and out of shape, not as fit as the girls. They had him, held him down. "Tell them to get off me."

"Not yet. We need to talk."

"You've already told me what you've done. There's nothing else to say."

"Yes there is." She paused long enough to pour two glasses of my finest Syrah. She carried them to Ty. Told Trish and Maggie to take him to the sofa, then wait at the door. Maggie got the knife, Trish the bat. They stood guard, Katie's personal soldiers.

I lay on the floor, certain that I would never get out of the study. That I was mortally wounded. I wondered at my lack of emotion. Shouldn't I be having some poignant final thoughts?

I thought of the wine, that I'd like some of the Syrah. That I'd never be able to drink it again. That I was dying passively. But that I must have accomplished something significant in my life. I tried to think of what that something might have been. Saw the world far below me, felt my body fly. Circus school? I was dying, and the best accomplishment I could come up with was circus school—during which I'd messed up, fallen, and dislocated my shoulder? I let go of the image and my mind became gray fog. I closed my eyes, adrift in mist but still conscious. Listening.

"I really owe it to you to say this, Ty." Katie paused. "Thank you."

"For what?"

"Well, for confessing. For taking the fall. I appreciate it, really and truly."

"Okay."

"I'm sorry you'll have to go back, but see, all this time, I figured you knew the truth and were being a protective big brother, confessing so his little sister wouldn't be sent away—"

"What?"

"—to juvey."

Ty was silent.

"I was sure you knew."

"That's not funny, Katie."

"I'm not joking."

"You're trying to tell me that you killed Dad. And you expect me to believe it."

"Believe what you want."

Ty hesitated. "No way. You were too little. Plus you were his princess. His little doll baby. He never laid a hand on you. You'd have no reason."

Katie was silent.

"Shit." Ty's voice tightened. "Shit. Shit. Shit. Katie, did he hurt you?"

"You bet he did. Son of a bitch."

"Oh God, Katie. I'm sorry. What did he do? Tell me." He was almost crying.

"He did tons of things. But the last one was what set me off. Bastard wouldn't let me have a cell phone."

"Dammit, Katie," Ty fumed. "Don't mess with me."

"I'm not. He seriously refused. He said I was too young."

I opened my eyes, peered through my haze. Ty sat slumped on the sofa, his head thrown back, hands covering his face. Katie sat beside him, eyes gleaming.

He sat straight, faced her. "Look, Katie. You were just a little girl. Too young to deal with what happened. I get it if you felt so bad that you invented your own story. But you didn't kill Dad. Mom did."

"The fucker was asleep. I took the knife in both hands and stuck him." She pointed to Ty's abdomen. "There. And there. And again up there. I'd have done it more, but the knife got stuck. I couldn't get it out. He opened his eyes and made gurgling sounds. Blood spilled out of his mouth."

"No way." Ty shook his head. "You were only eight years old. No, it had to be Mom—"

He stopped, eyes riveted on Katie, who returned his gaze. And smiled.

* * *

Ty's lips were bloody. His body deflated.

"I was sure you knew and I figured that someday you'd get tired of carrying the blame. I couldn't risk having you tell the truth about what happened."

Ty paused. "Katie. Dad's murder is the least of your worries. Look what else you've done—"

"Don't you get it? No one will suspect me. They'll think it's you, and not just because of the DNA in the hats. Because of motive, Ty. Why would I kill Mrs. Marshall? She loved me. Oh my God. She welcomed us into her office like we were her own lost children. Or Stephanie? Your beautiful ex. I never could understand what she saw in you. She was way out of your league."

"You wanted me to go back to jail."

"Ty. It's not personal. It's that I had to discredit you in case you decided to tell on me."

More silence. More disbelief.

I couldn't keep my head up. I rested it on the floor. Looked at my arms. The cuts had clotted. I thought about the cuts on the girls' arms, whether they'd bled a lot. And about pain, the different kinds. Stinging and burning, throbbing and screaming. Words floated around me.

Katie explained that, sooner or later, Rose would have told Ty she was innocent and Ty would have figured out that Katie was the only other possible killer. Katie needed him back in jail where he couldn't spill her secret.

Ty didn't argue with her reasoning. He kept asking questions. Why had she killed so many? Why not stop after Mrs. Marshall and frame him for just one murder? Katie dodged, said something about hedging her bets. But from the doorway, Maggie called, "Bullshit, Katie. Tell him why we didn't stop."

Trish's shrill giddy laugh jangled me.

"We didn't stop," Maggie went on, "because we didn't want to."

"It was cool," Trish said. "Like being high."

"No. Better. Like being high, having an orgasm, flying, and eating flourless chocolate cake all at once."

"Which by the way, is there any food here? I'm starving."

"Shut the fuck up." Katie stopped them. "Never mind why we kept going. You wouldn't understand."

"I'd like to try." Ty peered at her. "Tell me. What was it like?"

Was he serious? Did he really want to hear what it felt like to commit murder? Maybe he was stalling, convinced that they were going to kill me or both of us. Maybe he hoped that he could engage them and somehow convince them to let us go.

Or maybe his curiosity was genuine. Maybe Ty wanted to join them.

I turned my throbbing head so I could look around. Trish and Maggie had moved away from the doorway, had joined the others. Trish sat on the floor, her back to me. Maggie had probably gone to the kitchen, looking for snacks. I closed my eyes. Drifted, weightless. Soon, I'd be with Charlie. Dead like him.

I pictured it. We were on a sandy beach under a palm tree yet warmed by the sun. A gentle breeze brushed our skin. I leaned against him, and his arm was around me, holding me. He leaned close and I got goose bumps when his breath tickled my ear. He whispered something. I thought he said, "Fun." But a moment later, he repeated it more urgently, and I understood.

I had nothing to lose. So I mustered my strength, told myself to reject fatigue and ignore dizziness and pain. I checked to make sure the group was still huddled together, absorbed in their discussion of murder. I breathed "here goes" to Jerry's corpse. Then, slowly and quietly, spurred by Charlie's whisper, I climbed to my feet. And ran.

CHAPTER FOURTEEN

Maybe pandemonium ensued. Maybe I just imagined it. I half-fell, half-flew out the study door while behind me Trish and Katie screamed for Maggie to stop me. They chased me—I felt them behind me, the heat of their bodies like licks of fire, and I raced down the hallway with my arms outstretched, reaching for the front door where I would grab the knob, twist, pull, and thrust myself out onto the porch. I would scream and run down the steps into the street.

But Maggie got to the door first. She'd heard her friends yelling and sped from the kitchen to the door, where she crouched like a catcher waiting behind home plate. Why was I thinking of baseball? I never even watched baseball, had never played it. The others were maybe two arms' lengths back. They could lunge and grab me. My thigh screamed with pain, bleeding again. Images flashed in my head. Katie at my heels with claws. Maggie up ahead with fangs. No place to go, no choice except up. I veered left and flung myself onto the steps. Didn't care that I had no wind. Didn't stop to consider that I was weak and wounded. Adrenaline lifted me, carried me. I was steps ahead of them, felt myself breaking free. Instinct told me to avoid the guest room at the top of the stairs; they'd gain momentum and catch me before I could slam the door. Instead, I'd gain a few seconds by swinging left and sprinting to my bedroom. I had no idea if I was right but didn't stop to think about it. I just swung around the newel post and went. Slammed the bedroom door, pushed in the lock button, and stared at the door, panting and sore.

Fists pounded, bodies slammed. Female voices cursed and threatened. But where was Ty? Had they left him alone downstairs? Would he call the police?

They stopped shouting and banging, and I heard them whispering outside the door. They plotted. Conspired. The three of them would take the door down somehow, or they'd fiddle with the lock. Either way, they were going to come in. I had to keep moving.

But how? I looked around my room. Oh God. How had I never seen what a trap it was? Why hadn't I understood that I might need to escape quickly, that I might need a rope or extension ladder? Or an axe.

"Mrs. H?" Katie called, her voice sweet. "What are you doing in there? Come out. Ty needs to talk to you."

"Don't listen—" Ty's voice cut off and he grunted as if swallowing a punch or kick.

I rushed into the bathroom. Would my razor help? A nail file? Or a nail scissors—I had one somewhere. I opened a drawer, the medicine cabinet, couldn't find it. And why did everything come in soft plastic bottles? What was wrong with glass? Glass could hit hard, could break, leave sharp edges. I scanned the tub, the sink, the counter. Glimpsed the mirror. Found a ghost there, its hair rumpled, eyes raw. Skin stained with salt and blood smears, drained of color. A jagged bloodied rip on the shoulder of its t-shirt.

"Mrs. H. If you don't come out, you're going to force us to hurt Ty."

The ghost frowned. I turned away, also frowning. Weren't they going to hurt Ty anyway? Now that he knew what Katie and her friends had done, he'd have to die.

Except that his death would make him a victim, proving he wasn't the serial killer.

Unless they killed us both, staging it to look like I'd killed Ty in self-defense while he was killing me. Of course. They'd do something like that. Leave us with Jerry as the killer's final rampage.

My brain hurt. My body screamed. I limped out of the bathroom, holding my toothbrush and nail file. My bed looked fresh, innocent. I wanted to crawl under the covers but couldn't. Didn't want to get blood on it.

Katie was still talking, cooing, making promises and threats. I pictured her on the other side of the door, her pretty smile. Hellfire in her eyes. The others were quiet. What were they up to?

Softly, I heard someone count to three. On three, with great yelling and a crash, the door almost burst off its hinges. Chips of plaster fell off the wall.

"Let us in, Mrs. H!"

I went to the windows, the only way out. An outside ledge circled the house, but it was only a few inches wide. Not enough to stand on. I looked down. How far was it? I tried to do the math. The front steps were about six feet high, making the first floor six feet off the ground. The ceilings were, what, twelve feet high? And the ceiling itself might be a foot thick. And the windowsill was two, maybe three feet off the floor. So what was that? Twenty-one feet? Twenty-two? Why was I bothering to calculate—the height made no difference. I had to jump anyway.

Katie was counting again. One. I unlocked a window. Two. I pushed it open. Three. Even though I expected it, the slam jolted me. I thrust myself at the screen and it fell away, made a small thud on the path below.

I checked the door. The hinges had loosened, and the lock wouldn't withstand another ramming. I eyed the windowsill.

Doubted that, with my sliced thigh, I'd be agile enough to climb onto it on the first try. Or that I'd survive the jump without breaking my legs.

I hesitated, looked back just in time to hear a crash and see the door break free. It came down awkwardly, slowly like a falling leaf, and landed not with a bang, but a crunch. Katie stood in the open frame. For a moment, we locked eyes. Hers were, as usual, smiling. She didn't look away when she said, "Go."

Maggie and Trish burst into the room, Katie behind them, pulling Ty with her unbroken hand.

In a heartbeat, I was crouched on the windowsill. I didn't remember jumping or climbing onto it, but I must have, because, damn, I was there.

"Jump," I told myself. But I didn't.

I glanced down. The ground looked far away, certainly more than twenty-one feet. Not that I knew what twenty-one feet looked like. Still, I didn't move.

Behind me, Maggie and Trish stumbled over the fallen door.

"Ouch—my ankle. Dammit, Maggie! Watch out."

"Me? You watch out!"

"Shit, look—"

"Fuck, she's jumping!"

I had no time. In a heartbeat, they'd be on me. I closed my eyes, held my breath.

Didn't jump.

"Hup. Force out." I heard the words clearly.

It was Shane. We were on the platform together. "Hup!" he repeated. "Force out!"

"Hup," I said aloud.

But I didn't jump. Might have if I'd had a trapeze.

"Got her?"

"Yup." The voice was too close to my ear.

I held onto the window frame, wobbled to my feet.

"Push her!"

A breeze threatened to blow me off the sill. My head pulsed. The house shimmied. "Force out," I heard. Was I still talking out loud? "Now," the voice commanded.

I obeyed, sort of. Not jumping into the air, but edging off the windowsill, sidestepping onto the narrow concrete ledge. Barely balancing, clawing at bricks, twisting my feet. Not looking down.

Behind me, Maggie and Trish called my name.

* * *

The world swirled and blurred.

Maggie's head poked out the window. "I'm gonna get you, Mrs. H," she cooed.

An arm extended, a hand reached for me. I inched further away. Thought of circus school. If only we'd gone back and finished our lesson, maybe I'd have gone on and learned tightrope walking.

Maggie climbed onto the windowsill, reached for me again. I looked back. Her hand was maybe an inch from my leg.

"I've got her," she panted.

She did? How was she going to close the gap? Was she going to follow me onto the ledge?

"Keep moving," the voice told me. Seriously? I didn't dare. Any movement at all might destroy my tentative balance.

"Trish, grab my legs," Maggie said. She knelt on the windowsill, reaching for my leg with her left hand, clutching the knife in her right.

I skittered sideways, barely eluding her. The muscle in my slashed thigh threatened to cave, but I kept inching away from the window, and Maggie kept easing further out onto the sill.

"Don't look at her," the voice told me. Was that my voice? It sounded deeper, more like a man's—was it Shane's? Or damn, Charlie's again? Why did I continue to conjure him up? I needed to let him go, stop depending on a dead man. Good God, what was I doing? I needed to focus. But a thousand fragmented thoughts stampeded through my mind, kicking up dust clouds.

"Focus," the voice repeated. "Look ahead at where you're going, not back at where you've been."

Really? The voice was a philosopher? No matter, the advice was good. Slowly, I turned my head away from Maggie and her flailing and looked ahead.

That's when I saw the tree.

The old oak at the corner of the house. The one that dropped tons of acorns and shed truckloads of damned leaves every fall. The one whose branches had been trimmed because they'd grown too close to the house.

The one that might save me now.

"Can you get her?" Trish called.

"Almost. Hang onto me."

If I made it all the way to the tree, I could leap for one of those branches and climb down. Or swing like on a trapeze. "Keep going," the voice said.

"Just another inch and—"

"No, wait—Maggie!"

Maggie's fingers brushed my leg. I heard a thud. Slowly looked. Maggie lay facedown on the ground. She didn't move.

Nothing moved, not even the breeze. For a moment the world was silent. Then Trish began to scream.

* * *

How come Maggie wasn't moving? Was a drop of twenty-ish feet enough to kill someone? Maybe she'd hit her head, gotten knocked out?

My legs felt rubbery, refusing to support me, and I held my breath, tried not to fall.

"Maggie!" Trish called.

Maggie didn't respond.

Trish climbed onto the windowsill as if it were easy, smooth as a cat. Coming after me.

Somewhere nearby, Ty shouted, "Katie, don't!"

Time to move. I looked back at the tree, took cautious steps sideways with my back to the bricks. Estimated the distance to the branches. Held my breath. Glanced back at Trish.

She was moving fast, seemed undaunted by the height or the narrow width of the ledge. Her steps were long, quick. In seconds, she'd have me.

I hustled, hurried, almost hopped along the wall, hurrying to the corner of the house. I was just steps from the tree. Trish barreled into my peripheral vision. She was close enough to touch me, not quite close enough to knock me down. But I wasn't going to think about Trish. I was going to think about trapeze. About swinging safely to the ground.

"You got nowhere to go, Mrs. H," Trish breathed. "You're at the end of the wall."

I looked at the tree. Selected a branch.

"I got you!" she growled, lunging.

But she was too late. "Hup!" I cried, and I forced out, flying to my branch, taking hold. It was more flexible than I'd expected. It sagged under my weight, didn't support me, and I dropped fast, gripping it, aware that I'd made a mistake. The branch wasn't breaking my fall; it was falling with me. I was going to hit the ground hard, breaking my legs while gripping a flaccid limb. But a moment before impact, the branch stopped yielding. It jerked to a stop like a bungee cord, and I clung to it, dangling a few feet from the ground, swaying in the breeze.

A voice—was it Shane's?—yelled, "Bravo!" and someone clapped with enthusiasm.

I let go of the branch, landed on my feet, and remained on them despite the excruciating pain that reverberated through my thigh.

Above me, the tree rustled. I looked up. Trish stooped on a branch, stepped to another, climbing down. I had to hurry, keep moving. I could make it to the neighbor's. Or flag down a car. I spun around the corner of the house.

And ran smack into Katie.

She was still clapping, but stopped to position her knife at my neck. "Amazing, Mrs. H. You were like Tarzan—or his ape. What was the ape's name again?" She looked at Ty.

Ty was beside her, dazed, his hands bound with torn cloth. An ugly wound on his head. "Cheetah," he mumbled.

"Right. Cheetah." She waved the knife, pointing the way. "Let's go."

Ty stumbled and I limped. Katie led us to Maggie.

"Maggie?" She nudged her with her foot.

Maggie didn't respond.

"Shit. She's still out. Roll her over, Ty."

Maggie didn't make a sound. Ty, hands tied, rolled her onto her back, and we saw the surprise in her wide-open eyes, the blood stains on her clothing, and the handle of the knife protruding from her belly. She'd been holding it when she fell.

* * *

Katie stared at the body.

Run, I told myself. *Take off while Katie's still stunned.* She'd come after me, but Ty might intervene and slow her down. Could I count on Ty?

"Damn." Katie turned in a circle, repeating the word. She slapped her forehead. "Damn." She looked up at the tree, where Trish perched on a branch, watching.

"Oh, God," Trish called. "She's dead?"

Katie nodded, nostrils flaring. She took a breath. Steeled her jaw. "This is Mrs. H's fault." She turned to me. "If you hadn't made her chase you out the window, this wouldn't have happened."

Her eyes glowed, and she hunkered, her knife ready to strike. I stepped back. She stepped forward. We moved that way together, in a grotesque cha cha, until Ty grabbed her from behind.

"This stops now, Katie."

She whirled, swinging the blade at him. I lunged, grabbing her arm, blunting her blow. Ty lifted his wrists, lowered his bound arms around her, and she sagged, cursing, in his grasp. For a moment, still reeling, I thought we'd won. Maggie was dead, Trish was up a tree, and Ty had Katie. But I was wrong. Ty didn't have Katie; it was the reverse. Cradling her broken hand, she threw her weight and knocked him off balance, shoved him to the ground. They tumbled near the tree, rolling and grunting. Katie's uninjured arm was pinned, but still holding the knife.

I hobbled over to help, not a clue what I was going to do. Grab her wrist? Step on her broken hand? Something. In my haste, I forgot about Trish and, as I passed the tree, a dark shadow swallowed me. The impact of her crashing onto me sent us flying to the ground. We hit hard, Trish on my back, panting hard. I arched my back to knock her off of me, but she grabbed my waist and held on. I spun around, faced empty eyes and bared teeth. I lay back, took a breath, then slammed my forehead against hers. Felt a blinding crack as if I'd cleaved my skull in half. I braced myself for a punch, even a bite. But Trish did neither. Her grip slackened, releasing me, and I struggled to my feet. Too fast. I teetered, unsteady, and stepped back, taking the weight off my bloodied injured thigh. Trish got up, too, and for a moment we stood facing each other. Then, she opened her mouth and came at me, roaring. I spun around and sprinted. Heard Ty yelling, maybe saying, "Look out"? I looked back, glimpsed Trish closing in, and flew forward. No, not forward. Down. My foot was caught and I stumbled. Saw grass, the stone walkway, a bloody shirt and knife handle. I flung my arms out to break my fall, and landed on top of Maggie.

Once again, Trish was on me. I wriggled, sandwiched between a dead woman and a fiend. Trish took hold of my throat and squeezed. I tried to pull her hands away, loosen her fingers, scratch them, but they wouldn't relent. My face got hot, wounded cheek ballooned, eyes popped, tongue swelled. I heard the ocean roaring. I thrashed, I kicked. I realized I had no chance. She had me. I was going to die. I craved air. Any kind of air—cold, hot, damp, stinking, polluted—it didn't matter. Just air. How long was it going to last, this pain and craving? Would I lose consciousness or agonize until the end? Charlie appeared, dim and distant, and I ached, remembering when I could open my lungs and feel air rush in without effort or thought. My strength was gone. I stopped struggling, let my hands fall limply beside me.

And found the handle of Maggie's knife.

* * *

My mind was dark, shut down. But some primitive part of my brain must have functioned well enough to signal a survival response, sending a message to my fingers.

And, even in their weakened state, they must have responded, closing around the hilt and tugging.

Later, I remembered the shuddering of Trish's body. The release of her hold on my throat. The heaviness of her collapse, her dead weight crushing my chest.

I remembered gasping, coughing, struggling to breathe. The raw pain of my throat, and brutal stiffness of my neck. The endless time pressed beneath her, her hair falling across my face, her breasts smashing mine. And the relief when finally I managed to slither out from under her.

I remembered looking up to see Ty's bludgeoned face and, once I was able to sit up, seeing Trish's body, the knife handle protruding from her back.

* * *

I crawled to Ty. He couldn't get up to help me. He was a mess, his hands tied, eye blackened, forehead cut, lips split, and besides, he was sitting on Katie, holding her down.

I flopped beside him on the grass, used the knife to untie his wrists. I couldn't talk, could barely breathe. We stayed together near the oak tree, wounded and dazed and ignoring Katie's pleas and promises, her apologies, her threats.

The street seemed weirdly quiet. Cars drove past but didn't stop. I had no sense of time, though. Maybe an hour or maybe just seconds passed before a jogger noticed us and stopped, running in place. Staring at us.

Ty let out a single delighted, "Ha!"

"Christ. What the hell?" The jogger stopped running.

I tried but couldn't answer.

Katie lifted her head, whimpering. "Please. Help me!" She made herself sound frail.

"What happened here?" The man scowled at Ty.

He stepped closer, scanning the lawn.

"Please," Katie wailed.

"Shut up," Ty told her.

Katie began to cry as the man moved across the grass. He stopped when he saw Maggie and Trish. Must have thought that all three were victims, that Ty and I had assaulted them.

"Jesus." The jogger's mouth opened. He stood motionless.

"Help me," Katie begged. "They killed my friends!"

"She's lying," Ty spoke over her. "Can you—"

"And they're going to kill me!"

"—call for help?"

"No! Get him off me!" Katie squealed. "Please!"

The jogger backed away and stood near the curb, cell phone in hand, punching in numbers. Eyeing us. Reciting my address, describing mayhem.

A woman whose face looked familiar walked by with a Sheltie leashed to her stroller. She stopped near my front path, looking at me, at Ty sitting on Katie. The color drained from her face. I heard her ask the jogger what had happened.

He said he didn't know. He thought it must be a domestic thing, but it was bad.

Her hand went to her mouth, and she rushed off. I recognized the dog, thought the woman's name might be Pam, that she might have lived on the corner. Maybe Pam reached into her pocket for her phone. Maybe she called the cops.

Cars drove by without stopping. Time passed.

The jogger didn't force Ty to move, didn't rescue Katie. He just waited near the curb, watching the street for police while Katie pleaded and lied, and Ty told her she was full of shit. Then, boom, the street swarmed with cops, ambulances, news teams, spectators. EMTs lifted me onto a stretcher. I wanted to tell them about Jerry but couldn't talk. When they wheeled me to an ambulance, cops were putting crime scene tape up around the house, blocking off the For Sale sign with its bright yellow button that said SOLD.

CHAPTER FIFTEEN

The floral arrangement was too big for either the nightstand or the windowsill. Bursting with white and yellow roses, daisies, some exotic orange-colored tropical blooms, unfamiliar purple flowers, and lots of what I thought was called baby's breath, it sat on a chair, taller and wider than Becky, who was sitting next to it. Jen fiddled with the flowers, picking at the petals. "The chrysanthemums got crushed. After what we paid, it's a sin."

"Let them be." Becky frowned. "They'll look like plucked chickens."

"I'm just pruning. Dead petals are depressing."

"So are bald-headed stems."

They went on, bickering.

Susan sat on the side of my bed, reading the message I'd typed on my laptop. "Thanks for bringing this."

"I figured you'd want to communicate." She squeezed my hand.

Trish had all but crushed my windpipe, and the doctors had said I shouldn't even try to talk for at least a few days. I also had a concussion, a broken cheekbone, and a huge bandage around my thigh.

Susan watched me, frowning.

"What?" I typed.

"Nothing. Just . . . I'm glad you're going to be okay." Her eyes shifted while she answered, hiding something.

"That's not it. Tell me." What could it be? Was Ty dead? Had they found another corpse?

"You scared me, that's all. You look like you've been through hell."

Oh. I hadn't thought about how I looked. I'd had been consumed by how I felt. "Mirror," I wrote.

"No." Susan set her jaw.

Oh God. Was it that bad? "Yes," I wrote. "I want to see."

"Wait until the swelling goes down."

Really? I started to swing my legs to get out of bed, but a surge of pain reminded me that my postsurgical bandaged thigh was supposed to remain immobile. Besides, there was a camera in my laptop. I could turn it on, see myself. I changed the screen, searched the desktop icons.

"You are so stubborn." Susan handed me a small mirror from her purse. "Okay, have it your way."

"WTF, Susan? Are you fucking nuts?" Jen swept across the room, diving for the mirror. "Why are you giving her a mirror?" She tried to grab it.

I shoved it under my blanket.

"She wants to look at herself."

"No, she doesn't," Jen said. "Trust me."

"It's up to her," Becky said. "But, Elle, I think you should wait."

The three of them crowded around me, watching, waiting to see what I'd do. Becky chewed her lip. Jen worried her hands. Was I that awful? I slid the mirror out of the covers, held it up. Heard a gasp, realized it was my own.

I looked like a losing prizefighter. No. A losing prizefighter would look better. My lips, especially on the left side, had ballooned, purple and cracked. One cheek and half my nose were scraped and swollen. The left eye was open just a slit, surrounded by bulbous ballooned skin an indefinable shade of bluish purplish yellow. There were stitches along my hairline. My neck was bruised purple, yellow, and green. My hair was clumped and knotted.

My friends were talking. "Don't worry. You look much better than when you came in."

"In a few days, the swelling will be gone."

I handed the mirror back to Susan.

"You're still a knockout," Becky said.

"She has eyes, Becky," Susan snapped. "She can see that she looks like hell."

"WTF, Susan. Don't say that," Jen said. "We need to be effing positive."

"Yeah. The purple around her eye isn't as dark. See? It's turning yellow," Becky said.

"Stop talking about my face," I typed. I told myself I'd heal. I wouldn't be an eyesore forever. The ugliness would fade. I hoped the memories would, too.

An awkward silence ensued. Susan replaced her mirror. Becky took her seat beside the floral arrangement. Jen opened a box of chocolates.

"So with Elle in the hospital," she said, "we'll have to put off rescheduling freaking circus school."

I typed, "No. It's fine. Go without me."

Susan read my message aloud.

"No way," Becky said. "You're the whole reason we're getting free lessons. We'll wait 'til you're ready."

I pictured circus school, the platform. Shane offering me the trapeze. My stomach did a flip turn, and the trapeze became a tree branch. "Really, why wait? Take the lessons. I don't mind."

"No. We made a resolution to do new things together. That means all of us."

I swallowed. Swallowing hurt. But fine, no point arguing.

"Besides, I scheduled a no-impact event for this month," Becky said.

"Hold on," Susan said. "Why are you scheduling events? You picked circus school. It's Elle's turn next."

I typed that I'd asked Becky to help out.

"Seriously, Susan? How's Elle supposed to schedule anything? I told her I'd do it for her."

Jen looked up from her chocolates. "So what's the frickin' plan?"

"Madame Therese."

Oh God. I typed, "Are you kidding?" On impulse, Becky and I had visited Madame Therese a year ago.

"What the eff is Madame Therese?" Jen asked. "Does she run a brothel? Cuz, honestly? I'm not into it."

"Sounds like a dominatrix," Susan guessed.

"Stop it, you guys. She's a legitimate fortune-teller."

Susan and Jen groaned.

"No, really. She's good. Ask Elle." Becky's eyes lit up. "Everything she told us came true, right, Elle?'

"Wait. You two have gone to her before? You went to a freakin' fortune-teller?" Jen's eyes popped.

I typed that it had been a long time ago, but nobody read what I wrote. I remembered what Madame Therese had told me, essentially that I attracted tragedy and death. And that I'd come back to see her again. Which apparently I would, if Becky had her way.

"That's a complete racket." Jen eyed Becky. "You don't believe in it, do you? Because fortune-telling is bullshit."

"Not Madame Therese. You'll see."

"Actually, Becky." Susan frowned. "We have a problem about that. Our resolution was to try new things together, but you two have already been to see her. So, in point of fact, this experience isn't new."

"Oh, let it go, Susan. This isn't a courtroom and you're not getting off on a technicality. She's coming to dinner with us the week after next."

Jen sucked melted chocolate off her fingertips. Her nails were blood red. She surveyed the candy box, making her next selection, picking up what looked like a dark chocolate butter cream. "What the hell. It's one dinner. How bad can it be?"

"Don't eat them all, Jen," Becky scolded. "Those were for Elle."

"Trust me." Jen examined the bonbon. "Elle doesn't give a shit about candy right now, do you Elle?"

I tried to smile. Aborted the attempt; smiling hurt. I thought of Madame Therese. I wasn't eager to hear what she'd predict, but at least I could avoid flying on a trapeze.

Jen sucked creamy filling out of the shell. "So." She looked up. "Susan, did you tell her yet?"

Tell me what? Becky and Susan scowled at her.

"Really, Jen?" Susan said.

Uh-oh. I typed, "Tell me what?" No one read it.

"Jen." Susan glowered. "No. I haven't told her. She has enough to worry about, so I'm waiting until she's stronger."

"But she'd want to know," Jen argued. "And she has a right to know."

"What's the hurry, Jen?" Becky asked. "It's not like she can do anything about it. So what's the point of upsetting her?"

Had they forgotten I could hear them? I typed, furiously. "What happened?"

"That's not the point," Jen said. "The point is that it's her life. Who put you two in charge of deciding what Elle should or shouldn't know?"

I kept typing, asking what they were talking about, saying that whatever it was, I wanted to be told. Nobody noticed. They went on arguing, Susan and Becky blaming Jen for being thoughtless and insensitive by bringing it up, Jen accusing them of ganging up against her and forgetting that, even battered and stitched, I was a big girl, and I had rights.

When I pounded on the tray table, my arm hurt, the laptop bounced, and the water pitcher splashed. All three of them spun and looked at me in alarm.

I typed, "Tell me."

"Go on, big shot," Becky said to Jen. "Tell her."

"I'll tell her," Susan said.

They exchanged glances. Susan cleared her throat, folded her hands, sat straight. Jen set the chocolates on the nightstand. Becky stepped over and took my hand.

Oh God, I thought. Someone else died. Ty? He hadn't seemed mortally wounded. Katie? Or Stan. Oh God, was it Seth? Or someone not related to the case—

"It's your house." Becky's voice was somber.

My house? They looked at me, three pairs of anxious, sorry eyes. Had it burned down—a gas explosion?

"The fact is your realtor got murdered there," Susan said.

"So the house has a history," Becky cut in. "Especially since Charlie got killed there, too."

"Charlie has nothing to do with it." Jen rolled her eyes.

"Of course he does. He's part of the house's history."

"Which they knew about when they made their offer. It's not a secret what happened with Charlie—"

"This is about Jerry," Susan said. "The buyers were upset when they found out what happened. But really, it doesn't matter why. What matters is—"

"Bottom line, your buyers effing bailed."

What? I looked at Susan who glared at Jen.

"I'm sorry, Elle," she said. "Jen's right. The sale is off. Your buyers backed out. They think the house has bad karma."

I repeated the last sentence in my head. My buyers backed out. What did that mean? I pictured people backing away from the house. Oh, of course. Why was I so slow absorbing information? No buyers. That meant no sale. So I wasn't moving.

I leaned back, letting the news roll around my head. Memories swirled. Katie and her friends in the house, dancing around me with knives. Maggie chasing me out the window. A shadow coming into my bedroom in the night, looming over me, pushing into me. Jerry dead in Charlie's easy chair.

And Charlie. Carrying me over the threshold as if we were newlyweds in some sappy old movie. Or surprising me with a bubble bath or a single rose. Or standing at the sink, splashing on aftershave. Even after two years, I sometimes smelled it near the sink. Or in the closet, the bedroom, the study.

"...pulling an Elle. You shouldn't have made us tell her, Jen. See how upset she is? Are you satisfied?" Susan scolded.

I typed. "It's okay. I'm just thinking."

"I'll help you find a new realtor," Jen offered. "Norm knows goddamn tons of them."

Oh Lord. Another realtor? I'd have to start over, staging the house, having showings. Keeping the place pristine and museum-like for new potential buyers who'd parade through, criticizing the darkness of the foyer, complaining that the cabinets were out of date. Leaving their shoe prints on freshly vacuumed carpets.

"There's no rush," Susan said.

"That's right," Becky said, "take your time."

"But seriously," Jen said. "Can you blame them? Would you buy a place where the realtor had just been butchered?"

"Jen!" Susan said, and Becky said, "Oh my God," and the bickering resumed.

I closed my eyes. Realized that it wasn't just the buyers who didn't want the sale. The house didn't want it either. The place had gone through a lot with me, and it wasn't ready to let me go.

* * *

When Stiles walked in, the others left, except for Susan. She declared that, as my attorney, she should be present.

He began by asking how I felt, saying he was sorry I'd had such a terrible experience. His eyes looked sincerely sad.

"How's Ty?" I typed.

He told me that Ty had a bunch of abrasions and a nasty concussion but was coming along.

I didn't know much about concussions, except that football players and boxers got them. Mohammed Ali got Parkinson's disease from them. And now Ty and I both had them. I saw Ty sitting on his sister, holding her down. Blood caked in his hair, and his gaze was off kilter.

Stiles sat beside the bed, admired the flowers. Asked if I was ready to tell him what happened.

I began typing. I wrote that I'd been ambushed and terrorized in my house. That Katie and her friends had killed my realtor, and that Ty had tried to help me.

Detective Stiles stopped me, asking questions about specifics. I had no answers.

Instead, I wrote that Katie, not Ty or his mother, had killed their father.

Stiles leaned away from the screen, unconvinced. "I don't think so. Ty Evans confessed to that murder."

My fingers responded, explaining why Ty confessed. That he'd thought it would be better for his family if he served a few years in juvenile detention than if Rose served the rest of her life. But that Katie had admitted killing her father.

Stiles rubbed his eyes. "So let me get this straight. You're saying that Rose Evans thought her son Ty did it, and Ty thought his mother, Rose, did it. But they were both wrong, because Katie did it. And when Ty confessed, Katie assumed it was to cover for her because she was his little sister."

I typed. "And when he got out, she was afraid he'd want payback, so she decided to frame him by killing victims connected to him and leaving evidence that led to him."

"But the father's case was closed," Susan said. "No one would believe him if he blamed anyone else for killing his father. Ty had been convicted and gone away for it."

I had thought about that. My fingers flew on the keyboard. "I don't think she was just afraid Ty would reveal that she'd killed their father. I think she was afraid Ty would get in her way. While he was in juvey, she got away with whatever she wanted. Rose had no authority, so Katie had no limits. Ty, though, would get in her face, so she wanted him gone. I think she framed him so she could continue her little power regime." She'd been the ringleader. Maggie and Trish had followed her lead, even cutting themselves with her, making the same pattern of wounds.

Stiles leaned back. "That's interesting. Except for one thing. If she just wanted her brother to get sent away again, she could have stopped after one murder. Framed him and been done with it. But she didn't. She kept on going."

"What are you saying?" Susan asked.

"Simple," he said. "Framing Ty was only a small part of it. Katie Evans and her friends killed people because they wanted to."

I didn't type a response. I was thinking about Katie's power. Over her mother, over her friends. Over Seth.

I pictured his bruises. Oh God. Why hadn't I realized it before?

I began typing. "Seth—Rose didn't abuse him—It was Katie."

That was why he'd hidden in the cubbies when she and her friends had come to walk him home. Why hadn't I figured it out? Why hadn't he told me? I'd seen how he'd cowered at the sight of them. How he'd run around the classroom to get away. That hadn't been a game. Oh God, he must have been terrified. I'd blamed Rose, reported her to the authorities, made sure Seth was taken from her, never suspecting that, even in foster care, he'd still be exposed to his abuser. Katie had been the golden sister, the charmer. The helpful cheerful leader and cheerleader. Was it during their walks home that she and her friends had hurt him? Or had they assaulted him later, at home?

Why wasn't Stiles saying anything? Why didn't he look surprised at my revelation?

I typed. "You knew?"

Stiles glanced at Susan, then met my eyes. Told me that Seth had confided in his foster sister. She'd found cut marks on Seth's arm, and she'd asked what happened. At first, he'd said they were from a cat. But finally, making her promise never to tell, he'd admitted that his sister, Katie, and her friends had used a razor on him.

What? They'd cut him, too? My chest tightened. I pictured little Seth. His whispered conversations to his dad. His angry red drawings.

Stiles continued. "Seth said that Katie and her friends chased him into the empty kindergarten, and the kindergarten teacher showed up. He was afraid they'd killed her."

Oh God. Becky had walked in on the girls terrorizing Seth. That was why they'd knocked her out.

Lord. I shut my eyes, saw Rose coming after me, punching my car windows, kicking my fenders. I'd messed up.

"Elle, stop it," Susan said. "I know you. You're blaming yourself. It's not your fault."

Stiles went on, said that Katie was being held without bail. That Ty, once out of the hospital, would go home and stay with his mother. Rose was in shock and denial about Katie, but finally beginning to understand the reason for Ty's confession and accept his innocence.

"And Seth?" I typed.

Stiles hesitated. "He's being looked after. His foster family is getting him counseling." He stopped.

"He'll stay in foster care?"

"For now."

"You might as well know," Susan said. "They've taken him out of Logan."

Out of my class?

"He's transferred to Edison. His counselor thought it would be good for him to get a fresh start someplace new."

I started to type, but stopped, not sure how to ask what I wanted to know. It wasn't just how he was doing or whether I could see him. What I really wanted to know was if I was at fault for what had happened to him, if I'd failed him. If he'd ever be all right. If he'd ever forgive me.

CHAPTER SIXTEEN

My first day back, I got there early, anxious about my class. The parking lot was empty except for Stan's pickup. Stan's truck was almost always at the school. Wouldn't surprise me to find out he lived in the building, in one of his custodian closets.

I'd been gone for two weeks. My stitches were out, but I still had scabs and bruises. I walked with a limp, and the skin around my eye was puffy and yellow. What would the children think? What did they know? What should I tell them?

I thought of Seth, wondered how he was doing. First his brother, now his sister was in jail, accused of murder. The body count that had begun with his father had grown to include Mrs. Marshall, Joyce Huff, Stephanie Cross, Patsy Olsen, Jerry, and Katie's cohorts, Trish and Maggie. Eight people, all dead. There had almost been ten, but Ty and I had managed to survive.

For two weeks, the media had exploded with stories of Katie's gang of sadistic teenage serial killers and their victims. Ty had been hailed as a self-sacrificing, misunderstood hero, a loving brother who'd been duped into confessing to his sister's first homicide, the murder of their father. Ty was praised for risking his own life to confront and stop his sister's murderous trio. Funds were being collected to help him get on his feet. A lawyer had volunteered to take his case and clear his name and criminal record. The owner of a local auto body shop offered him a job as an apprentice mechanic. I'd talked to Ty by phone a few times. He'd sounded tired and vague. Not ready to think about what he was going to do, let alone to accept a job. We agreed to stay in touch, promised to meet for milkshakes when he felt well enough. I doubted it would be soon.

I assumed that Ty had been bombarded by television and radio producers. They'd certainly bombarded me. I'd been invited to appear on *Dr. Phil*, *Good Morning America*, *Dateline*, and *Twenty-Twenty*. Some Hollywood agent had called to find out if I'd sold TV or movie rights to my story yet, indicating that he had an interested client. Not just the city, but the whole country seemed captivated by three smart, pretty, and popular young girls who'd murdered at least six people because, as the papers quoted Katie, they "thought it was fun."

I wondered what Seth knew of these stories. Had he seen any of the news coverage? Had his foster family shielded him? I worried about how he was, how he was adjusting to foster care. If his drawings were less bloody. If he still talked to the ghost of his father. I probably wouldn't find out, though. Mr. Royal had confirmed that Seth's foster parents had enrolled him at a different school in order to break all ties with his past.

In that same conversation, days before my return to work, Mr. Royal had talked about my position at Logan, suggesting that I take a leave of absence for the rest of the semester. I'd assured him that I was well enough to teach, but he'd been reluctant to accept that, even though I had my doctors' approvals. Maybe he doubted my ability to work. Or maybe he wasn't eager to have me back for another reason. Maybe he thought my presence—with my place in the headlines, my yellowed eye socket and still-visible wounds—would be a disruption.

I sat in the parking lot, wondering. Would I be?

Maybe I would frighten the children. I pictured them, Evan, Bobby, Stella, Millicent. Elana. I was eager to see them, but, in fact, I could still leave. There was still time to call a substitute. No one would have to know I'd even stopped by.

And then what? Would I go home to my no-longer-on-the-market house and watch reality television? Go to the mall? Join an online chat group?

No, I was a teacher. A good teacher. My students needed me, even if I looked like a losing prizefighter. I pictured their sweet faces. How was Chelsea doing on subtraction? Had Evan mastered carrying and borrowing? And Bobby—was he reading any better? Had the counselor scheduled his dyslexia test? Damn, I missed those kids, needed to make sure they were doing all right. Careful not to aggravate my still healing thigh, I climbed out of the car, pulled a stack of folders out of the trunk, started for the building.

But stopped.

The school looked different. Was it the windows? The doors? Something seemed altered. The place looked animated. Like a giant brick brown bear, protective, alert, watching for its cubs.

Seriously, what was wrong with me? The school was not a mama bear. It was a pile of bricks and steel. I had to stop dawdling, needed to go in and prepare for class.

But I didn't go in. I stood in the parking lot, watching the school as Mrs. Marshall appeared at a second-floor window, gazing down at the playground. Joyce decorated windowpanes with cutouts of flowers. Scores of children, faces I'd taught, passed me by, calling out to each other, playing tag, skipping, tossing balls, lagging behind. "Hi, Mrs. H," one called from behind.

I turned, but the student faded away.

A couple of cars had pulled into the lot. Colleagues were arriving. Some stepped over to welcome me back, ask how I was. I exchanged hugs and smiles. Asked how their semesters were going. Saw, over their shoulders, Duncan Girard pull his Jolly Jack truck up to the edge of the property, children running over to see him on their way to school.

Becky walked by, took my arm, and escorted me to the office. "You have lots of memos to look at."

Memos? "Not now. The kids are coming in. I've got to get to class."

Becky handed me a pile of mail. "You really should sort through this."

Really? I rifled through it, found brochures promoting teaching manuals, a newsletter from the teachers' union, forms from the PTA, memos about flu shots and staff meetings. Nothing urgent or even interesting. Why was Becky bothering me with old mail? I shoved the pile on top of my stack of folders. Started for my classroom. Mr. Royal stopped me, asked me again how I felt. I said I was fine. He tried to make conversation, but I hurried off into the hall.

And came face-to-face with Stan. Even though Becky and half a dozen others had just walked passed him, he stepped directly in front of me, blocking my way. He didn't look at me. "You can't go this way," he said.

"I'm sorry?" Stan was stopping me from getting to my classroom? I was already late. The children had come in. They were unsupervised.

"Floor's slippery. Wait a minute."

The floor was not slippery. A hundred kids and Becky had just stampeded over it.

"Excuse me, Stan." I stepped to the side.

Stan put an arm out, not letting me pass, towering over me. My stomach tightened.

"Sorry, Mrs. H," he said. "I can't let you."

What? I wheeled around, started back to the office. If I had to, I'd get Mr. Royal to make Stan move aside.

"No," Stan called. "It's okay, Mrs. Harrison. Never mind."

Never mind? I turned again. Stan had moved out of my way. I hurried to 2B, my classroom. Had a case of butterflies, eager and nervous. Stan lurked behind me all the way to my room. I dashed inside, looking at him over my shoulder.

Twenty-two voices shouted, "Welcome back, Mrs. H!"

A hand-decorated banner hung across the blackboard. Cheers and applause erupted, with lots of jabbering, running, and hugging.

"Mrs. Harrison, I fed the hamsters every day!"

"Mrs. Harrison, did you read my card yet?"

"Did you really catch the killer?"

"What happened to your eye?"

The children had brought juice, apple slices, and graham crackers. Two fifth graders had volunteered to help serve. Each student had written me an illustrated card, and they were hung on the bulletin board, each in its author's space. They clamored for me to read aloud. My class was pandemonium, and Becky's kindergarteners were filing in, coming to perform some songs in my honor.

Small hands grabbed for mine. Children called my name. My vision blurred, and I grabbed a tissue off my desk. Wiping away tears, I saw a dark figure in the doorway. Stan stepped inside the room. He didn't meet my eyes but, in fourteen years, it was the first time I'd seen him smile.

CPSIA information can be obtained at www.ICGtesting.com
Printed in the USA
LVOW08s0842191016

R11493800001B/R114938PG508709LVX1B/1/P

9 781608 091911